Mighty Old Bones

**Center Point
Large Print**

**This Large Print Book carries the
Seal of Approval of N.A.V.H.**

Mighty Old Bones

A Thistle and Twigg Mystery

MARY SAUMS

CENTER POINT PUBLISHING
THORNDIKE, MAINE

This Center Point Large Print edition
is published in the year 2008 by arrangement with
St. Martin's Press.

Copyright © 2008 by Mary Saums.

All rights reserved.

The text of this Large Print edition is unabridged. In other
aspects, this book may vary from the original edition.
Printed in the United States of America.
Set in 16-point Times New Roman type.

ISBN: 978-1-60285-247-1

Library of Congress Cataloging-in-Publication Data

Saums, Mary.
  Mighty old bones : a Thistle and Twigg mystery / Mary Saums.--Center Point large print ed.
  p. cm.
  ISBN: 978-1-60285-247-1 (lib. bdg. : alk. paper)
  1. Widows--Fiction. 2. Human remains (Archaeology)--Fiction. 3. Alabama--Fiction.
4. Large type books. I. Title.

PS3569.A78875M54 2008b
813'.54--dc22

2008010452

Mighty Old Bones

one
Jane Thistle
and the Bad Sign

*I*t wasn't the sight of blood that disturbed me. The gelatinous pool took me by surprise, yes, certainly, but I had seen that much and quite a bit more in my time. Still, coming upon it in the woods on my morning exploration gave me a bit of a start. I stopped, listened. Nothing but birdsong and the rustling of leaves could be heard. Weak daylight found its way through the canopy and down to the forest floor. Its dull reflection on the puddle of thick red liquid grew larger. As the shadows receded, something much more ominous came into view and riveted me to the spot.

I clicked on my flashlight to see more clearly. Its beam dashed all hope that the blood was due to the natural cycle of animal predator finding prey. As much as the thought of a rare prowling bobcat or coyote distressed me, I'd have preferred either to the evidence of a more dangerous species. Near the puddle, beside an exposed tree root, the impression of a large boot indented a patch of fresh mud.

I looked around me, slowly turning in all directions, remembering the early evening rain the day before. With another look at the shoe's imprint, I shivered. Sometime in the night, an intruder, a trespasser on my land, had left behind a grisly calling card.

I squatted for a closer look. Warm breath blew on my outstretched hand and a cold nose moved down to snuffle quietly around the footprint. "Good boy," I whispered to my trusty companion, Homer, a large black Lab mix whom I inherited along with this parcel of woods.

Since moving to this, my own private forest, almost eight weeks earlier, I must say I expected trespassers to come along eventually. Still, I hadn't expected them so soon. The hot summer days stretched into October, cooled for a night or two, and returned to eighty- and ninety-degree temperatures, thus making me forget that hunting seasons would be here soon. My woods would be strong temptation for the unscrupulous.

Settling into my new home at the edge of a wildlife refuge, which itself borders Bankhead National Forest, had taken on a most welcome sameness. Small rituals of exercise and relaxation, my daily excursions through the woods, the beauty of nature that surrounds me, all these things were so new and wonderful that I'm afraid I allowed them to lull me into a state of complacency.

No more. The blood served as a reminder that I must be vigilant in my duty as caretaker of this wood. I watched Homer move away, slowly at first then picking up speed, his nose still to the ground. He moved left to right and around one spot before trotting off in a straight line.

"What is it, dear?" I said, and followed to see what we might find.

A few minutes later, it became clear our search would be in vain. We found nothing else. My flashlight alone was not enough to see well so early in the morning. For all I knew, Homer and I were stamping about over the very things we might be looking for. I shone the light on my watch.

"Ah, well. Come, Homer. We'll try again this afternoon." He pretended not to hear me speak or turn and walk back the way we had come. I laughed. "Stay if you like, then. But I need to shower before I go to Phoebe's house. She has quite a morning planned for us."

His large head, barely visible in the early dawn, rose and swiveled in my direction, the rest of his body completely still. He understood the operative word, as I knew he would.

Phoebe. My best friend. How she puzzles Homer. He loves everyone and wants so much for her to like him. But I'm afraid it is not to be. She tolerates him for my sake but has no wish to become overly fond of any animal.

We're quite different in that. I love all animals, particularly those on my own land, from the families of deer down to the smallest bug. It isn't that Phoebe is coldhearted, not at all. The problem is she is fastidious. She keeps her house in spotless condition. Throughout my life, I worked in the dirt, on archaeological digs around the world, wherever my late husband, the Colonel, might be stationed. Dirt and sweat, and now leaves and mud from my walks with a bit of dog hair mixed in, don't bother me in the slightest. Pets and the natural world in any form cause great concern for Phoebe so she avoids them as much as possible.

At sixty-five years old, she's two years younger than I am and has lived in Tullulah all her life. Her personality might be described as that of a typical redhead. For her age, she has a remarkably thick head of hair, which she wears pulled up with curls on top. It's quite becoming.

Her best quality is her ability to make me laugh. She tries to hide her soft heart behind a sarcastic façade much of the time. I see through her though, and she knows I do. She kids me quite a bit. What great fun we have together. And in our short acquaintance, it has already become clear she is a strong ally. I trust her with no reserves, for she has proven herself to be as honest and brave a person as anyone I've ever known.

"Ah. There you are." Homer, having given up his search, bumped into my leg and kept pace on the trail that would take us home. He looked up at me, his teeth gleaming inside a wide smile. Poor fellow. Dogs are such optimists. I hoped he wouldn't be too disappointed that Phoebe wouldn't be coming to visit.

It was odd for me to have a best friend. Something new, possibly since I was a teenager. The frequent moves that my husband's job in the military required, never staying very long in one location or even in one part of the world, meant my friends were never close. I also held a part-time government job that, for the most part, was solitary work. The persons I did happen to meet in that line of duty, sadly, weren't around for very long.

After the Colonel's passing, I came to Tullulah to retire and quietly fade away. To my surprise, the town and the woods rejuvenated me. At sixty-seven, I am stronger and more at peace than any other time in my life. From the age of eighteen, when the Colonel and I married, we traveled to places just as beautiful all over the globe. Yet it is only here, in a tiny secluded town in northwest Alabama, far from almost anywhere else, that I have found serenity in the deep untainted woodlands I love so much.

two
Phoebe Twigg and the Woolly Mammoths

*W*hen Jane knocked on my kitchen door, my hands were in dishwater, so I hollered for her to come on in. I didn't have to ask her what she had been doing that morning. Whenever she has a good walk through the woods she gets this look, like she has been snorting helium and is about to float up into the sky any minute.

I just don't get it. I mean, the exercise and fresh air and all, that part I get. My question is, what's wrong with nice, flat pavement where you don't have to sink your good tennis shoes two or three inches down in old mucky leaves and mud? Who wants to spend a half-hour scraping that gunk out of the treads with a toothpick? Why not walk where there are no trees so you don't have to duck and push back branches that whip you across the face from out of nowhere? That hiking and camping stuff is beyond me. No, thank you. I like my air conditioner.

Mind you, I'm not criticizing. I would never do that to my friend. I'm just saying. There's nobody smarter than Jane, and if she wants to deal with ticks and snakes, I say more power to her.

I let the dishwater out of the sink and then sprayed the last of the suds down the drain. I picked up a cup towel to dry my hands and said, "Looks like you've had a good day so far. Did you have fun talking to all the happy little animals and trees?"

Jane smiled. "I did indeed. They send you their best." She plucked a grape from the fruit bowl and tossed it in her mouth. If she wasn't gray-headed, she would've looked like a kid scooting onto the bar stool at my counter. She's tiny and has the face of an elf. Just looking at her, you'd never guess she's the type who could pick you off at a hundred yards. Yeah. She looks and talks like your sweet granny in England but she don't allow no foolishness. Anybody that messes with Jane is liable to get shot or smacked cross-eyed, Asian-style.

"Well, my morning has just been wrong." I told her all about it while I took my dishes out of the rack and dried them.

When it's pretty outside like it was that day, I like

to walk down to the town square, which is just a few blocks down the road. The square is the regular kind. Old buildings, I'd say from the twenties or thirties, and the same shops like you see everywhere. We've got some furniture stores, a bakery, the City Grill, and Lloyd's Drugs, where you can still get a mighty good soda-fountain cherry Coke or milk shake. In the middle of the square, we've got the courthouse where the sheriff's office is and the jail underneath.

I was on my way to the hardware store. When I got to Fein Brothers Real Estate, I stopped to read the flyer in their window about our library's Halloween party. That's when I heard a deep voice go "Oof!" and the next thing I knew, a Saint Bernard the size of an elephant planted his big fat body right in front of me. He *oofed* again and before I could take a breath or a step backward, he reared up and smacked his muddy paws on my shoulders like this: one, two, blap, blap, just like that.

Before I could push him off or holler, that Saint Bernard had licked my face plumb clean. His tongue was so wide it only took him three swipes to get me from ear to ear and forehead to neck. And here I'd spent twenty good minutes, all wasted, putting on my makeup.

"Get your smelly self down off of me right now!" I hollered. His mouth closed and his big sticky nostrils went into overtime, sniffing real fast all around my face.

"Brutus, heel! Heel!" a man said. I couldn't see who he was since he was on the other side of the woolly mammoth.

"I'm sorry. Oh, Mrs. Twigg, it's you. I'm so sorry. He's never done that before. I apologize." It was a scrawny guy in a jogging suit. I couldn't think of his name right off, but I knew his face. He used to bring his little girl to the library every week for story time.

"They all do it," I said. "Every one of them. Not to anybody else, just me. Dogs know I can't stand them and so they come straight to me and get all over me."

"He didn't hurt you, did he?"

I rubbed my shoulders and rotated both arms around. "It depends on whether or not that slime is full of diseases and soaks into my skin and kills me in the night."

Brutus, who had settled down next to his master, must have misunderstood me because he started smiling real big again and panting with his tongue hanging out. He lunged at me, both paws hitting with one big *blap,* right back to my shoulders like he was going to start hugging and kissing me.

I screamed. This time, his owner yanked him down, apologizing over and over, and the two of them took off down the sidewalk. I was happy to see the back end of Brutus, wagging his big tail as he trotted off with his nerd master.

I took my pack of antibacterial wipes out of my purse and used every last one of them. The drugstore was right there, so I went in and used the mirror behind their big long counter to fix my hair back into place and dab on some more powder and lipstick.

"Hey, Phoebe."

"Hey, Betty." Betty Raines works the cash register there full time, has ever since she caught her husband with another woman last spring. Betty didn't divorce him. She decided she would rather work at the drugstore. That way, she would either catch him buying that Viagra or keep him from buying it since he wouldn't want her to know. He quit the other woman so I reckon it worked. Sure, he could go out of town to get his pills, but at least Betty made her point.

"Can I help you with anything?" she said.

I don't believe I've ever seen Betty when she wasn't dressed up and fully accessorized. She always looks like she stepped out of a magazine ad from the fifties. She keeps her hair dyed strawberry blond, flips it up on the ends and lacquers it to death, just like we all used to do years ago. She still favors those tight cashmere sweaters and pointy bras, which says something else about that kooky husband of hers.

"Well," I said, "now that I'm here, I may as well get some more antibacterial wipes. The purse size, if you've got them."

I thanked her and went on to the hardware store for a new fluorescent bulb to replace the dead one over my kitchen sink. After that, I walked on around the square to get a little exercise.

I kept an eye out for the Saint Bernard. It was a good thing. I saw him up on the next block. He saw me and jerked against his leash, like he was fixing to charge across and down the street to me. I made a quick right and cut through the alley behind Braxton's Furniture Store and took the long way home.

I got to within a block of my house before I came upon the second dog. I was admiring Julie Huntsinger's pretty red maple tree and thinking how all those leaves would be on the ground the next day if we got the storm the weatherman was predicting. All of a sudden, a howling commenced. I nearly jumped out of my skin and swirled around to see where it was coming from because I did not want to get slimed again.

There it was, in front of the Reeds' house. A big solid-white dog about the size of a Shetland pony stood in the yard, facing the house. The sight of it must have made my body's instincts flip on because I had jumped sideways behind the nearest tree before I even realized it. I didn't remember the Reeds having a dog. I thought it might be a neighbor's, though I'd never seen it before.

Whoever it belonged to, it was as big as Brutus. And Lord have mercy, what a howl that thing had, like nothing I'd ever heard. I wished I had a tape recorder on me. It would've been a good spooky sound for the Trail of Terror at the library's haunted house that would be coming up soon. I ran the other way over to another tree.

But it was the funniest thing. When I turned to look at him again, he was gone. That was one fast dog because he didn't have time to run away, not without me catching sight of any part of him either in the street or off on the other side of the yard. I didn't hang around. I cut through and made for the Nelsons' yard because I knew it didn't have a fence in back.

Across the alley was old Mrs. Ensley's house. I cut through her yard, too, and though I didn't see her, I knew she would be peeping through her living room window to see what I was up to, so I waved in that general direction as I passed and stepped onto my own street, Meadowlark Lane. I couldn't wait to get in my house and bolt the door behind me.

Jane laughed through the whole story up until the part about the white dog disappearing. She went from a big smile and twinkling eyes to a dead stare, first like she was thinking hard and then like she remembered something. She wouldn't tell me what. Said she was thinking of something unrelated and tried to laugh it off. I know one thing. Whatever it was, it was a bad memory, and it scared her.

three
Jane and the Disturbing
Incident at the Pig

J looked at my watch as I climbed into Phoebe's car. It was just past eight and already the morning had been quite eventful for both of us. I decided not to tell her about finding the boot print and the fresh blood on my walk, not yet. It would only have upset her unnecessarily. I planned to talk with Detective Daniel Waters, a nice fellow with whom I'd had dealings, about the trespasser though I doubted the detective could do anything about it.

My land, you see, has been off-limits to the locals who might like to hunt there for many a decade. The former owner, Cal Prewitt, was a cantankerous old hermit and a dear friend. He refused to let anyone come on his land and enforced his wishes with a shotgun. Though he hunted himself, he did so to eat. He didn't believe in killing for sport. From the day he died and left his private forest to me, I knew hunters in the area might do as they pleased. A little old lady like me wouldn't be seen as an obstacle.

With fall almost upon us, it was hardly a surprise that someone was already testing the waters. Actually, on three previous occasions, I found smaller bits of evidence that uninvited humans had been in the woods in the past two weeks. The blood I'd found that morning, however, changed things, for it was the first to point specifically to hunting activity.

"So, you don't mind if we stop off at the Pig first?" Phoebe said as she reversed out of her drive-way. The Piggly Wiggly is where we always buy our groceries.

"No, not at all. We have plenty of time, I think."

"Loads. I figured I might as well use it to get my baking supplies. The weatherman predicted we might have tornado warnings this week, so I need to stock up and get busy. I like to take food out to the workers when the electricity goes out, which it usually does when the least little wind blows around here."

We chatted on the way, Phoebe doing most of the talking since she was excited about the real reason for our outing. She had scheduled both of us for hair appointments at the Beauty Barn that morning. It would be my first visit.

"Somebody has got my place," she said. She referred to a large motor home that took up a substantial number of parking spots, among them one Phoebe called her own. I knew immediately that the motor home did not belong to a resident of Tullulah.

We walked inside amid a flurry of excited conversations. A number of customers stood about, most with paper cups in hand beside a table of breakfast rolls and coffee, compliments of the Pig. One customer tipped his hat on seeing me, a patrolman in uniform whom I had met not long after I moved here.

While Phoebe got to the bottom of things with the group, I noticed a young man watching us. He stood at the clear plastic window of the manager's station, an elevated platform by the last cash register. He turned away when our eyes met, or perhaps the manager or a clerk spoke to him at that moment. I didn't know him, but I had seen him when we parked. I noticed his car behind us earlier when we turned onto the town square as well.

Phoebe rolled a shopping cart to me and we began our trek through the aisles. "That trailer belongs to those movie people. They were in here buying snacks and told the regulars they were thinking about doing some of their filming in Tullulah, rather than doing all of it in Hamilton like they planned."

Almost every edition of the local newspaper devoted some space to the "movie people" who were working on location just south of Tullulah. Their project, an independent film, required much greenery and rolling hills, both abundant in the countryside that surrounds and spreads out from the bottom of Tullulah's mountain.

As Phoebe shopped, she moved faster and faster through the store. I managed to keep up but couldn't understand why she hurried. "What's the rush? We still have plenty of time."

"I know, but I want to get back outside before they leave. They might need some local actors. Or actresses. I thought I'd stop and say hello, tell them we're so happy they're here and then ask, you know, real casual-like."

I kept a straight face.

Once through the checkout, I took my purse out of the cart. The automatic doors opened for us as Phoebe pushed the cart outside. She turned to say something to me when suddenly I felt my arm pulled down. At the same time, Phoebe was knocked to the side by a figure that put me off balance as well. All I saw was the torso of a young man in a maroon T-shirt with another shirt, plaid and worn open, over it. The next instant, I saw the back of his dark curly hair as he turned to run away.

"What the . . . Jane! He's got your purse!" Phoebe screamed.

I managed to grab the tail end of the open shirt that he had kindly left untucked and pulled him closer, just enough to grasp his arm. I swiveled and used leverage to turn his body slightly and bring him down on his back with a loud thud.

He didn't move.

Phoebe sucked in a loud startled breath. She held her hands over her mouth and stared down. "I believe you've killed him."

"Don't be silly. His eyelids are moving."

"Hey, somebody call the funeral home."

"Phoebe, don't be ridiculous, he is not dead."

"He will be when I get through with him. The very idea, robbing a decrepit old lady. And in Tullulah. No, sir, buddy. This here young'un is not long for this world. Jane, help me get him up and then come show me how to flip him. Just one time, that's all I ask. Oh, shoot, here comes the fuzz."

The patrolman she had spoken with earlier walked out the Pig's door, coffee cup in hand. He didn't see us at once. An older gentleman who came outside with him looked like he was telling a joke.

The boy moaned a bit and looked groggy as he sat up. Phoebe clucked her tongue. "Too bad. They should have plenty of room for him down at the jailhouse. I guess we should step back so Junior has room to cuff him and haul him off."

When Phoebe called to the policeman, and while our

attention was slightly diverted, the thief took a chance. In an instant, the young man jumped to his feet and sprinted across the lot and out of view, my purse held firmly under one arm. The policeman threw down his cup and gave chase.

He had no luck. After a few minutes, he came back, out of breath and dispirited. He had radioed for backup while looking about for the thief. He didn't stop to talk with us but hurried toward his vehicle, asking us to wait until he or another officer could take our statements.

Twenty minutes later, the police took our report, but I knew it would do little good. It was the last thing any of us expected.

Phoebe kept looking at her watch. She held up a finger. "Okay, fellows, you've got one minute to wrap this thing up because that's when we're leaving. Right, Jane?"

Before I could speak, Phoebe locked eyes with the officer taking notes.

He let us go. Her face returned to normal, to the nice church lady and former children's librarian that she really was. She grabbed my arm and pulled me along, inviting all the policemen in hearing to her house for cake anytime they wished to stop by.

The curls on Phoebe's head flopped as she ran, bouncing on the top rim of her new all-black fashion sunglasses. When we reached the car, she slung her purse into the backseat. She turned the ignition before fully settling herself behind the wheel. With the shifter in drive, she put the car in motion without waiting for me to shut my door first. I pulled with all my might, managed to close the door, and grabbed the dashboard.

Her foot gunned the accelerator. We jerked out of the Pig's parking lot with a screech, grinding black rubber marks in the asphalt. I managed a weak apologetic smile for the policemen who watched our departure.

We zoomed to the town square and around it three quarters of the way, taking each corner at a skid. I felt as if we tilted on two tires the whole way round. Looks of horror from pedestrians had no effect on Phoebe's speed nor did their cries of disapproval break her concentration. Used to Phoebe's driving, I remained silent as I fought gravity to keep my seat.

She spun the wheel as we turned onto a side street and, taking another turn sharply, the car bumped into the driveway of a gravel parking lot. Beside it sat a very old log building, its front door and wide porch facing the main street. Phoebe stomped on the brake. The back end of the car fishtailed a few feet to the right and the car jerked to a halt as the rear tires sprayed rock and plumes of white dust.

Phoebe pushed the gearshift into park. She turned to me, adjusted her Hollywood shades, and said an enthusiastic, "Yeah, baby. Call me Bullitt." With a cackle and a rearview mirror check, she hopped out of the car, waving for me to follow.

The Beauty Barn was neither a barn nor a beauty in the usual ways. Its appeal was in the primitive look of its exterior, like something from bygone homesteader days of the West. And, of course, if it had been built in the last days of the 1700s, as it looked, this part of northwest Alabama had been considered the West not long before. The dark, almost black, weathered beams stood out in contrast to the more modern buildings surrounding the odd-shaped patch of grass that comprised the Barn's lot.

We walked up the steps into the porch's deep shadow. Phoebe shoved the door open to a brightly lit room. The heady scent of fruity potpourri rose from a number of large wicker baskets set about the floor of the reception area. Farther in, we were met with the unmistakable smells of hair salons the world over: shampoos, hair sprays, and the chemicals of hair dyes and permanent waves.

We had only just stepped past the vacant reception desk when a loud voice hailed us from the back of the single large room. "Hey, Phoebe. Y'all come on in." A tall dark-haired woman wiped her hands on a towel as she walked toward us.

On the way, she checked the progress of other ladies' style preparations in various stages of completion. She waved the towel in the direction of a row of bubble-headed hair dryers and gave orders to one of her assistants. "Sherry, would you check on Mrs. Thompson's wave rods for me? Sometimes she curls fast. Especially in front. But check all over, please. Laura, you can go ahead and get the mix ready for Jennifer's blond highlights."

She stood before us at last and smiled. "You must be Jane. I'm Bonita. Nice to meet you," she said as she put her hand out to shake mine. "We're ready for both of you. Come on back."

Phoebe and I followed her through the middle of the floor, with a row of stylist chairs to our left in front of a wall-sized mirror. To our right, we passed Mrs. Thompson in her dryer chair, wincing as she endured Sherry's careful but apparently painful inspection of the tight curlers. Other ladies under the dryers' bubbles beside her waved to us and smiled.

When we reached the back of the room, Bonita ushered us into an alcove that contained four sinks for shampoos. Only one was in use. Its occupant raised her head, ignoring the strong spray of water intended for her rinse, letting her medium-length hair drip down her back.

"Phoebe! It's about time you got here. And you must be the famous Jane. Welcome to Tullulah. I hope you like it here. I'm Glynnis Brown. My husband runs the hardware store on the square, so if you ever need anything, anything at all, all you've got to do is give him a holler and he'll fix you right up."

"Glynnis, you're soaking yourself," said the young woman who held the sprayer. She smiled up at the two of us, giving us a wink while she snapped the wet towel from Glynnis's neck and replaced it, quick as can be, with a dry one. "Okay, lie back where I can finish."

Another teenaged girl came around the corner and

introduced herself. "I'm Teresa. We're so glad to have you in Tullulah, Mrs. Thistle. I hope you're getting settled in all right."

"Oh, yes, quite well, thank you. It's very nice to meet you all. And what a lovely shop you have here. I've been looking forward to coming in. Phoebe has told me so much about it."

Once our own towels and capes were fastened into place and the shampoos begun, we were able to relax at last after our morning's ordeal. With Bonita taking care of Phoebe and Teresa taking care of me, the soothing process of shampoo and scalp rub combined would have lulled me into a semiconscious state had it not been for Phoebe's recount of events at the Pig.

Bonita leaned Phoebe's chair back to the sink. "You're a little agitated, Phoebe girl. Has it been an exciting morning?"

"Ha. I'll say." Phoebe only needed a few moments to wiggle her body into a comfortable position before she began the first rendition of our adventure. "Bonita, honey, you're not going to believe what just happened to us. Jane and I were mugged."

"Mugged? You are such a kidder," Bonita said. Upon seeing Phoebe's serious expression, she said, "You're joking, right?"

Phoebe shook her head. "Nope."

"Where?" Bonita turned off the water sprayer.

"In the Pig's parking lot." After many exclamations of disbelief, Phoebe continued. "Never saw the guy before and probably won't ever see him again."

Phoebe's story was something along the line of a practice run, a bare bones framework on which she could build and add to in future tellings. She touched on all points of the event, yet it was a truncated version in comparison to the saga she related once we were finished with our shampoos and walked into the main styling room.

There, within hearing of a larger audience, she began again. She stretched and flourished the details in a way that suggested a more grand and dangerous plot. It was a most admirable effort. I'd have been impressed had I not witnessed the silly boy's theft myself.

"There we were, minding our own business," she said. "We got through the checkout lane and I pushed our buggy outside. All of a sudden, we hear this *whoosh.*"

I must say Phoebe is an excellent storyteller. I quite enjoyed the manner in which she pitched her voice and paused for effect. Bonita didn't seem to mind Phoebe's frequent jerks as she punctuated her words with hand and arm gestures. In fact, she was able to feel when Phoebe was about to move forward. Quite patient Bonita was, waiting with towel in hand to resume her ministrations whenever Phoebe might sit back. Phoebe did so for a while and appeared to have settled down. Bonita shook a plastic bottle and prepared to spray its clear liquid contents on Phoebe's wet hair just as Phoebe suddenly leaned forward again.

"And then," she said, "he stuck his arms right in between us and plopped his hands smack on top of Jane's purse."

A collective gasp of astonishment came up from the roomful of ladies. "Right down the street? At the Pig?" they said in various high pitches.

"Yes, ma'am, he sure did."

"I can't believe it," Bonita said.

"Believe it, sister. We were attacked in broad daylight right here in Tullulah."

Various mutterings of shock and disapproval followed. The manicurist in the far corner released her patron's hand. "What did y'all do?"

Phoebe moved slightly but, feeling the resistant tug of Bonita's comb, she sat still. To compensate, she spoke in a louder voice, moving her head as much as she could, left and right, to make eye contact with her audience. She pointed to me. "That one right there got him and got him good. Jane put the hai karate on him."

The resultant murmurs coincided with Bonita's release of Phoebe's hair. Phoebe hopped up out of the styling chair. With a flip of both arms, she flung aside her plastic cape and began to demonstrate.

"She sure did. She done like this here, 'Eeee-yah!'"

Her hands cut through the air with fast movements in a way I'd never before seen and certainly had not done myself. She scissored her hands, the edges out straight, and paused, as if frozen, in a stance she must have copied from one of the martial arts videos of which she has become so fond lately.

"He looked shocked but only for a split second before he started fighting back, like this." She moved from her stiff pose into a series of jabs with her fists. "What kind of a boy would fight a little old lady? No offense, Jane."

"None taken," I said. "But actually, he didn't really 'fight' in exactly that way." No one paid any mind to me, nor would I have done, with the much more entertaining spectacle Phoebe enthusiastically provided.

"And then Jane did like this, 'Ooo-waaah!'" Phoebe accompanied her remark with a supposed grab of the wrist and twist of the arm to her invisible attacker. "Right into his breadbasket. He doubled over and then she karate-chopped him on his neck with a *ka-whap, ka-whap* down on both sides, one right after the other one." This she portrayed with quick slices downward, another embellishment of the truth. I had done nothing of the sort.

Phoebe stood looking at the floor, her fingers splayed, her hands and feet apart in a gesture one might see on a Broadway stage, or after the death of a Shakespearean character. I half expected a soliloquy.

"Phoebe," Bonita said, "you're dripping water everywhere. Here, sit back down."

"And there he lay," Phoebe continued, still staring downward, before coming out of her thespian reverie. She looked up. "He looked like he was going to be napping for some time. I thought he was out cold. Which is why we all relaxed and weren't paying close enough attention. One minute he was still as could be, and the next he jumped up and took off, running like a streak of lightning."

She swiped the wet strands of hair that had flopped down over her forehead to either side of her face. At last, she complied with Bonita's request, let her cape fall back into place, and stepped up once again into her chair.

Laughter and applause broke out, with the ladies' heads nodding in their towels and pink curlers. They seemed to be directing their approval at me as well as Phoebe, for they smiled and spoke kind words, congratulating me on the attempt to stop our thief.

In that, I had failed. He got away with my purse, after all. I didn't look forward to renewing my driver's license and getting a new credit card. Still, I was thankful neither Phoebe nor I were hurt. It could've been much worse. At the time, I thought that was the end of it but it was, in fact, the beginning, a relatively harmless event that presaged more dangerous ones to come.

four
Phoebe Takes Jane
to the Bookstore

There are people in this world who are attracted to nuts. Jane Thistle is one of them. I don't mean she *is* one of the nuts. She's as sane and smart as all get out. What I mean is, she likes folks who are not altogether right in the head better than those who are normal.

I would be the one exception. You couldn't find a more normal person than I am. But other than me, she goes for the weirdos. I can prove it. Her only other close friend here so far was Cal Prewitt, the local hermit, and he was the weirdest person who ever lived in these parts.

Cal's dead now. He owned all the woods next to Jane's house out there in the sticks. That's how they got to be friends, because he was as much of a nature freak as Jane is. He turned out to be all right, but still, that boy was mighty strange sometimes.

Whenever I introduce Jane to an ordinary person, she's always polite and friendly. But when we happen upon one of Tullulah's basket cases and I can't steer her away, Jane goes beyond polite. She gets extremely interested in whatever strange obsession is rattling around in the other person's head.

It embarrassed me at first. I thought she did it to make me feel better, like she wanted me to know she loved Tullulah no matter how many crazy people lived here. Later, I realized that's not it. She honestly likes them all. She would stand all day long and listen to them tell one wild story after another.

After we got our hair fixed at the Beauty Barn, I asked Jane if she would mind if I stopped at the bookstore before going home. They get magazines in earlier than other places in town. It was about time for one of my monthly favorites to come in, one with recipes, so I hoped to get it before I started baking that day.

But back to the nuts. What I was saying was, when we left the Barn, we went over to the square. From where I parked, we had to walk past Ted's Barber Shop where two benches sit outside. Old geezers in their overalls congregate there on the weekdays, usually in the mornings. Their wives won't let them laze around their houses, so they come downtown to do it.

They're the kind of guys you say hi and wave to while you run past. Jane wasn't having any of that. I tried to pull her on along with me. She stood her ground like a stubborn old mule. The harder you pull on mules, the deeper they dig in. Seven of the old guys sat there that day, and every one had a silly story or joke to tell. Not a single one of them has a lick of sense. Jane stood there laughing and nodding and generally egging them on.

She did the funniest thing. I still don't understand it. She walked down the row of them, talking to each one, shaking their hands as she went. When she got to the last one, I thought I'd finally be able to drag her on to the bookstore but doggone if she didn't keep talking. She stuck her hand out, straight into the middle of nothing, at the end of the bench where nobody was sitting. It shocked me so, I'm not sure I understood what she said, but part of it was something like, "Oh, dear. You are, aren't you?"

"Jane, honey." I said it real gentle because, honestly, my first thought was that she had done flipped her wig from what happened with that thieving boy. Like she was having a delayed reaction. So I said, "Look, we need to run on and get you inside out of this heat. It'll be nice and cool in the bookstore. Okay?"

She stared at me a half-second, still looking a little frazzled. Then she closed her eyes and smiled. "Yes. Good idea." And then she was back to her normal self. For a little while.

McGaughey's Books sits on the corner of Main and Third. It's the prettiest store on the whole square. Bill and Cathy McGaughey fixed it up on the outside to look like one of those fancy Irish pubs you see on calendars. They painted the front a deep forest green with white and black trim, and their name runs across the top in giant gold letters. Very classy.

It's the only bookstore in Tullulah. The population here, about nine thousand, isn't enough to attract one of those big super chain stores like in the Shoals or Birmingham. It would be nice to have one, but we don't really need it. Cathy can order anything I want if it's not already on the shelves. She hardly ever has to do that. She and Bill have that building stuffed with books. A special kids' room, the magazines, and all the travel, history, and other nonfiction books are on the ground level. The second floor is all fiction.

Besides the books, she keeps a line of homemade items, like local honey and jellies, on display along with other fancy specialty gifts, crystal doodads and the like. On the other side of the store, three small tables are for having a cup of coffee or tea and visiting with friends, or you can take your coffee cup over to the fireplace and sit in one of the overstuffed chairs around it that are so comfortable for reading. I like the chocolate fudge cake. Jane always gets a plain croissant. It's a nice place to rest after a hard day of shopping to get your blood sugar levels back up.

When Jane and I came through the door, Cathy stood up from behind the counter. "Well, hi, ladies," she said. "How you?" Her hair used to be blond in her younger days. She used to be thinner, too, but didn't we all? Me, especially. Cathy's lilac silk blouse complemented her skin tone. She still looked young, though she must be near fifty now. She took her glasses off and let them hang on their chain around her neck.

"We're fine," I said. "Those old men on the bench tried to bore us to death but we escaped."

"Good," she said, giving me an earnest look. "The *Southern Living*s aren't here yet."

"Well, rats."

"But I do have some other things I want you to look at." She turned around to a bookshelf behind the counter, ran her finger over the backs of several books, looking for something. "Here we go. I set a few back for you. Ones like we talked about. Action or with guns or both. Have a look." Cathy, and a lot of other people in town, knew about my new interest in guns. Since Jane moved to town, she has been my inspiration as far as self-defense. Because of her influence, I bought two guns, a handgun and a rifle. They're the first I've ever owned.

I caught my breath as Cathy fanned the new books out. "Ooh-wee. Jane, would you look at all of them."

"Oh, there's a lot more than that," Cathy said. "I picked these so you could see which kind you like the best. Then we can order more. All of these have had good reviews. Now, this one is about a former Marine who works security for celebrities in Hollywood. He has a little bit of a mental problem."

"In Hollywood? You gotta be kidding." I took my reading glasses out of my purse to get a better look.

"No, for real," Cathy said. "And this one here is about an international female spy who shoots for hire, kills people all over the globe. She was a fashion model before the government recruited her. She's got an eating disorder from all that killing affecting her mind. Plus bad arches from wearing high heels so many years on the runway."

"Excuse me," Jane said. "I think I'll browse." She headed to nonfiction.

Cathy told her about some new nature books that came in and where they were and then turned back to me. "And this one is about an ex-SWAT team guy who is working undercover in a bakery in New Jersey. I've read it. It's really good." The cover had a gun barrel sticking out between a platter of cannoli and a wedding cake. *Sniper in the Pastry: A Dirk Striker Action Thriller.*

"Hmm. Has he got a problem, too?"

"Yeah. He's allergic to yeast. Bad. It's got a lot of suspense, what with all the sneezing and itching and white flour floating around in the air all the time. His eyes water so it affects his aim when he has to shoot."

I flipped it over to the back cover. The *Chicago Tribune* said, "Action-packed . . . 629 pages of pure adrenaline." The *New York Times* called it "Riveting . . . a masterpiece of a thriller."

"Pretty impressive," I said. I looked at the last few pages. "Hey, and it's got recipes in the back. I want that one for sure."

Six more paperbacks fanned out next to Dirk Striker. I looked from one to the other but just couldn't decide. "I'll take them. All of them."

Cathy smiled and started ringing those books up quicker than a jackrabbit on hot asphalt. While she did that, I looked through the greeting cards and picked out a few. You can never have enough get well or sympathy cards in the house.

Meanwhile, I noticed Jane's face scrunched up funny, looking at a particular book on the shelf. She reached out slowly, like she was afraid of it or thought it would electrocute her or something. She touched it, kept her hand on it a while, and then finally pulled the book out.

"You find some?" I said. When she raised her head to look at me, her expression changed.

"I think so," she said, all smiles. "Yes."

She didn't fool me. She was doing the same thing she did outside before, acting like everything was all right when it wasn't. She proved I was right with the very next thing she did. She took two other books off the shelves without even looking at their titles. One was up high, and the other she had to stoop to get off the bottom shelf. She slung them in her arm, still not looking at what she picked out, and met me at the counter.

I didn't say anything. I played along, figuring I'd eventually be let in on whatever the deal was. Meanwhile, she wanted to hurry on and run some errands so she could get home to the sticks and go bond with the forest. Again. You'd think she would've had her fill of that by now, after being here for weeks. I believe she was actually getting worse. I had plans of my own that involved bonding, with a pillow and a down comforter while being unconscious. A little nap never hurt anybody, especially me after being mugged at my very own Pig.

five
Jane Has a Confession

Throughout my adventures with Phoebe that morning, my mind kept returning to the footprint and the blood in the woods. My stomach knotted each time. The forest's well-being is the most important thing in my life. I'm obsessed with it. Now I had to think of the next logical action to deal with my uninvited guest.

After leaving the bookstore, Phoebe and I returned to her house. I didn't stay. I had other stops to make before going home. All the while, as I drove from one to another, I found myself giving quick glances to the passenger seat. On it sat the bag that contained the three books I had bought. They were a problem. Or rather, part of a larger problem.

Not for the first time in recent weeks, I feared my usually logical mind was going soft, perhaps influenced too much by the unique qualities of either Tullulah or the forest or both. I don't mean the beauty of the place or other physical attributes. I'm talking about another aspect, one that became apparent the first time I visited the area some years ago, one that is a bit hard to believe.

A peculiar talent I had as a child, you see, has come back to me here. I experience it nowhere else, only when I am near Tullulah and its woods. They possess a certain magic, I can think of no better word to explain, that grants me an odd ability. I see, and sometimes hear, people who are not there. That is, they are there. I see them. It's only that no one else does.

It happened that day as Phoebe and I walked along the square together toward the bookstore. We came upon a familiar sight, one seen the world round in every community. Old men sat upon benches at the hub of the town's activity that, at that time of day, was in front of the square's barbershop.

The men filled two benches that looked like church pews under the shop's awnings. All wore overalls. All had rough weathered skin from a lifetime of outdoor work. Most sipped from mugs of steaming coffee while they listened to their friends' various opinions on the day's coming weather. They nodded jovially as we approached, though Phoebe paid them no mind.

A man who must have been in his eighties leaned forward from his seat on an outstretched cane and said, "Excuse me, ma'am, aren't you Mrs. Thistle? The lady who bought the Hardwick place?"

"I am indeed. Jane Thistle. How do you do," I said.

Each man introduced himself as I walked by, all quite friendly. Most remarked on my British accent, though it is hardly noticeable as such anymore, I am told, after over forty years of living with an American husband. Phoebe fidgeted impatiently, so I moved more quickly down the line. I enjoyed a few pleasantries with the seventh gentleman and turned to shake hands with the eighth. It was only when I reached out my hand that I realized there was something different about him.

He shimmered. One moment he looked as real as could be, and the next his entire figure wavered a bit, like a television image distorted and blinking off for a half-instant, then back on again.

Silence fell over the men on the benches until the seventh man spoke. "We lost one. Recently. Gilbert Entrikin." Down the line, the older man with the cane said, "We've been leaving his regular seat there open. In case the old codger ever wants to haunt us."

Laughter erupted and broke the solemn mood. Mr. Entrikin, the one I could see but apparently wasn't there or, I should say, wasn't alive, looked more amused than them all. He held his belly as he shook.

A low chuckle came from deep inside him and grew to full-throated laughter. His eyes squinted shut and his cheeks looked as rosy as if he were in perfect health. I suppose he was, now that he no longer had an earthly body with its aches and ailments to bother him.

I couldn't help myself. His laughter was contagious. I grinned and laughed along with the eight of them. Until I caught sight of Phoebe.

She looked at me as if I were daft. Her expression changed to concern. With a gentle tug, she pulled me away toward the bookstore. As I said my good-byes, I trotted along to keep up with her but turned when one of the old men called to me.

"Wait," Mr. Entrikin said. "Somebody's got a message for you." He shimmered, leaned his head to the side as if straining to hear. "He says to get the blue ones." He shrugged his shoulders and looked puzzled.

"Who? Blue what?" A glance at Phoebe told me I should say no more.

He shrugged again. "It's Cal, I think. Not sure. I'm still new at this." Mr. Entrikin suddenly gave me a wide smile and a hearty laugh. He waved before turning his attention back to his friends' conversation.

Phoebe stared. I remember wondering at that moment how I would explain this time.

We carried on into the store, and it was there I understood Mr. Entrikin's message. While I browsed through the nonfiction section, Phoebe stood at the counter with the bookshop's owner. A few volumes interested me enough to take them down and leaf through them. I continued along, looking for nothing in particular. When I turned a corner, I stopped short. I couldn't believe my eyes. I immediately knew I would be buying precisely three books, all with a most obvious and extraordinary quality.

They glowed. The books emitted some sort of energy, mild though it was, in the form of color. A two- or three-inch thick blue translucence wrapped each of the books and pulsed, something like a force field in a science-fiction movie.

In my short time in Tullulah, such occurrences have happened with more frequency. I'm not sure if it is the town, the forest, or my house that causes this. I only know that the longer I live here, the more these abilities increase.

When I was a child, I often talked to people while I was out playing in the fields around my grandparents' farm in Wales. This worried my grandparents as it became clear that the people I encountered and described to them were former neighbors, all long dead.

The problem disappeared when I grew older. However, it came back to me upon my arrival in Tullulah. As time has passed, this new phenomenon of seeing auras seems to have added itself to my repertoire. At least, I suppose they are proper auras. Being an amateur, I'm not certain it is the same type of color that New Age aficionados see around people and objects. I only know that I see something there.

I've learned from other experiences that those things

I see in colors have some importance to whatever my present situation might be. Usually, a small thing. I've come to think of it as a phenomenon somewhere between instinct and premonition, an extension of my thoughts that somehow manifests in color. At least, that's my present theory. Who knows what might lie ahead as I spend more time in this place?

It began with seeing what I believe are ghosts nearby when I first moved here. As time has passed, what I see has become clearer and, with this peculiarity, more colorful.

Around the house, I sometimes see spots of various colors. At first, I found I couldn't see them except in special photographs, ones taken by Riley Gardner, a young man in the area who fancies himself a ghost hunter. Later, I could see them with the help of a pair of Russian-made infrared binoculars from my former part-time work. Since then, somehow, my eyesight gradually adjusted to see several locations within the house, at varying times and without aid, where colored pockets of air hung around areas of, perhaps, supernatural importance.

As to my new books, they were behaving properly inside their bag in the car. No glowing blue spilling out. I turned left and parked in the post office's lot. Short gusts of strong wind sent leaves flying past and pushed me along toward the doors for my final errand.

My mailbox was quite full. I subscribe to various archaeological, science, and history journals, and noted happily that several had come that day. I would have plenty to read by candlelight if the power went out.

The wind whipped around me as I returned to my car. I could see darker clouds at the edge of town coming this way. To the east, blue skies and sunshine prevailed but not for long.

I worried about Phoebe. She doesn't have a basement. Mine is large and quite comfortable. I decided to make a last stop at her house, to see if she wanted to stay with me, in case a tornado did come into the area.

six

Phoebe Has a Visitor

When I got home from the bookstore and Jane left to run her errands, I thought I'd be ready for a nap. Hah. I was so wired up I couldn't sit still. I had to get out and do something, so I visited the rest home even though I'd already been once earlier in the week. Also, a couple of people from my congregation were in the county hospital, so I stopped there to see about them.

By the time I got back home, I was plumb wore out. A shower and comfortable clothes made me feel better. A movie I wanted to watch was about to come on, so I flipped on the TV, hoping the storm would hold off until the show ended.

Now that I am armed, I watch more shooting movies. I relaxed on the couch with Sylvester Stallone and we both went into a hot, dripping wet jungle with nothing but our will to survive. I took out my CZ 75, a hefty black handgun made by the fine people of the Czech Republic, and held it out toward the TV. Anytime I watch a good movie with some shooting in it, I like to grab the CZ, unloaded of course, and practice aiming like they do in the movie.

Usually I get this one because my other gun is bigger and mounted on the wall. It's hard to get it down and back up again without climbing in a chair. Besides, I prefer being able to look up at it when things get rough in the movie, you know, like when the bad guys get entirely too ugly with innocent people, or they're fixing to get ugly and the scary music is playing. Times like that, it's a comfort to have one gun in your hands and one looking over you. It's a security thing.

However, with this particular movie, I probably would have to get the big gun down to hold when Sly started taking care of business with his AK-47. That's what my rifle is. Well, it almost is. Mine is an AK-46 and a half, the ladies' model. It's smaller overall with smaller handgrips and magazines. I got it airbrushed in a pretty apricot color and had its name, Smokahontas, written on it with smoke coming off the end. It matches my living room, not just the colors but also with the Native American décor. I'm pretty white, but like most people in and around Tullulah, I have a little bit of Indian blood. I haven't actually looked it up or anything. Some things you just know.

I'm still learning how to shoot my guns. Jane gives me lessons every now and then at her shooting range. We pick off cans and bottles set up on rocks out by the bluff on her place.

These days, a lady has to find comfort where she can get it, especially when murderers and rapists are running wild all over the country. Everywhere except here, I guess. Tullulah, Alabama, has got to be the dullest spot on earth. But that's a good thing. It's so dull, none of those mobsters would ever come here. And if they did, they wouldn't last a minute. They'd take one look, see there's no sushi or Italian restaurants unless you count the Pizza Hut, and there's no beer or liquor stores for miles and miles, so we don't have any bars. They'd go around the town square once and keep on going out of town.

I don't think they'd like the women here, either, since mobsters seem to favor the hubba-hubba kind. Tullulah's only got two choices, sweet homemakers and cranky spinsters, and neither one of those talk nasty or let their boobs hang out of their clothes like doll-face arm-candy women do.

So bad guys have no reason to come here. Which is fine. It makes for a peaceful life, and I am thankful to be so blessed as to have lived here all my years. It also makes for stone-cold boring, though, so I have to make up for it with my action hero movies.

I'll tell you which new action heroes I like, all those young hunky Asian guys in the fancy new kung fu movies. I like how they fly through the air. That's what I'd like to do, fly in slow motion with my legs stretched way out in front of me, my hands cocked and ready to deliver about a hundred karate chops sped up so fast it only takes a second or two. I'd be through with the chopping before I could finish saying, *"Hi-yah!"*

The doorbell rang right when Sylvester Stallone was about to smack the living daylights out of a perp. I stuffed the CZ under the sofa cushion while I waited for Sly to deliver his line. The doorbell rang again.

"Phoebe?"

"Oh, for heaven's sakes." It was my youngest sister. "Keep your drawers on, Corene. I'm old and it takes me longer to get my joints working than it used to." I took my time and kept watching Sly. "You got that right, son," I said to him. "You show those bad guys who the boss man is."

Corene had her fist reared back to knock again when I opened the door. "Oh, there you are," she said. "I was afraid you'd fallen down and broken your hip or something."

I'm sorry, I told you a lie a while ago. There is one other kind of woman in Tullulah, but only three times a year, which is when a tall, skinny, redheaded, Camel-smoking, whiskey-drinking, man-chasing hussy, even if she is my sister, comes to call. The rest of the time, the Lord only knows where she's at or who she's leading around by the nose ring.

I love my sister. Of course I do. That's why I said, "Corene, what a surprise," instead of "Corene, what kind of a crazy mess have you got mixed up in this time that involves me giving you money?"

"It's good to see you," she said while she gave me a hug.

Something was up. She had on her Liz Taylor perfume so I was automatically put on alert. "You going out on a date?"

"I'm going on a trip!" She squealed it and hopped up and down a couple of times like a six-year-old.

Did I mention she is fifty-three? Well, she is. "What's that you got in your bag?" I said.

"It's a present—for you!" She set the bag on the floor and unzipped the top. A ball of fur with a face in the middle popped up.

"No," I said, "that's not a present for me. I know it's not a present for me because you know how I hate dogs. You know I've always hated dogs, since we were children, and that's why I don't have one now and don't plan on ever having one."

"But this one's special. Look how cute it is." She lifted it out of the bag and kissed that nasty thing on top of its head.

I took a step backward and said, "They're unclean. It's in the Bible."

"Oh, hush that, you old stick in the mud. It's adorable."

The fur face shook its head back and forth real fast. It didn't help. Its hair still flopped down over its eyes.

"It's a mess," I said. "Goodness, all that hair. I can hardly tell which end I'm looking at."

A car horn honked outside. I went to the window

and drew back the sheer. A yellow convertible Cadillac sat in the drive. A skinny dude wearing a cowboy hat was behind the wheel. He waved. I smiled and waved back. I let the sheer fall back into place and crossed my arms. "So you're going on a trip. And you don't want to take your dog so you tell me he's a present? You beat all, Corene."

"He's not mine, exactly. I have been keeping him the last couple of weeks but I had to. My next-door neighbor, Miss Maggie, croaked and so somebody had to feed the poor thing. But now, something has come up."

"So I see. But I can't help you this time. Anything else I'd do, but not this. I can't have a dirty whatever kind of dog that is in my house."

"Lhasa Apso."

"Is that cowboy teaching you Spanish?"

"It's the name of the dog breed. They're very lovable and practically no trouble at all."

I closed my eyes, shook my head real slow from side to side, while I motioned toward the door.

Corene huffed and started whining like she always does. "For goodness sake, Phoebe. It's such a sweet little thing. Look, it wants to give you a kiss."

The blamed furry munchkin stretched its dirty little neck out toward me and started licking its mouth and nose.

"Get that nasty thing away from me, Corene, before it slobbers boogers all over me. I am not taking that dog. Forget it."

She jerked the little varmint back just as the car horn tooted outside. "All right then, missy," she said. "If that's the way you feel."

"It is."

"And all I was doing was trying to brighten your life up in your old age when you ain't got nobody to share it with." The horn honked again. "And I've got to run, so I'll just take little Rowdy with me and say la-di-da to you."

"No need to get all hissy. I've always taken care of you and done whatever you asked but a dog in my house is going too far. You can drop it off at the vet's on your way out of town. They board animals, I hear."

"Huh. I may just do that."

"Yeah, and they can give it a good bath and a haircut while it's there."

Corene's face relaxed. I reckoned she thought that was a good idea and would be two less things she'd have to do herself for the mutt. She smiled. "Phoebe. Darling." Her orange lipstick was creeping up the vertical lines over her top lip. "I understand. Really, I do. And I appreciate the tip about the vet. Thank you. That will solve my problem. I knew I could come to you for help. Just like always."

It was true. All my life I'd looked after her, ever since she was a baby and all the way through four (so far) divorces.

"Not mad at me?" she said with a little hurt look in her eyes. "All I'm doing is going to have a little fun, that's all."

"Fine. Whatever. Knock yourself out. Now, do you want to invite your boyfriend in for me to meet him? I've got coconut cake or some pot roast, if y'all want to eat before you leave town."

"I appreciate that, but we need to get going to beat the storm. Can I use the little girls' room before we head out on the road?" She turned before I could answer. As she walked, she stuffed the mutt back in the quilted carrier. Its head popped out of the top again and shook. I pictured dirt and fleas and rabies with a hundred legs apiece flicking out and spreading all over my rugs and furniture.

As much as Corene gets on my nerves, it was good to see her and see her happy. Still, I sure would be glad for her to be gone. I had already missed a good fight scene in my movie. Plus, Jane had asked me to go out trekking through the woods the next morning with her. I wanted to get my supplies together and needed to think about what I'd need to fight off the elements.

Corene came out of the bathroom and said a quick 'bye as she crossed through the living room to the front door. I gave her a side hug, the hairball's carrier on her other hip, and said, "You be careful."

"I will," she said. "We won't be gone long, but if you need something, you've got my number."

Truer words were never spoken. "I sure do."

She went through the screen door and ran down the stone walkway to the Cadillac convertible. I heard it shift gears as she opened the passenger door.

The Caddy's tires thunked over the end of the drive

and they were gone in a flash. I breathed a sigh of relief. Or of something. You'd think I'd be used to her wild shenanigans by now.

I walked inside, closed the door and locked it, ready for some peace and quiet. I don't like people ruining my serene lifestyle with surprise visits and mangy mutts and smelling the place up with Liz Taylor and such. Oh, well. Corene would be all right. She always was.

A commercial was on, so I headed to the kitchen. Some coffee and a piece of pie would hit the spot. When I went through the hallway, I noticed Corene had shut the bathroom door but left the light on inside. Sometimes I wonder if that girl has got a brain in her head. I opened the door, reached in and cut the switch off without really looking in, and went on toward the kitchen.

I took two steps and stopped dead in my tracks before putting my rear suspension in reverse. I cut the light back on. And stared at the floor. Two beady black eyes stared back.

"Why, you dirty dog, you."

The mutt whimpered.

"Not you. That no-account sister of mine. Oooh, when I get my hands on her . . ."

Rowdy looked a lot smaller out of the carrier. He was about as big as a rat. He tippy-toed on the bathroom tile. His whole little body shimmied across the floor toward me. I couldn't tell if he was scared to death or doing the Hully Gully.

"If I was you," I said, "I'd be tickled pink to be shed of Corene."

He whimpered again. His eyes went all wet and gooey.

"Oh, for goodness sake, don't you start with that mushy stuff. What in the world am I going to do with you?"

He inched closer, put his front paws up on my legs. His silly tail wagged and all that long hair on it waved back and forth like a hairy flag on a stick.

"If you're going to touch me, you've got to have a bath first. And son, I've got to be honest with you. That hairdo has got to go."

I did the best I could. I wore my Playtex cleaning gloves that go up to the elbows. All I had was regular shampoo, so I used it on Rowdy and hoped for the best. He did look cleaner. He even looked grateful. He wouldn't have felt that way if he could've seen his hair. It was a sight. I brushed it and tried to get the knots out. If he stayed long, I'd have to get some crème rinse for the tangles.

Outside, the heat was a killer. You can't imagine the humidity unless you've lived in a place like Tullulah where there are more trees than are good for a person. They make it sticky around here. I'd had all the miserable summer weather I wanted and was good and ready for a break. Shoot, it was already October and close to Halloween, and high time for some cool air.

The storm on the way made it even hotter. On the news, they said a few tornados touched down in Mississippi. The scary yellow line on the weatherman's screen was headed this way.

I knew they were coming, even before I turned on the TV. The sky had that weird green look and hard gusts of wind blew stuff all over the streets. When I went outside, it was hard to breathe. The coming storm was already sucking the air out of the air, if you know what I mean.

You might wonder what in the world a grown, intelligent woman like me was doing out in the yard anyway when there's fixing to be a tornado. Yeah, that's right, I was out there so that orphan rug rat could do his business. Let me tell you, he took his sweet time about it. He had to go sniff everything out there first, even with the wind whipping his ears and long red and white hair all over the place. Picky, that's what he is, and wasn't worried a bit that I might get swooped up in the sky or struck by lightning.

"Look here, Rowdy. Get down to it or the next thing you know, you might be pooping in Kansas with Toto."

He seemed to get my gist. I turned toward the door, acting like I didn't care if he followed me or not. By the time I got the screen door open, there he was coming up the steps.

"After you," I said. He swept by me like the king of England and went straight to the bowl of water I'd set out. "Hey. Watch it. Don't you drink too much of that, you hear?"

seven
Jane Braves the Storm

*L*arge raindrops splatted on my windshield as I drove from the town square to Phoebe's house. A broken branch fell across the glass as I steered into her driveway, the leaves completely obscuring my view for a few moments. Thank goodness I was off the street and could brake quickly without causing an accident. A strong gust of wind rocked the car back and forth. With an even stronger surge, the wind whistled and picked the branch up and hurled it across Phoebe's front yard.

Leaves and debris weren't the only things flying through the air. As I looked forward through the windshield, I saw one of Phoebe's windows at the side of her house being raised up in spite of the storm. A bare white arm emerged. It cocked and threw a square object with great force into the wet grass, then retreated inside to close the window once more.

I felt under the passenger seat for the folding umbrella I kept there. "Oh, drat." I muttered at my foolishness. The week before, I'd put it in the trunk along with a few other stray items when I vacuumed the seats and floorboards. I had forgotten to return it to its usual place. No matter. In this storm, it would probably only fold inside-out the instant I stepped out of the car. Instead, I emptied the contents of a plastic shopping bag, took my keys from the ignition, covered my head as best I could with the bag, and ran for it.

I spared a glance in the direction of the object Phoebe had tossed out the window. It was a paperback book. To my surprise, I noticed it had joined two others in what now constituted a small pile. The latest addition had landed on top in comparatively pristine condition to the others that were waterlogged and dirty, as if they had been in their present position some time. I think perhaps one of them had also been torn. It looked as if it had been ripped in two. I assumed Phoebe did not share the bookstore owner's enthusiasm for her recent purchases.

Phoebe had already opened her door when I reached her screened-in porch. "Thank you, dear."

"What are you still doing out in this mess?"

"I shopped a bit more than I intended." My clothes dripped on the green Astroturf mat. I held the plastic bag close to me so it wouldn't drip on the floor.

"You don't have to stand there like that, Jane. This porch is used to rain. Come on in here before we get blown away." I did as she asked, though I didn't intend to stay. I slipped off my shoes and set them by the door just inside her living room.

"Phoebe, I only stopped to see if you wanted to come home with me to wait out the storm. I heard tornado warnings had been issued."

"Yeah, we get a lot of those this time of year. We don't usually get actual tornados, though. They like to skip over Tullulah. But I sure wouldn't want to be in the valley in a trailer right now." She spoke as she walked away from me and into the hallway that led to her kitchen. "Let's go get you a towel."

"Really, I shouldn't stay. Why not come along with me? My basement is quite comfortable. We'd be safe there."

"Aw, relax. Nothing's going to touch down. Why don't you just stay here with me until it passes?" She paused at the bathroom door and turned to me. "No sense in getting back out in that mess, Jane. You don't know what might come flying through the air or down the road at you."

"You're right, but I need to get to the house. I'm worried about Homer. He has been out all afternoon and I want to get him inside."

"You want another one to take with you?"

"Another what?"

In answer, she merely pointed downward toward the interior of the bathroom. "Another mutt to keep Homer company."

I stepped closer and peered inside. There on the white tile floor sat a small dog. "Oh, my. Hello, dear." It returned my gaze and gave a single yap. "Phoebe, I had the impression you didn't particularly care for dogs."

"I don't."

"And that you said you'd never allow one in your house."

"I did. My flighty sister dumped this fleabag on me."

The little dog was adorable, even in its present state. He reminded me of another dog, though I couldn't remember where I had known one like him. Someone close, though I was too scatterbrained at the moment to think. The dog's hair, normally long, silky, and flat against its body I presumed, now stood on end, thick and fluffed out. It looked as if it had been styled into a red-and-white Afro. I presumed Phoebe had just given it a bath from the citrus and lavender scents that hung in the air.

"It's certainly clean," I said.

"I'll give him this, he didn't mind taking a bath a bit. Though I'm afraid I might have put too much styling gel in his hair. All I had was a thickening formula."

Loud sheets of rain lashed the roof. "Phoebe, please. Do come home with me. You and . . . em . . ."

"Rowdy."

I arched an eyebrow. "You and Rowdy would be most welcome."

She shook her head. "We're fine. But if you intend to get home, you better go on. It's looking bad out there."

"Yes. All right. I'll call you a little later tonight, okay? If the phones work."

"I'll be here."

Once again braving the rain with my plastic grocery bag as umbrella, I hopped in my car and closed the door with relief. The rain beat steadily on my way home, pounding the car and the streets until I reached the outskirts of Tullulah. Then the wipers that had worked so feverishly to keep the windshield clear were suddenly scraping across almost dry glass as I passed through spots where no rain fell at all.

The road to my house cut through a flat area with fields on the left and a marshy bird sanctuary to the right. Its waters drew close and almost as high as the road. Ahead, black clouds loomed over the forest in disturbing, striated patterns that moved more swiftly across my view than any I had ever witnessed. Just as disturbing as their color and speed was a sudden realization. They traveled north to south, when normally they should be going west to east. Their fast churning terrified me.

Though I traveled in a rainless pocket at the moment, I could see a wide gray swath of dark clouds in the distance, striped with white and silver from cloud to horizon that looked as if it now stormed beyond my property. Perhaps if it stayed there a little longer, I'd get inside the house without getting drenched after all. Now if only Homer was near enough to hear me when I drove up, all would be well.

The column of rain and the foreboding striations of fast-moving clouds mesmerized me as I drove toward them. Deep darkness lurked behind the silvery sheets of rain. Between watching them and trying to keep my eyes on the road, I almost missed an even more unusual sight off to my left.

I'd passed the edge of the marshes and now drove up through a series of small hillocks. They were bright, almost emerald green in the oddly green-tinged air, due to shafts of the burnished late-afternoon sunlight peeking through on my far right. Out of the corner of my eye, I caught a glimpse of something moving. I turned to see what it was, and had to do a quick double take to be sure my eyes weren't playing tricks on me.

It was a man, walking in a field beside the county road. The rain flattened his dark shoulder-length hair. Water dripped off the long tunic he wore and soaked his brown boots. He carried something on his back, a cylindrical bag of some kind. When he turned, his eyes dazzled me, for they were young, yet deep, as if an old soul peered out of them.

I braked and stopped to offer him a ride. Just as I motioned through the window, a crash of thunder deafened me and a brilliant light split the sky. A second crash, louder and more resonant, followed immediately with another blinding flash of light. I looked up and to the left. Both lightning strikes still etched jagged lines of light in the dark as I watched. They and numerous other bolts struck from a whirling mass of black-gray clouds down to the top of the bluff, the highest point on my land. Their white and purple flashes danced on a large outcrop of rock, electrifying the surrounding trees.

The clouds moved swiftly forward, as what sounded like a long, slow ripping of the very sky tore at my ears and sent a chill of fear through me. The ripping ended suddenly in a crash, a low bass boom like a ship's cannon fire. It echoed down into the valley and rolled outward in a wave that made my bones shiver.

I brought myself up quick. I had forgotten the man. He had not come to get in the car. I looked out all the windows but didn't see him. Rain pouring down the glass made it difficult to be sure. I braced myself and opened the door, ready to be soaked.

He was not in the field where I'd last seen him. I ran toward the back of the car, looked down the road behind me, then around the other side, scanning fields there and back to the driver's door. I was completely alone. The man had disappeared.

eight
Phoebe and Rowdy
Tough it Out

I had to fight the screen door a little bit to get it closed against the gusts of wind that were coming harder now. This was going to be a big one. Rowdy sat on the floor, watching my every move, like I was his entertainment for the evening.

"For my next number, I believe I'll go get some candles and matches so we won't be sitting in the dark."

Rowdy yapped and wiggled his tail. Sarcasm didn't seem to work on him. He came over and followed right at my heels. There was a flashlight in the same drawer as the candles so I grabbed that, too. I don't have a basement or we'd have gone down in it.

I unplugged all the appliances and lamps all over the house. When I came through the living room again, I grabbed up my craft basket and carried it to the dining room where I'd set the candlesticks. That was the middle of the house. I figured if a tornado came, the two of us could run to the bathroom and jump in the tub. I snapped my fingers.

"That tub is still wet from your bath. Let me go wipe it out good." He trotted along with me again, watched me grab towels off the rack and rub down the tub. I took some clean towels out of the linen closet and spread them out inside. "We might as well be comfortable, huh?" He looked at me like he approved.

A big clap of thunder boomed right over the house. Rowdy yelped and lunged for me. He nearly knocked me over, even though he couldn't weigh more than five pounds.

"It's okay, it's okay." He shook like a leaf in my arms and started whining. "Look here, shhhh, we're okay." He whimpered as more rumbles followed the big one. His little wet nose snuggled up under my chin and he started kissing me.

"Honey, darling," I said trying to calm him down. I couldn't believe I said that. My mouth moved and I heard the words, but it was like somebody else took over my body. "Okay, now, here's the thing, just so you understand. You're gonna have to stop that licking stuff. I can't stand it. But you're not too bad for a little fur ball, and if you can stop kissing me, I can put up with you, okay?" I sat him down on the floor. "For a little while. Just until Corene comes back off her whirlwind romance trip. So don't push it." I went into the kitchen and looked around to see if I'd forgotten anything. Through the window over the sink, I saw a mimosa branch bobbing up and down, up and down.

I hated to see Jane drive off in that storm. She would have been perfectly safe here in my house. I've ridden out many a tornado in my lifetime. You get used to it. Like I told her, the actual tornado funnels never touch down up here on the mountain. They like to skip over and jump down into the valley to follow the river. I felt sorry for anybody down there. They're the ones who get most of the damage.

I heard the patter of little toenails coming toward me and looked down.

"You still here?"

He sat, polite as he could be, like a kid who had been taught to mind its manners, though I knew my wild sister wouldn't have had anything to do with that. The old lady who croaked trained him right. Even as much as I despise dogs, I felt a little sorry for this one. It wasn't his fault that he got tangled up with Corene. He just got unlucky and had no choice, kind of like me being her sister and all. I could relate.

"Let's get a comb going on that hair," I said. It had relaxed some and was laying down flatter, more horizontal now instead of vertical like it was doing earlier. I hoped Corene would come back from her love trip before I had to give Rowdy another bath. Otherwise, I would have to buy some special combs and brushes. Or maybe just doggie hair-cutting scissors. He might look good in a burr.

That's when I remembered that a lady I see at the

Beauty Barn told me she was a dog clipper and had a new business down on the town square. If worse came to worst, I could always drop the little mutt off there. No sense in buying stuff I wouldn't ever need again.

That thunder was something else, let me tell you. It rumbled and raged like the end of time. The munchkin shook all over just about the whole night, even after I wrapped him up in a nice warm towel I heated up in the microwave. I held him up close to me like a baby but he still nearly shook his little self to death. I'll say this, I didn't see one flea on him or any scabby places where he had been scratching. It didn't look like he had any health problems now that he was clean. He was just a squirt. Not even hardly big enough to be called a dog.

I had just set the comb down when all of a sudden, *boom*. The electricity went out, like I figured it would. I reached over to the left real slow and clicked on my flashlight. The squirt shook.

"Don't worry. It's nothing," I told him. "In ancient times, they didn't have any lights at all, and lived in the dark. That's why they named it the Dark Ages. They survived, and we'll survive. We don't need a TV or an oven. For now."

I wished I hadn't said that. Thinking about the oven made me hungry. Rowdy whimpered a little bit and nudged his cold nose against my face and then licked me. "Look here. What did we decide about that already? Now you just quit that right now," I said, though, to tell the truth, it wasn't so bad and actually kind of sweet, like he was trying to make me feel better.

"Hey, I've got an idea. You hungry?"

He wouldn't have been able to hear me if he hadn't been so close to my mouth because outside that rain was flat beating the roof. The whole inside of the house lit up from the lightning flashing outside, on and off, one right after another like you see in war movies when the soldiers are down in the trenches waiting for the bombs to stop.

I'm into war movies. I used to just like action adventure types, like the Stallone I watched this afternoon. But here lately, I have been getting into war. For two reasons. One, because I bought my guns and because Jane and I got into a somewhat war situation ourselves not too long ago. So my mentality has flipped. Two, they've started showing a new program on TV where this retired sergeant, real life I'm talking about, not an actor, gets on there and talks about military stuff. My favorite part is when he tests out different guns and other weapons like bows and arrows, and he uses watermelons for targets. What a great idea. The man is a genius. Next summer when the watermelons come in, I fully intend to buy up a truckload and do some target practice.

What an inspiration Jane has been to me. I feel like I'm a new person, now that I'm armed. It has opened my eyes. It's a little weird. She has enough guns in her house to arm the military of a small nation, but does she care? Not really. She doesn't give a flip about those guns. Her husband collected them all through his life and, from the looks of them, never sold or traded a one. I know for a fact that Jane has two armoires, nice antique ones, with fancy military rifles stuffed like sardines in there, all styles, serious rifles, and two antique trunks stacked full of handguns. I've seen them. No telling what else she has hidden in that big house, which has two floors plus a full basement and a full attic.

Just the other day, I was over there after Jane and I had been shopping. She opened her closet door to put the new shoes she'd bought inside. When she pushed her hanging clothes out of the way, I saw three huge metal cases stacked on top of one another. These things were heavy duty, like something you'd transport an atomic bomb or plutonium in, only bigger. She saw me looking.

"Those are some mighty fine hat boxes you've got in there," I said.

She laughed. "Not hats. More of the Colonel's acquisitions for his collection, I'm afraid."

She closed the door and changed the subject. I didn't ask. I didn't have to. The sides had military-looking stencils that told what was in them. I made a mental note to look up "MP5" and "vz.61 Škorpion," and when I did that night, I found out what they were. Submachine guns.

The first box looked like it was U.S. military. The second one had the words "Česká Zbrojovka," which

I recognized because they are also on my CZ 75 handgun.

The third box was different. First of all, it looked military but the writing wasn't in English. Squiggly slanted foreign lettering covered the side. Even though I couldn't read that, I did recognize two stenciled words in English. "Israel" and "Uzi." My jaw like to hit the floor. Didn't need to look up either one of those. I'm as pro-Israel as you can get without being an actual Israelite. Don't I wish. Nothing could have impressed me more.

Jane is my hero, even if she doesn't ever go to church. She can't help it. She was raised Church of England over yonder, and I don't think they believe in attending services, so it's not her fault.

I'm thankful we don't have much call for self-defense here. But with the TV spreading sick minds nationwide, it's no wonder things just keep getting worse everywhere. I hope it never spills over into Tullulah. We're too small of a town and already have our quota of crazy people. If any nasty psycho city fool strolls into town and starts cussing on the street, buddy, I am there. I'd take Smokahontas down off the wall and the two of us would go have a little talk with him on his way out of Dodge. Son, I am sitting on ready.

Thinking about shooting and fighting made me even hungrier. I walked in the dark to the kitchen, holding Rowdy in one arm and aiming the flashlight beam out in front of us with the other. There was cold chicken in the refrigerator, leftovers that I'd cubed to put in salads. I looked at Rowdy and said, "Who knows how long the power will be out. We better not let this chicken go bad."

nine
Jane Makes it Home

*A*t my house, the car's headlights moved across my front lawn and porch in an arc, highlighting leaves and other debris that flew past in the weird, stormy green atmosphere. With my plastic shopping bags looped around my wrists, I ran for the shelter of my porch.

I'd no more touched the first step before the skies emptied and rain fell down even harder as if from great vats. To my relief, Homer shot past me, up the steps to the door. In his eyes, I could see that the thunder boom terrified him but, courageous boy that he was, he stood his ground at the screen, then shook himself from his head all the way down to the tip of his tail, spraying water in all directions. As soon as I opened the door, I dropped the bags. The light switch didn't work. The electricity was out.

I grabbed several towels from the linen closet. I wiped one across my face and eyes and rubbed it quickly across my head. "All right, then," I said as I reached into a drawer for a flashlight. "Into the basement with you." I stuck the flashlight in my pocket, the towels under my arm, and found candles and matches. We hurried down the basement steps as the thunder seemed to roll straight across the shingles of the roof.

Once the candles were lit, I dried Homer off as best I could and told him to stay. I returned upstairs to get his water and food bowl then made another trip to pick up something to read. I found the bag that contained my book purchases and the day's mail. The windows rattled furiously around me in the front room. I returned quickly through the darkened hallway and kitchen and to the den at the back of the house.

Outside of the bay window, I could see all had turned gray in the torrent. The flowering bushes that border my rose beds whipped violently about in the wind. So much rain fell at such speed that it sounded as if a train roared past. Lightning flashed through the large multipaned window and illuminated an old cardboard box I'd brought out and put on the floor. I walked to it, hesitated, and gave in with a sigh, carrying it downstairs.

Homer explored the basement, checking the perimeter with a cursory first look to be sure nothing dangerous lurked in the shadows. His second sweep was a closer inspection of all box corners, the hot water heater, and the other various cast-off articles of my previous life. Since moving, I'd found no use for them, though I was hesitant to get rid of the past so completely just yet.

I set the cardboard box next to the lit candles. I'd placed them on the desk my late husband, the Colonel, had used in his office for many years. From beside it, I pulled an old but not quite antique end table from out of the shadows by the basement wall to the couch.

On the far side of the room, constant hard sprays of rain buffeted the outside door and its glass panes. Steps led down to it from the backyard. At the bottom of the steps, a drain in the concrete kept the area just outside the door from flooding, thank goodness. I aimed the flashlight beam toward the door to be sure no water came inside underneath it.

A loud crack of thunder splintered the relative quiet. Homer bolted for a corner to hide under a dinette table. As the rumble subsided, his bravery returned. He slid out and trotted quickly to my side.

"There, there, dear. Thunder scares me as well. But we're all right. Here, come sit with me a while." I threw an old blanket over the sofa for him. I sat down and patted the cushion beside me, arranging a chenille throw over my knees. Homer obliged and jumped up. More thunder boomed, like distant tanks rolling and crashing into one another.

Directly in front of me across the room sat the box with what felt like an expectant attitude. Silly. I stared. Though it and the desk were in the dark, I saw it clearly. It didn't dance or wink or send sparkles in the air like something from a Disney movie in order to draw my attention, though none of those things would have surprised me. I've witnessed more bizarre occurrences than that in this house. Still, it wasn't ordinary. Just as the new books I bought that day possessed an unusual quality, so did this bent and crumpled cardboard box that sported a tomato sauce logo on the side.

It glowed in the shadows with a slightly gold aura, not a metallic one but more of a creamy golden color. I brought it to the couch. Homer hopped down for a thorough sniff around the edges of the box. His old master had inscribed it with "#2" in bold red marker. I wondered what memories the box and its smells brought back to Homer. Once satisfied, he jumped up on the couch to settle next to me again.

The #2 box is one of many I inherited from Cal Prewitt. I keep them stacked in an extra room. No furniture there, only boxes. They contain information about Cal's land in the form of notebooks and scribblings on many loose papers compiled throughout his life.

Each box contains notes on one important aspect of the forest, according to Cal, all things I should know about and could find by using the crude maps he drew and included. He numbered each box according to importance. The first one, which I went through not long after my arrival in Tullulah, provided a treasure hunt of sorts, one that led to a more beautiful place than I ever imagined I might find here.

I had hesitated in the subsequent weeks to begin exploration of the next box. For all the joy brought by box #1, events related to it had turned to tragedy. I consoled myself with my daily walks since then, immersing myself in the forest and its everyday wonders. Now, as those bad memories began to fade a bit and life returned to normal, my curiosity about the remaining boxes returned as well.

Cal originally ranked this box as one of lower importance. He changed his mind somewhere along the way, using a black marker that almost obliterated the "#8" underneath. He moved it up to the number two spot before he died, printing with bold red strokes and question marks on the box's side.

It rattled a bit as I moved it. I unfolded the cardboard flaps to peer into the musty interior. On top, a large used mailing envelope contained loose papers and photographs. I set the envelope aside, for below it, I saw a sheet of yellow legal paper covered with Cal's familiar scrawl. I smiled at its loops and trailing letters. How I missed him. As I read the words, they became his slow, scratchy drawl in my mind, spoken as clearly as if he were there with me.

"This in here may be more than I thought it was at first," he began. "Inside are some pictures I want you to look at and a map of how to find the place. Take Homer, he knows the way. I go there quite a bit, to ponder on it. There's some books in here, more on the shelves with general things about Indian writing, but these in here are ones with the closest markings.

"There's rocks and cave walls with old writing on them similar to this all over the woods. So me and Daddy and Granddaddy always figured this was just more of the same. The last few years though, I've realized that may not be so. Not sure. Have a look yourself.

"What I'm thinking is it is the work of some sister tribe to the Cherokee or Creek or maybe one we don't know about—so many different ones came through here since this was good hunting grounds. There's not too much to go on in books I've been able to get ahold of, but you might have better luck. With the trouble we're having now, I've gone and put some brush and limbs around the place to be sure nobody would find it. But the map has got clear directions so you won't have no problems finding it."

The map was next, a crude but clear diagram drawn on the back of a paper grocery sack. In the bottom of the box, the contents that had rattled together were not as interesting as I had hoped. In fact, on first glance, they were rather disappointing. I set the two small objects side by side on the table.

The first was a large arrowhead. I didn't know much about arrowheads, only that there were many types and that they were easily found here in the hills that surround the Tennessee Valley. In this area, numerous tribes shared hunting grounds over the centuries. What little knowledge I had of arrowheads in general made me believe that, no matter how much I researched, little if anything conclusive might ever be known about this specimen, other than a general time period in which it was most likely made or used.

The second object wasn't so ordinary as the previous one. It puzzled me. I had no idea what its use might be, only what it looked like. It was a stick.

When I centered it in the flashlight's beam and turned it this way and that, it became more intriguing. Some sort of cutting device had shaped it. The cutter had used a planing motion to make four flat sides so that it looked something like a squared dowel rod. Each side measured probably an inch wide, with the whole stick about four inches long.

Then I saw something interesting. On two sides, faint markings had been carved that could barely be seen or felt, symbols of some type. Cal's library had several books about native symbology used to mark trails in the forest or to leave as messages. Some are found in artwork in rock carvings. I could use one of his books for comparisons. Perhaps if there were a match or two, I could ascertain the stick's meaning or use.

I ran my finger over the strange symbols. A little shiver went up my spine as I imagined many other hands doing likewise, probably the reason they were worn almost invisible. This was something I could dig into, something to research. The arrowhead, though ordinary looking, might also yield up some information.

I leafed through the dozen or so sheets of loose paper in the used manila envelope. Cal's notes were nearly illegible. Even those I could read were hard to understand. I put them down and turned my attention to the photographs.

"Drat," I said. Homer raised his head. "Sorry, dear. Didn't mean to shout." He blinked his acceptance of my apology. "It's just that these are no better than the trinkets." Homer touched his nose to the photo as if he might make sense of it if only he could get close enough to see it more clearly.

"You see? Cal has gone to great lengths to provide us with pictures of bushes. Ah, here we have dirt. And another nondescript bush. What a lovely close-up of a rock. And here . . ."

I stopped. The next shot showed a rock with markings. At least, I thought they were. The shadows and light in the photo could be fooling my eyes. But why else would he have taken the picture? I glanced through the few remaining photos but none were any better.

"In that case, my dear friend," I said as I lay my hand over Homer's head and scratched, "we shall have to have a look ourselves, eh?" He seemed to smile, his mouth open and a happy look in his eyes, probably thinking of Cal.

I kept reading the jumbled, incoherent notes. In one of the notebooks, Cal said that the arrowhead and the stick were found in an old bowl. This is why he kept them, he said, because their placement seemed to indicate an importance or a relationship he had yet to figure out. Another small thin object had been present at one time but had eroded to nothing more than a rusty ridge at the bottom of the bowl. The bowl itself had broken. Cal had discarded the broken bits. He said the bowl had no special markings as some of his other native keepsakes did. My heart sank. How I wished he had kept the pieces. There might have been something helpful there.

I sighed. Next to having those bits, it would've been nice if any other information could have been passed down as to the exact location of the bowl when it was found. I didn't blame Cal, of course, for putting the objects in the box this way. They probably had been long removed from their original places. Cal and his forebears did the best they could, with no knowledge of how digs worked, of the importance of preserving what they found.

Even so, Cal may have inadvertently left me something useful as to the bowl's original location. In the box, a number of older black-and-white photographs with dates on them as far back as 1955 showed a half-buried object that might be the bowl in question. I couldn't tell in such bad lighting and without my magnifying glass. With any luck, that was why Cal included these particular photos. And, with quite a bit more luck, I would actually be able to find this place if I could decipher Cal's scrawls that passed for a map.

In the photos, it looked to me as if water erosion had caused a furrow to form at the side of the rock overhang that contained carvings. Water must have run down the little gully, then it appeared to have caused a wide circular indention in front of the rock that would have flooded and become a pond whenever it rained. Over many years, the water must have washed the soil and underlying rock away, perhaps six inches or so into the earth, as best I could tell from the picture. That might account for the sudden appearance of the bowl in that spot.

I picked up Cal's letter once again. Bless him. He said he believed I might have a special expertise in these particular objects. Wishful thinking on his part, I'm afraid. It's unlikely I would know anything at all concerning any native subject that Cal himself wouldn't have known much better.

I'd been so involved in these new puzzles, I forgot I was in the basement. The storm had given way to a much lighter pattering of rain against the high windows. I decided to go upstairs for a look.

Homer jumped down from the couch when I gathered the chenille throw and stood. I put it in the box then put the box on my hip, got the flashlight, and blew out the candles.

Upstairs, Homer and I ventured out to the porch. The winds and rain had all but stopped, and left a nice evening breeze, wet and fresh, as well as a dramatic drop in the temperature. Now true fall was in the air with the coolness usually associated with October weather. Just as Phoebe had told me some weeks ago, it would be summer in Tullulah until Halloween. She was only a few days off.

Homer and I made a circuit of the yard with my flashlight in the near darkness. Leaves and small branches covered the property. I half-expected to see large broken limbs hanging down from the trees in the yard. What a relief that none had been struck.

We crunched over the fallen twigs and branches, circling the entire house. I saw no damage, thankfully, to the roof or gutters. The rockers on the porch lay over-turned, along with the geranium pots and the small table they usually sat on. Once I was satisfied that no telephone wires were down nearby or within sight on the road, we went back inside. Tomorrow we would walk through the woods across the road for further inspections.

I tried to reach Phoebe to make sure she was all right, but to no avail. Neither landline nor cell phone services worked. I took a short but very nice hot shower by candlelight, using as little of the water heater's reserves as possible, and went to bed.

The night sounds of the forest, once unfamiliar and distracting when I first moved to the outskirts of Tul-lulah, had become a wonderful lullaby. As I settled into the down comfort of my bed, I realized the storm made the woods much more quiet. I sat, enjoying the rare treat of almost total silence. A paperback mystery kept me company for the next hour or so, thanks to a book light I had received as a gift. When my eyelids would stay open no longer, I drifted toward sleep, snuggling under the cover with the thought I'd soon need the housewarming gift Phoebe had given me, an electric blanket for the coming winter.

As I crossed through the in-between world, a silly dream of rocks dancing in a ring came to an abrupt end when a sound downstairs brought me fully awake. Not a loud noise. Something small and light, like a dropped coin. I stared into the darkness. Had I really heard anything or was it merely a part of the dream? I lay still and listened for some time. Whatever it was, it hadn't roused Homer from sleep. I relaxed. The wind continued its song, wrapping around the walls and traveling on through the countless leaves of the surrounding forest.

THE MORNING DAWNED WITH A COOL CRISPNESS IN THE air. As I took my morning run, I watched the sun come up behind the nearer mountaintops, sparkling still with water from the storm. A thick fog shrouded the road, allowing only glimpses of empty fields and stands of trees as I passed.

Homer, who had taken to accompanying me on my run of late, stood up ahead in the road, listening, his strong black body framed in mist. It pleased me so to see him healthy. Not long before, he'd given me quite a scare. He had escaped death, but his owner and my dear friend, Cal, did not. How we both missed him. Homer looked fully mended now. Our daily run strengthened us both. Going through those terrible days, the importance of keeping myself in tiptop shape became a priority. I hoped no more confrontations of a dangerous nature would ever occur again. Yet I knew the possibility was there. I needed to stay strong for that, just in case.

We raced the last hundred yards or so to the house. As always, I finished second. We caught our breath on the patio then walked to the right boundary of the yard to a small clearing between several tall oaks. It had become a ritual to do a tai chi routine there where the ground was flat. It was a place of great serenity. The vista of rolling green mountains and morning clouds streaked with the sun's first rays was a lovely way to start each morning. I breathed in the cool air with gratitude.

Once done, Homer and I made our way inside for our breakfast. I started a pot of coffee. Homer walked to the center of the room to inspect a bit of dirt or perhaps a bug. While the coffee brewed, I gathered eggs and cheese from the refrigerator for an omelet then walked across the kitchen floor to the pantry closet where I kept potatoes and onions, with the thought of making hash browns.

I stopped. Homer sat in the middle of the floor, his front legs stretched out as far as they would go. He was staring at me and, now that he had my attention, he gave a soft *woof,* moved his head downward, and touched his nose to the floor a few inches from a small dark object that lay there. He raised his head and gave another softer *woof.* He sat still, continuing to stare at me as if waiting for orders.

"Good boy," I said. I stroked the wide stretch between his ears. "Now, what have we here?"

Just beyond the black ends of his claws, the small gift glinted on the kitchen floor. I picked it up. And smiled.

"How lovely. I wonder what it is." I bounced the little blue piece of glass in my palm. It weighed hardly anything.

There was no doubt that my housemate had left it for me. I looked all around, though I didn't actually expect to see my benefactor. "Thank you, Boo," I said to the air. "You're a dear."

Boo, my resident ghost, is a shy teenage boy who died in the house many years earlier. I frequently find lightweight gifts from him here in the kitchen.

I turned the blue object this way and that in the light. It most resembled a button in the shape of a flower, only it had no holes for thread. I placed it in the center of the kitchen table where the low-hanging overhead light cast a circle around it. From there, I could frequently ponder its use and where it might have come from. I resumed my plan for hash browns and made our breakfast, much to Homer's relief.

I used my cell phone to try Phoebe again when I thought she would be awake. Her home phone was still out as well. I called her cell number and was relieved to hear her say the storm caused no major damage there. She and Rowdy came through it unscathed.

"Are we still on for a walk later?" I said. "I've found another of Cal's maps. I'd like to follow it to see what he was on about."

"Sure," Phoebe said. "I'll bring an apple danish ring. I baked four yesterday. Actually, I baked quite a bit of other stuff to take around this morning, too. I'll make my rounds and then come over. So don't fix anything much to eat, okay?"

We agreed on a time and I hung up without telling

her not to bother with the pastry. I couldn't. She takes such pleasure in her baking and in giving her creations to everyone. I hadn't the heart to tell her I rarely eat sweets. I only indulged when she brought me something on such an occasion as this. It would hurt her feelings so, if I refused on any grounds.

She doesn't particularly care for nature. I sense that she only tolerates my ramblings about this or that historical connection on my land. I'm afraid she doesn't share my enthusiasm for the unique plants and other natural wonders of the woods. She walks with me out of friendship, accompanying me in the forest when I ask, though she much prefers being in town.

If she had not wanted to come with me, I would have understood. I thought she might be helpful, however, in assisting me with photographs. I have to admit, as much as I love exploring on my own with only Homer, I also enjoyed sharing the little discoveries on my property with Phoebe, even if she was less enthusiastic than myself. This she also understood and tolerated. I'm so lucky to have such a friend.

ten
Phoebe Goes to the Library

The morning after the storm, after I talked to Jane on the phone, I pulled the food I made from the refrigerator and wrapped it all up to take around to the workers. I always do that when the power goes out. Even a few hours without electricity makes me appreciate it more. What I do is, I bake up something that carries well, and then I go down to the police station and the electric department to pass out goodies. Sometimes, I stop on the road and hand things out to the ones on duty. Those poor guys and gals work hard in awful conditions, all through the night sometimes, to get things back to normal.

Oh, don't get me wrong. It's not like I think I'm Florence Nightingale or Mother Teresa. All I want is for folks to know I appreciate their work. Plus, it would not do to let Rita Underwood and Gladys Orr and several others of the better cooks in Tullulah show me up. We have what you might call a friendly competition.

Like for instance, what a coincidence that Jody Wilkes suddenly decided to join Grace Baptist, right when they announced they were putting together a cookbook so they could buy choir robes. Especially when everybody knows Jody is a hardcore Methodist from way back. And then there's Shelby Ferguson, who moved here from Meridian, Mississippi, where Joe Ferguson found her after his first wife died. Shelby was used to winning cooking contests before she got to Tullulah, and honey, let me tell you, the Gillispie women, seven of the South's finest cooks, didn't like it a bit when Shelby swooped in and stole first place in a pie-baking contest.

Several instances such as that have made some friendly rivalries among the ladies. That's why none of us pass up an opportunity to try a new recipe on somebody, preferably several somebodys who can talk amongst themselves about which dish they liked the best. So that next morning, when the power came back on, I jumped into cooking mode to add to what I'd already fixed the day before. What I do is I make up two recipes, one with some kind of meat, and one dessert, and I do several batches of each.

While they were in the oven, I went out in the yard. The mutt came with me. He didn't try to run away at all, but stayed fairly close while I picked up sticks. He explored, sniffed all over the yard, and every now and then would look at me to make sure I was still there.

I made a little pile of branches at the far corner of the yard by the curb. Muttface inspected everything I set down there. I looked over at him one time and he was headed for a flowerbed I'd cleaned out, which was now a big bed of mud.

"Don't even think about it," I said. "I am not having you track mud in the house." He stopped, gave it a look, and trotted back over to me. "Good. That's good." I hated to admit he was smart, but if he could understand what I said and then would do it, he was better than most of those kids I wrangled with at the library.

That's what I did before I retired. I got married when I was a junior in high school, and then as soon as I graduated, I started working part-time at the library and never quit.

That was another place I went that morning. Having a storm didn't necessarily put my friends at the library out, but I don't need very much of an excuse to take them some goodies and catch up on the latest gossip. That's why I always save them for last when I'm out and about.

I like to take my time when I visit with Grace. Grace Taylor is just like me except she's younger than I am by a good fifteen years. I'm guessing there, because she never would tell me the exact year she was born. But other than that, we're just alike. Except her hair is black with just a sprinkle of gray, where mine is red with a lot of gray sprinkles. Well, if you want to get technical, her skin is black and mine's not. But otherwise, we are just alike. We wear the same size clothes, and though we don't do it as often as when I still worked, we get together for lunch and a clothes swap every now and then. We have the best time. That girl knows how to have fun.

I hadn't seen her since we drove down to Birmingham together when her sister was sick. One of my sisters lives down there, too, so I visited her while Grace was at the hospital. Of course we went shopping. You can't go to Birmingham without a stroll through Brookwood Mall. We had us a big time. If we stopped at the wine store on the way home for pantry stock, it wasn't anybody's business.

The Tullulah library is fairly good-sized. We may not have a lot in Tullulah, but what we've got is done right. We missed out on the Carnegie buildings, back in the 1920s. I reckon we were too far away from the big cities. That kind of ticked off Lorna Todd, whose daddy owned the timber company and had scads of money. In those days, Lorna liked to think of herself as both the tops in high society and also the intellectual leader of Tullulah, if you can imagine either thing around here.

She went to one of those ritzy colleges up north, some woman's name, not Agnes Scott but something like that, and up there, she got the wild idea that she was a queen. All she needed was some royal subjects. That's where Tullulah came in. She'd sworn she'd never come back, but I reckon there weren't any towns up north that would let her tell them what to do, so she came home. This is just what I've heard. That was way before my time, of course.

Anyway, Lorna went around starting clubs. Guess who was always the president? She started a local history club, a gardening club, a wildlife club, a charity club that raised money for various causes, and a literary club. Notice I didn't mention a Bible club. She knew that would be a lost cause. She knew any six-year-old in the county could quote more scripture and out-preach her heathen self any day of the week.

She called her literary club a salon. This wasn't like the other clubs because it was by invitation only. She held it at her house, and then when her parents died, she decided to make their house—which was and is Tullulah's closest thing to a mansion—a museum, library, and local civic center. She had nice glass cases made for doodads passed down through her family. It grew as she added local historical finds. Then people started donating things, including personal libraries. So we don't have one of those ugly government buildings for our library. Ours is classy. It has what they call grandeur. I never tire of walking in and taking a deep breath. The marble entrance, the sweeping staircase, all the wood polish, and the smell of old books are things I miss being around every day.

But now, I was telling you about Grace. That morning, when I walked in, Grace saw me coming and her whole face lit up in a big smile. "You took your sweet time, Chi Chi," she said. "What happened? Did that new lineman from Memphis take one bite of cupcake and propose?"

I gave her the eye. "Hush your mouth. That boy ain't never getting near my cupcake."

She threw her head back and laughed and then slapped my arm. "Give me that basket," she said. She took it and the cake carrier from me and led the way back to the break room.

Our voices echoed off the walls when we walked by the checkout desk, past the computer room and the microfilm room, and on into what had once been the kitchen of the old house. The back windows and old crown molding were the only things left of the original. Everything else shone like a New York kitchen, all metal and nice counters big enough for several cooks to work. The library rents it out for things like political to-dos and even wedding receptions.

"So," I said while Grace took the green plastic wrap

off a tray of chicken fingers, "how long was the power out at your place?"

"Only four hours," she said. "Took two trees down in our backyard."

"No damage to your house though, I hope."

"No, just a big mess in the yard and the driveway. One tree missed Al's car by about three inches." She went over to a phone on the counter, one of those office kinds with lots of buttons. She pushed one of them and when she spoke, her voice went all over the building. "Attention, everyone. One of our favorite patrons has brought us some fine-looking snacks. Come on back to the break room and help yourself."

It wasn't a minute before three library workers and one customer had already fixed themselves a plate. They all said, "Hey, Phoebe" except for a young boy I didn't know. He smiled and nodded hello. He said he was Brian and was twenty-five years old but he sure didn't look it. I would have guessed sixteen. "Now who is your mama?" I asked him.

"Darlene Miller."

"Oh, goodness. Are you her youngest boy? I'll say, you sure have changed since I've seen you. How is Darlene? I saw her about two weeks ago as they were wheeling her out of the hospital."

"She's better. Cranky, but able to get around some. My sister took care of her a while until I was able to move back."

"How nice that you'd move in to help out." His hair flopped down in his eyes as he shrugged.

"I was able to get a temporary job here until I have to go back to school next spring, so it's no trouble. I would have done that anyway."

"What, are you on one of the work release programs?" Everybody laughed. Which is so rude. I have no idea why people do that all the time and then don't explain themselves like I've said something stupid when I have made perfect sense.

"Something like that," he said.

Lucy Watts, the oldest employee at the library, was the only one who didn't laugh. But then, that's not her thing. I don't think she can hear anymore, either. She was old when I started working and that was over forty years ago. She refuses to retire. She usually sits in the back and toddles around doing who knows what. The only time she ventures out onto the library floor is to shelve books. She can do that fine since she can use the cart as a walker. Taking corners is a little tricky because she wears those slick soled Mary Jane slippers all the time. That makes it hard to get any traction and sometimes they fly out to the side. But she hangs on to that little cart for dear life and does fine.

Jim English pecked me on the cheek as he left with his plate. "I've got some paperwork I've got to finish by noon, so I've got to run. Thanks, Phoebe."

I love Jim. He hired on not long before I retired and was always doing such nice things for all of us. He came over and put in a new bathroom sink for me to save me money. Stuff like that.

As he went out the door, I overheard the library's only customer talking to Grace. He wasn't bad looking for an old guy. Grace saw me looking and got that twinkle in her eyes that I knew meant one thing. Trouble. She was putting her hand on his arm and steering him toward me.

"I don't believe you two have met," she said. Her lips turned up at the corners and her dimples crinkled which was yet another sign she was up to no good. "This is Mr. Jay Gould. He's working on a little research. For the production company doing the movie in town."

I shook his hand as Grace introduced me. While he was complimenting my cooking, Grace took a step back and mouthed, "He's single," real big from behind his shoulder.

It took massive willpower to hold my tongue. I really wanted to stick it out at her but I knew Grace would do something to make me laugh. I had to admit, he wasn't bad. Seemed nice. White hair, no bald spots, and a white beard that he kept very neat. He had pretty blue eyes that are normally not what I like. If I was looking for a man, that is. He had a trim figure but not bony. He had a little bit of a funny accent. That was to be expected of a Hollywood movie person, I suppose.

"Where are you from?" I asked him.

"Originally from Peoria. Lived in California until my wife died four years ago."

"Oh, I'm sorry to hear that," I said. "So, all the way from Indiana and California, huh?"

"Actually, Peoria is in Illinois."

"Silly me. Of course it is." I smiled and giggled, you know, to show him how good and silly I am. Strike one, Yankee boy. Not that I was counting. He did have a very nice smile. "So your company is thinking of filming in Tullulah?"

He looked away. "Thinking about it, yes."

"If you do, Grace and I would make good extras."

He laughed and promised to call us if they needed anyone. And then he just looked at me. He sure wasn't much for conversation.

"Well," I said, "I've got several more stops to make, so I better get going. Nice to meet you, Mr. Gould. Grace, would you come walk with me to the door, please, ma'am?"

Mr. Gould waved and turned back to the table for another oatmeal cookie. Grace and I didn't say a word until we got outside the library with the front doors closed behind us. Then we both busted out laughing. I grabbed Grace's elbow and walked her to the side where nobody could see us from inside.

"What are you, nuts? The last thing on earth I need is an old man for a boyfriend."

She put her hands on her hips. "Feeb, he is three years younger than you."

"No, he's not. He's older. A lot. And how would you know his age anyway?"

"Looked on his driver's license, of course."

"What, are you a pickpocket now? There's no reason he would have showed it to you."

"He didn't know that. I told him I had to see it to let him use the microfilm. How else am I going to screen men for you?"

I shook my head. "Lord help my time, what am I going to do with you? Now quit that. I'm happy by myself. I don't want some fancy husband, wandering around my house, wanting me to cook something."

"Oh, yes, you do," Grace said. "I don't know who you think you're talking to. Like I just walked up out of the blue. I know you better than that, Chi Chi."

"Whatever. I'll see you when I fit your costume. How about Friday night?" We were already getting ready for Halloween.

She said that would be fine. She'd stop by on her way home from work. Grace is a doll. She does her best for me. It's slim pickings in my age group, I realize that, so I had to cut her some slack for trying. But I'd still get her back.

Before I went home, I stopped at the drugstore again. I thought I might pick up some food for Rowdy, rather than go to the Pig. I wasn't ready to go back in there yet, after the trauma.

You wouldn't believe all the stuff for dogs on the shelves in that drugstore. I picked up a can of dog food and slapped it down again when I saw the price sticker. What was in there, Russian caviar? They had to be kidding. I saw Betty coming toward me.

"Betty, don't you have a little dog?"

"Sure do." She wasn't chewing gum, but I could smell Juicy Fruit. I understood. We're both old school.

Our mamas taught us that ladies may not chew gum in public. It's trashy. She had a wad stuck in the roof of her mouth. I've done it a thousand times myself. The wad would also explain the slight lisp when she said, "Sure."

"What kind of dog is it?" I said.

"She's a Yorkie-poo."

"Oh," I said like I was impressed. I had no idea what she was talking about. "What's her name?"

"Peekie-boo."

Good grief. I forced myself to keep a straight face. "And about how big is a Dorkie-poo?"

Betty held her hands out about a foot apart. I told her about Rowdy. You would have thought I told her I had a new baby grandchild from the way she carried on. She showed me what kind of food Peekie-boo liked. I bought what she suggested, which I was happy to see had a much better price tag than the other stuff, and also picked up a few other little things, like a special comb. I figured I might as well make it easier on myself even if Rowdy wouldn't be staying with me very long.

eleven
Jane Finds Another One

When I heard the kettle rattle, I rose and poured myself a cup of tea. Phoebe wouldn't be arriving for our walk for some time yet. I thought I'd read the previous day's newspaper while I waited. I was about to take a sip but, slowly and with great care, I set my grandmother's china cup into its saucer with a slight tremor. I stared at the front page. I blinked hard and blinked again.

"Good heavens," I whispered. Homer, lying by the door, raised his large square head from atop his front paws and gave me a questioning look.

"Sorry. It's just that the newspaper is behaving strangely."

He rose and walked to me, sitting before my chair and cocking his head. He gave me an incredulous look. "Yes, you're quite right," I said. "Actually, it isn't the newspaper that's misbehaving at all, is it, love? It's me. I'm afraid it's happening again, dear."

I set the newspaper down and sighed. I rubbed my eyes. What should have been simple print in black and white on the page was something completely different. Part of the print had a yellow glow, as if a ghostly hand had highlighted the text.

I tried to ignore it. I got up and started a load of laundry. I dusted the living room and dining room. Finally, armed with another cup of tea, I faced the paper once again.

Enough dithering, I thought. What I needed was an objective opinion. I picked up the newspaper and turned it toward Homer.

"You see? No matter how I turn it, this section is yellow." He gave a single bark that sounded more like a word. I was unsure if it was one that confirmed or denied my own assessment.

I gave the rest of the paper a glance, turning through the pages in search of other highlighted passages. There were none.

"Well, then. I suppose I should give attention to the article. On the off chance that it is actually yellow, you understand." He blinked. Since he remained seated there beside me, I thought it a small courtesy to read aloud for his benefit.

"'Local Man Missing,' it says in the heading. 'Sheriff John Bailey has phoned us here at the *Day-Herald* to let everyone know that Junie Reed has reported her father, Brody Reed, is missing again. As you all know, Brody frequently goes off into the woods for days on his own. This time, Junie is a little worried since we have storms predicted. This wouldn't ordinarily be of any concern to her. Brody is probably the best woodsman in these parts. "This time," Junie says, "I'm worried because Daddy has been getting forgetful lately." This is a valid concern, as some readers will remember his last spell got him lost in downtown Tullulah. Junie asks that if anyone has seen him in the last few days to please call her or the sheriff's department. "He knows these woods better than anybody, and has survived in a lot worse conditions outside. At his age though, and with the bad weather coming, I'd feel better if he was home."'"

I set the paper down and sipped my tea. Homer returned to his rug. Puzzling. Why was that name familiar? I'd ask Phoebe about it. No doubt she could give me the names of all Brody Reed's family members, their ages and occupations, and what his life had been like since birth. Her knowledge of personal histories in Tullulah astounds me.

I had almost finished reading the paper when Homer uttered a soft growl. He was on his feet without a sound and off quickly. This wasn't unusual behavior. In the last few weeks, he'd taken to staying inside with me after our breakfast. Quite often, at about the same time of morning, he'd done just this, perked up his head and padded off to find the source of a noise I had yet to hear myself. In the first few instances, I followed him to the kitchen door. He always sat and looked at me expectantly, asking, I assumed, to be let out. I obliged, and every time he trotted down the porch steps and to the old shed twenty yards or so behind the house.

Nothing ever came of his searches. I would watch him sniff around the small building where I stored tools and sundry items. He never flushed a small animal out, and he would trot back to the door a few minutes later, his imaginary search as security guard done.

This time, I walked outside with him. We still had fog, but it now lay like a thin covering over the grass. As he made his way across the grass, I, too, heard a sound. It was faint, but unmistakably a voice. Or so I thought at the time. I couldn't make out any words, only the emotion behind them. Fear.

Homer's sleek figure moved quickly through the ankle-high fog, his nose touching the ground as he made a circuit around the shed. We stood, waiting. Nothing but a slight stirring in the wind moved until Homer's ears swiveled forward.

He padded slowly to the shed's door without a sound. His body went rigid, like a pointer showing his master the hidden prey's location. I froze as well. Homer was right. We heard something quiet, almost like a sob.

I told myself it was surely nothing more than a mouse or wild rabbit caught in the shed. Or perhaps it was a dove or some other bird. Still, I hesitated rather than opened the door to see the perfectly good explanation for the sound we heard. I could believe I might be imagining things, but surely Homer was not.

"Is anyone there?" I said softly. "Are you all right?"

Homer, still locked in his stance, suddenly jerked forward, less than an inch, toward the door. His hunting instincts held him back to await my command.

Gathering my courage, I flung open the door. The total darkness inside made it impossible for me to see anything at all at first. There was no electricity to the shed. I made a mental note to bring a flashlight out to set inside the door.

But then, as I stared into the darkness, I saw it, hunched behind a packing crate. I realized the shed's intruder needed no light to be seen. A choked sound, a cry, came from it, just before it stood quickly, made a run for it, and disappeared. Straight through the wall.

Homer gave chase around the side of the building. I managed to catch a glimpse of the figure, a man who looked real and solid one moment but shimmered like a phantom of smoke the next, a mixture of green and white clothing, running toward the creek that runs near the edge of my backyard. There, he vanished, dissolving into the thicker and much higher fog that enveloped the stream.

Homer barked, confused, circling and walking back and forth at the creek's bank. He looked side to side, just as I did. He sniffed the ground but with no luck. The apparition was gone.

PHOEBE ARRIVED AT MY HOUSE WHILE I STILL GATHERED the tools I thought we might need on our trek. She tapped on the door as she opened it. "It's me."

"In the kitchen." She entered, carrying a plastic Tupperware container filled, I presumed, with her apple danish ring. She wore a deep purple top with matching paisley stretch pants. Her earrings dangled with purple and yellow pansies on the ends. Her red hair, piled on top of her head in her signature style, displayed a hairpin with a small gold ornament amid the curly lockets.

"What a lovely pin," I said.

"Why, thank you. I bought it in Pigeon Forge when Ronald and I went up there for his uncle's funeral."

"I can't quite make out the ornament. A tiny shell?"

"No, it's a roly-poly bug. They take real ones and dip them in gold leaf or paint them in bright colors.

After they're dead, of course. The gold ones are more expensive."

"Fascinating. How, um, artistic." We made our way out of the house. Homer joined us from his ramblings in the backyard. He came up as we crossed the main road that leads into the Anisidi Wildlife Refuge. My own private refuge lay ahead of us.

My benefactor, Cal Prewitt, had left it all to me. We were not related, had not known each other for more than a few weeks, yet he knew that, in me, he had found a kindred spirit. I swore to preserve his woods, just as Cal's ancestors had preserved them for many generations and as he had done all his life.

He trusted me to find a way to ensure its future, though as yet I didn't know how I would accomplish such a task. I had no children of my own. It was difficult to know whom to trust, how best to protect it, not just for a few years or decades but forever. We walked across the front meadow toward the woods up ahead.

"When are we going to do some more practicing?" Phoebe asked as we crossed the first stream, one that marked the beginnings of the forest. She inclined her head to the left. There, some one hundred yards away, a number of boulders stood about chest high. Behind them, grass stretched another ten yards or so to the edge of the bluff. Phoebe and I call the boulders our shooting range. I gave her a few lessons when I first moved here and when the land still belonged to Cal. We've only been able to practice a couple of times since.

"Whenever you like, dear. I'm still getting used to the fact that I'm the boss now."

"Yeah, you've got full run of the place. You could weave flowers in your hair and hop and skip buck naked around here all day long and nobody would ever know."

"True. But unlikely."

Phoebe certainly knew how to surprise me. Prim and old-fashioned one moment, earthy and unpredictable the next. A staunch churchgoer with a hidden wild streak. Her thinly veiled reference to me as a dancing pagan wood sprite who worshipped the forest in the nude made me chuckle. I could see the light of mischief in her eyes. She had managed to combine the two favorite topics she uses to kid me, religion and my love of nature.

Though I haven't attended a proper church service since I was a teenager, I suppose others here see me as quite conservative. I am British, after all. Rather quiet as well. As to a hippie or naturist wild streak, no, though if Phoebe knew the truth of my background, she might think me decidedly "far out."

"What have you done with your little dog?" I asked.

Phoebe watched the trail closely as she progressed through the woods. "It's not my dog. It's temporary. But he's fine. He's in the house. I hope I don't come home to find my sofa and chairs ripped up with stuffing floating in the air. Boy, this place is a mess," Phoebe said as we picked up branches that lay across our path. "Now, tell me again what we're looking for."

"Cal calls it 'Rock Wall' on his map. His notes say it is the highest point of the forest. Depending on which of his notations are correct, we will be looking for a wall. Or a rock overhang. Or a hole in the ground. Or possibly a tree."

"Well that narrows it down. Did he not know himself? We need to take into account that we're talking about a guy known to take a nip or two."

"It's puzzling. Yes, he did know where it was because he said he covered part of it with brush. Still, he seems to be calling one spot all those things."

From what I could tell, the site of the rock wall on Cal's map was not far down the main path, actually wide as a road at this point. Farther along, it narrowed on the map and led to an offshoot cut away to the right and not far into the woods. A main trail that ended at "Rock Wall." Cal drew a line of dashes, and then showed the main trail picking up again on the other side of whatever "Rock Wall" was. An arrow indicated it continued off the page. At the edge, his shaky lettering spelled a name I recognized.

Above the arrow, the words "Smuggler's Run" gave me pause. It served as a highway, a major trail that traversed many states from North Carolina to Louisiana. Both it and the side path we turned on were passable by car now, but only just. Cal must have driven this way often, for it was quite wide and remarkably clear—other than the storm debris—for a road so far into the woods.

I was thankful Cal had been so ardent in keeping the

trails clear and easy to follow. The land rose gently at first, but as the woods thinned, we steadily climbed, higher and higher, until we reached a ridge. We stopped there and found ourselves looking across a wide clearing, one that appeared both natural and designed. The rock floor of the clearing stretched out to an overlook to the valley far below. The view took our breath away. The green flat pastureland looked tiny and miles away. Sometimes I forget how high in the mountain both the town of Tullulah and my own place here on its outskirts sit.

"Is this the place?" Phoebe said.

We each looked across the clearing at the same time. Both of us saw the remains of a low rock wall to the left of the clearing and continuing out of sight. As we looked in that direction, we saw the other map feature a distance behind the wall where the tree line began, an angled indention of solid rock that created an over-hang about twenty feet high.

Yet the site of the rock overhang, which we saw at a different angle than that in Cal's photos, did not occupy my mind at the time. It temporarily took second place to the gigantic root ball of a fallen tree beside it. From where we stood, I could see two large burned areas on its trunk, blackened by lightning.

"Heavens," I said. "I think I saw this happen." I turned around, walked to the rock wall, and looked down into the valley. Yes. I could see the road and the place I stopped during the storm.

"It smells smoky here," Phoebe said as she sniffed

the air. "Look right there at that burn mark. And another one."

She pointed to the lower burned area. Lightning had struck at the tree's base, toppling the trunk to the ground and upending the roots. The tangled wood tendrils now rose in the air, at least ten feet high, perhaps higher.

"The same tree struck twice?" I said. "In one night? Is that possible?" In addition to the blow, which appeared to have knocked it over, a long and wide black mark charred much of the tree on either side of a great split in the wood. More than two yards separated this burned area from that at the tree's base.

"Sure it could happen," Phoebe said. "My brother Gerald got hit three times, right in a row."

"Good heavens. Is he, that is, did he survive?"

"Oh, yeah. He's still bugging the fire out of me every chance he gets. He was playing golf in a thunderstorm like a fool. He got zapped, then he ran, then he got zapped again and it knocked him down, then it hit him again while he was flailing around in the wet grass."

"How terrible. And no lasting effects?"

"Unfortunately not. No improvement whatsoever."

"Amazing."

"Not really. I think the Lord was sending him a message to quit being so mean. Didn't work out like that. Gerald kind of absorbed the shocks and got meaner. Like a battery being recharged."

"Goodness. You certainly have an interesting family."

"Honey, you don't know the half of it."

We walked to the base of the tree, the heart of the lightning strike. A black rectangle approximately three feet long and perhaps a foot across at its widest point covered the tree's side. Phoebe put her hand over the blackened bark, rubbing it back and forth, then both hands, prying into the cut and studying it from all angles.

From where we stood, we could see a slight indentation in the ground beside the huge upturned root ball, just beside the rock overhang to which Cal referred. I took out one of the photos he had taken of the area to compare. Phoebe looked over my shoulder.

"Looks like the place. Except now the hole in the ground is a whole lot bigger." She touched the photograph then pointed. "Now you can see that rock that's jutting out better." She walked toward the overhang. I had no idea it was so large from the photograph. Nor had I grasped the amount of engravings. They covered virtually the entire front slab that faced the downed tree.

"Hey, Jane." I looked over to see Phoebe at the far edge of the cleared area that sloped upward. "Over here. I bet this is it."

I caught up with her and followed her gaze down into a small hollow. She pointed her finger and moved it across. "Tree. Or it was. Bushes. Indian stuff. Hole in the ground. Maybe there's a cave down in there somewhere."

Several flat rocks lay spaced just so between the tree and the overhang. I saw more on the other side of the huge tree trunk, following the line from the overhang to where the clearing was covered entirely with more flat rocks.

Phoebe wouldn't let me walk on the flat stepping stones until she had used a fallen branch with its leaves still attached like a broom to sweep them clean of wet leaves.

"We don't want to fall and break our hips and then have all my friends call me feeble. That would be the pits."

"Quite right." With ginger steps across the slippery floor of mud and leaves, we made our way to the overhang, forming a small cave-like space beneath. Its underside was above my head with perhaps another five feet of room to spare. Phoebe and I used our fingers to wipe away dirt and pieces of leaves that covered some of the "Indian stuff," which was revealed as three lines of many symbols each, and a fourth shorter line of different markings, all wondrously strange and completely undecipherable.

The cool air, the earthy smells of wood and smoke, the warning chips of territorial chickadees, the ancient wonder beneath my hands as I wiped moss and wet dirt away, all blended together in a heady mixture, akin to draughts of strong incense, that transported me above the ground and into another world. I was in heaven.

Phoebe brought me abruptly out of my reverie. "Are you feeling all right, Jane? You've got a freaky look on your face. You're not about to have a heart attack or anything, are you?"

"No, dear. Quite the opposite. This glorious place makes me feel euphoric."

Phoebe stared at me, her eyebrows raised, her head of red curls leaning closer to my ear to whisper, "It's a rock, Jane. Covered in mud. The wind is going to give us both earaches, and that bird that just flew over missed splattering my arm by less than an inch. Euphoric, it ain't."

I laughed. "Oh, stop teasing. You're not fooling me, my girl. You can't tell me these etchings don't interest you. Not with your love of all things Native American."

Her face changed in a snap from incredulity to smiling mischief. "Ha! Okay, I give you that. I do like the writing."

Once done, we saw two rather nice petroglyphs nearer the broken wall of rocks. The rock drawings were small ones that Cal had indicated on the map with arrows and a notation of only one word: "Carvings."

While Phoebe walked slowly around and under the overhang, I took out my notebook to jot down my observations about the two rock carvings, then we photographed them. One was the familiar circular spiral often seen in many ancient sites throughout the world. The other required more concentration in my rendering, several lines containing a number of native symbols that would require one of Cal's Cherokee dictionaries to decipher.

Despite her usual revulsion for being outdoors for very long, Phoebe certainly enjoyed the carvings, going back and forth from one to the other. "Here, take a picture of me next to this one," she said as she wrapped her arm around it.

I obliged then set the timer for a shot with both of us in the frame. We also posed by the charred hole in the fallen tree. We moved farther down the tree and skirted the great upstanding roots carefully to explore the "hole in the ground" they had enlarged.

"Hey, take a picture of this here," Phoebe said. "It can be like an art picture, like they show in fancy galleries." She held her arms out straight, her hands squared as if she were a movie director framing a scene. "Right like that. See how the roots look?"

"Yes. An excellent idea. I like that. I wish I'd brought a camera with black-and-white film."

Phoebe stood aside, moving her framed palms out to find more potential art subjects. "Get this, too," she said with her director's frame held down to the ground. "See that? It looks like an arm, kind of. And a hand, with little fingers on the . . . Yaaaaah!" She screamed as she leapt backward, grabbing my arm in the process and dragging me away from the tree roots.

"Your foot! Your foot!" she yelled.

I looked down at the spot she had forced me to vacate. At first, I couldn't make sense of what was before me. A slight indentation in the wet, brown earth was all I saw. Judging from Phoebe's agitation, I'd thought she must surely have seen a snake. Instead, what I saw held no danger, yet chilled me through and through just the same.

Within the bare patch where the tree's giant root-ball had been, a pattern of small yellowish white cylinders protruded from the wet brown dirt.

"It is!" Phoebe said. Her voice trembled in a higher pitch than normal. "Tell me it isn't, but I know good and well it is."

They were bones. No question. Nor was there any doubt they were human bones. One eye socket of a skull peeked at us from out of the mud.

Phoebe didn't move, only stared at our discovery. "Well, Jane. I cannot believe we have gone and done it again. Except this body is a whole lot deader than that last one."

twelve
Phoebe and the Bones

Jane had shivered all over her body like a herd of possum had run over her grave.

"Are you all right?" I said after we both realized we were looking at somebody's bones. Unlike me, Jane is the delicate type. I worried that she'd faint or have a heart attack or, worse, go all bananas on me like she did that last time we found the dead guy.

"Of course. I'm fine. I've seen many a bone in the ground in my day."

"Huh." I looked her up and down. She put on a good act, I give her that. "I suppose you have. So now what do we do? You want to have another one of those Indian ceremonies?"

"Perhaps that would be a good idea later on."

"Because I've been thinking about it for a while, in case we ever needed to do one again."

"Oh, yes?"

"Yeah. This time, I want us to smoke something. Like in a pow-wow. With a peace pipe. I don't have a real one yet. But I do have some of my granddaddy's old pipes. We could use one of those, if it's an emergency bone thing."

Jane squatted to have a closer look. "I'm not sure what to do next," she said. "I suppose the first thing to do is call the police."

"What for? Whoever it is, he's not on the missing persons list. He's been in the ground a while. The police don't care about nothing from ancient times. Besides that, the writing over there on the wall is probably like the tombstone, don't you reckon? So it was an official burial. Whenever it was."

"Possibly. Probably so." Jane knelt beside the bones, eyeballing them all over, left and right. She didn't touch them, but she did put a fingertip on the dirt at the edge of the hole left by the tree trunk.

"What we've got here is an Indian cemetery. Only, I don't think this is like the trees where we did the smudging," I said. "This body isn't right up under the tree. See, it's too far away. Unless he had his arm way back like this." I reached backward as far as I could like I was doing a backstroke in the air.

Jane nodded. "I believe you're right. He, or she, was most likely buried farther out in the tree's shade. Though the bones could have moved into strange positions. See how the roots have grown and shoved those aside."

I bent down beside her. "What is that sticking up over there?" I reached toward a bump but Jane stopped me.

"Don't touch it. We must leave everything as it is. Everything must be documented, just as it lies. Both for the police and the state."

"The state?"

"Yes. The state archaeology office. We will want a full dig." She looked up. Her face looked like a kid's at Christmas.

"Wait. Don't tell me," I said. "You're euphoric."

Jane laughed and said, "Yes, my dear, I believe I am. I think I'm going to cry."

Lord, give me patience and preservatives. I gave her a hug and patted her back. "You just go right ahead, hon. I understand. I know how you like dirt and trees and old dead bones. And now you got some of your very own. Go ahead and blubber, I won't tell any-body."

We took a lot more pictures before we headed out of the woods and back to Jane's house. Homer went on ahead of us like he thought he was leading the way. I have to say that, for a dog, Homer is pretty smart. He got the message quick that I did not want him slob-bering all over me. He has kept his distance ever since the first time I met him.

As soon as we got in, Jane went to the phone that hangs on her kitchen wall to call the police. "Oh, bother," she said. She tapped the button a couple of times. "Not working."

"I thought you got that fixed?"

"I did. More likely the phone company is still catching up after the storm." She hung up the receiver and got her cell phone.

I hung around at Jane's house until the police got there. They came a lot quicker than I expected. They were already out on other business, due to the storm damage.

I had no interest whatsoever in going back out into the sticks. Besides, I had a lot of other stuff that needed doing, so I excused myself. It was good to see Detective Daniel Waters again, though. I've known him since he was a boy. I had him in my Sunday school class I used to teach for five-year-olds. He is a good one. His poor family never had two dimes to rub together, but they raised him right. Every time I see him, I feel so proud that he turned into such a fine young man and has made something of himself.

Right as I was telling Dan good-bye at the door, I heard Jane call out to us from the den. Her voice didn't sound right. It was tight and higher than usual. Something was wrong.

We found her opening and closing her armoire and

then the lids on her two antique trunks. She kept going around the room, looking up and down her book-shelves. When she got to her desk, she opened all the drawers and flipped through files.

"Someone has been in here. This morning. Since we left for our walk." She spoke in a calm voice, but I could tell she was rattled.

Dan looked around the room. "Is anything missing?"

"Yes. A couple of primitive figurines from my shelf. And I can tell someone has looked through my desk."

I looked at my watch. "We've only been gone an hour and a half. They must have been watching. They did quick work unless they're still . . . Surely they're not still here and hiding somewhere!"

Dan and Jane exchanged a look. Dan whipped his gun off his belt and said, "Stay here. I'll check."

In the time it took him to say that, Jane had already grabbed a mean handgun, had it in her hand ready to go, and was on the way to check the closet. "I'll help," she said as she jerked the door open and pointed the gun around inside the closet.

In no time, the two of them searched the house, upstairs and down plus the basement. You should've seen Jane. The way she walked and moved her gun up and down, her arms straight out, the way she went around corners. She looked like Emma Peel on a serious mission.

Nobody was there, thank goodness. Jane said nothing else was missing. When Dan checked the

doors and windows, he didn't find any of them jim-
mied.

"I usually lock the doors," she said. "I don't
remember doing it this morning. I was too anxious to
take our walk, I suppose."

It didn't sound like her. She's pretty cautious about
safety. But, we all mess up every now and then. It was
just rotten luck that someone took advantage of it.

thirteen
Jane Takes the Police
to the Bones

*D*etective Waters and I walked outside to his
vehicle, a forest green, mud-splattered Jeep
Cherokee instead of one issued from the police department. A gentleman sat in the passenger seat.

"I brought our coroner with me. This is Dr. Mark
Jenkins. Sorry it took us so long, Mark." The doctor
stuck his right hand out the window so we could
shake. "We were on the same scene when you
called."

"A pleasure, Mrs. Thistle." Dr. Jenkins had silver
hair and looked about my age or perhaps younger.

Homer came bounding across the road from his old
home, picking up speed when he saw the detective. As
he did so, Detective Waters lowered himself to a squat
and clapped his hands together, calling Homer to him.

While he scratched Homer's ears and patted him,
the screen on my front door squeaked open. Phoebe

walked over, her purse in one hand and her car keys in the other.

"Hey, Mark," she said.

"Phoebe. What a surprise to find you right in the middle of things," he said with a laugh.

She put both hands in the air. "Don't blame me. I haven't done a thing. There's your troublemaker right there," she said, indicating me with a nod of her head. "May I go now? You don't need me since Jane can show you out there, right? Because I have a lot I need to be doing today rather than traipsing around out there. And then wait and wait for Mark to say something like, 'In my expert opinion, he's dead and has been for a long, long time.' "

"That's fine," Detective Waters said in a light voice. "If I need to ask you something, I'll come by your house. You don't happen to have any of that good strudel made up, do you?"

Phoebe smiled. "Not lately. Come on, anyway. Anytime. I imagine I can rustle up something whenever you're hungry." Off she went, turning her car down Anisidi Road and waving good-bye out her window.

Detective Waters gave a few last pats to Homer's side. He stood and stretched. "Let's go have a look. From what you've told me, Mrs. Thistle, you've most likely come upon an Indian grave." He put a hand to the back of his neck, rubbing and smoothing his hair. "Even so, if you don't mind, I'd like to keep this as quiet as we can."

"Certainly."

He looked as if he had more to say on the matter. Whatever that might be, he kept it to himself for the moment.

I gave directions as we drove through the woods, making slow progress over the bumps and holes in the old road. "Park here. This is as far as we can go. We'll walk from here. Up the ridge," I said as I pointed up toward the clearing where Phoebe and I had found the bones.

When we crested the rise, we saw a family of squirrels chase each other around the fallen tree. They stopped to look at our little troupe before scattering away through the brush and up various trees to safety. Detective Waters walked across to stand beside the upturned roots and earth, two or perhaps three times his height.

He unbuttoned his jacket and hiked his pants at the knees to bend down beside the bones. As I mentioned, we could see part of the skull and part of a forearm and its once-attached hand and finger bones. Another dry whitened object about the size of a half-dollar also lay exposed perhaps a foot from the arm bones. If I were to guess, I'd say it was also bone, but with so little visible in the dirt it was impossible to say for certain.

Detective Waters turned to me, laughing as he shook his head. "I'm amazed you found this place. Out of all the woods, you and Mrs. Twigg just happened to walk by here, right where you could find me another body."

The three of us laughed. "Cal's map led us here. To

see this overhang shelter." I showed them the crude drawing. They walked with me to the overhang to see its carvings. We walked further around toward the bluff and the pieces of stone, fallen now but surely once stacked on top of one another to form a long wall. The men gazed out across the valley for some time, marveling at the view.

We retraced our steps over the large clearing. At the site, the coroner took out his camera and began photographing the bones. He dug away some mud from around them but gently and only enough to see a little better. "I'd say they are well over the seventy-five-year range. I'll email these pictures to Dr. Norwood. She'll want to come out to have a look."

I looked at Detective Waters. "Dr. Norwood works for the state. She's our area's forensic anthropologist," he said. His black eyes, deep and sparkling with humor and intelligence, stared into mine. "Like I said on the way in here, I want to handle this exactly right, just as much as you do." He explained he wanted to get the coroner's opinion on whether the remains were of someone recently deceased or were, as we both suspected, much older. In that case, Dr. Norwood would take over. "She will make the final determination."

Dr. Jenkins and Detective Waters told of many such discoveries in the area that, upon study, were found to be two hundred to three hundred years buried. This particular section of northwest Alabama was home to mainly three tribes, Cherokee, Creek, and Chickasaw, before the United States government removed most of them in the early 1800s. Bones uncovered in recent years were the parents and grandparents of those removed to the West.

Dr. Jenkins knelt and nodded his head. He ran a finger down the length of the ulna and tapped it a bit before speaking. "Old," he said, looking up to the detective. "Like the last one we did over on McRaes' place."

He took a tiny recorder out of his pocket and spoke into it. "October twenty-eighth, in company of Detective Daniel Waters, on property owned by Mrs. Jane Thistle, approximately one half-mile off Anisidi Road and southwest of the Anisidi Wildlife Refuge. We find an area approximately eight feet by eight feet unearthed by roots of a large tree struck down in previous night's storm. Within the area a skull, full ulna, and the bones of one hand lay exposed. Bone color and condition indicate the individual most likely lived over one hundred years ago. In close proximity is evidence of native burial as seen in previous finds of this nature. Suggest corroboration from Dr. Norwood before proceeding with reburial or extraction." He clicked his recorder off and stuck it back in his pocket before standing to go.

Detective Waters also looked ready to leave. "I'll let you know what Dr. Norwood says, Mrs. Thistle. Her office is in Huntsville. She tries to come out fairly quickly on something like this. We'll see."

"Certainly. Anytime is fine."

He hesitated again, as if unsure and choosing his

words carefully. "In the past," he said, "we have had a few instances of Indian activists from out of state who get interested when this kind of situation comes up. I don't want to alarm you. I'm just telling you so you'll be prepared in case any show up."

"Is that likely to happen?"

"Hard to say. Sometimes yes, sometimes no. I'll go out and talk to the local chief to let him know what's going on."

"There's a local chief? I had no idea."

"On the other side of the mountain. The north Alabama tribe is small, compared to North Carolina and Oklahoma. Good folks. You'll like them. Dr. Norwood will notify the state Indian Affairs office. Sometimes that brings outsiders."

"We're talking about protestors?"

He nodded. "I'm just saying there's a chance. One or two fellows have been known to come down and take it upon themselves to keep an eye on the white man."

He looked deep into my eyes and gave a hearty laugh. And that was the first time I realized what was right before me. How silly of me not to have seen it earlier.

"That's right. The protestors are usually whiter than me."

It was so clear. His eyes, his strong native facial bones, the quiet calm in his movements and speech.

"As I say, they're not bad guys or anything. Well, most of them aren't," Detective Waters said. "They only want to be sure full respect is shown. I want that, too. My job is to make sure the law is followed, and that the right thing is done all around. So don't worry about anything. Especially that anyone in the police department will mess things up on the site. I'm not going to bring a jackhammer out here and tear up a grave or anything like that."

We laughed as we took a last look around. Detective Waters lingered at the overlook. "Those bones have rested right where they're at for a long, long time. They'll keep. Since they're on your land away from town, and from what I know of you, I assume you also want a dignified re-burial, I don't think the protestors or NAGPA will have anything to worry about."

The Native American Grave Protection Agency often made the news in the archaeological journals I read. I knew their policies in a general way, but made a mental note to go online and read them carefully.

"They'll want to make sure the remains are re-buried and the area left undisturbed," the detective said. "You don't plan on clearing any of this or building a set of condominiums out here, do you?"

I laughed. "No, of course not."

"Well, then, there won't be any problem."

As we made our way back to my house, I explained that I'd like to undertake a full dig at the site myself. "I'd like to study it. Do a complete analysis."

The medical examiner and Detective Waters exchanged glances. I told them of my previous experience and assured them that I would consult experts more knowledgeable than myself.

"Let's see what Dr. Norwood says first," Detective Waters said. "I'll explain your situation. You two can talk about it when she comes out. Meanwhile, we need to leave everything untouched, okay?"

"Of course," I said. "I'll put a tarp over the pit to protect the area. I have a canopy I can rig over it as well. Just in case there's more rain."

I was relieved that neither Dr. Jenkins nor Detective Waters had an inclination to move or disturb the bones in any way. That would give me time to organize my thoughts. Already my mind reeled off the old digging and preservation procedures, trying to remember all the equipment I'd need, the order to do things.

And I needed help. While it's true I had much experience on archaeological sites, I knew I was rusty after being away from that life for so long.

Once more, I considered the need for a confidante, an advisor upon whose judgment I could rely without question. This was an area of deep concern, one I'd turned over and over in my mind since acquiring this land. The decision of whether or not to trust another person, anyone at all, with its potential historical value as an untouched piece of wilderness, was not an easy one to make. Now, however, I knew that I must bring in a consultant, someone I was sure I could trust. I needed someone with a wealth of experience in excavations. Perhaps more importantly, someone who might be free, in respect to both time and what he might charge me.

Michael. He would be perfect. Now that he was officially retired, he might be interested, if he wasn't working for someone else on a digging project. And if I could find him.

A half-hour later, Dr. Jenkins and Detective Waters said good-bye and left Homer and me to our chores. We went to the shed in my backyard where I found several plastic tarps. I gathered the tall poles and the large tent canopy I'd kept long after the Colonel and I no longer held outdoor parties. I placed them in my car then gathered other things I might need. With a hammer, several stakes, a ball of twine, a tape measure, my camera, my leatherwork belt, and a sketchbook in tow, we set out to cover the exposed bones.

Homer kept me company as I took more pictures. Once the tarp was in place, we moved our attention to the fallen tree and the overhang's carved symbols. Homer explored while I sketched and made notes. The sun sank lower as I finished the last measurements between carvings and burial place. Even so, I found it hard to pull myself away, to stop staring in the near darkness at the area surrounding the fallen tree, the blackened, somewhat star-shaped wound where lightning had struck on the trunk, and the wide gash low near the roots.

I'm rather a skeptic. In spite of my experiences of a supernatural nature since moving to Tullulah, I found it unlikely that unusual recent events had happened coincidentally. Lightning strikes a tree, Cal's box provides a map to it that very day. Unlikely in the normal world, yes, but not so upsetting here. This appeared to be Cal's modus operandi, to send me explanations in some form to help me understand. Yet the two other coincidences worried me.

I find blood and a footprint on my land then a local woodsman goes missing. I had forgotten to talk to Detective Waters about the blood. I felt certain it was that of a deer, one an eager hunter bagged illegally. Still, I should consider the yellow highlighting of the newspaper article about Brody Reed. Did that indicate a relation to the blood?

The final coincidence had taken on a new twist. My purse was stolen then my house was burglarized. It's true that the two items I reported as missing in my house were of little real value, other than sentimental. I bought them in South America while on a business trip through my part-time government work many years ago. The villager who made them wisely set his adorable little girl, about six years old, next to his wares to sell them. I couldn't resist.

However, the burglar took something else that I did not report. I couldn't. Though I didn't purchase them myself, the Colonel owned many military-grade guns and other weapons that he collected over the years we were married. Now they were mine. Unfortunately, they were not all legal. Somehow, I couldn't bring myself to tell the detective I hadn't locked the antique trunk in my den that holds approximately forty handguns of all makes, as well as a variety of other tools from which our burglar selected the topmost item, an olive metal box that contains flash-bang devices and a small handheld flamethrower used by military personnel. They were probably all the thief had time to grab; perhaps we interrupted him, or much more would have been taken. Or perhaps he didn't have time to look at the trunk's contents and didn't know there was still much of value there.

Now I would have to move everything and hide it all very well, just to be sure. How foolish of me to become lax at something so important. If the burglar had seen the other valuables, I could expect another visit.

fourteen
Phoebe Keeps the Boys

*O*n occasion, I keep two little boys who live down the street overnight. Jason is eight and his little brother, Mark, is five. Their poor mother died a couple of years ago. Several of the ladies on Meadowlark and also some at church take turns looking after them. This gives their daddy a break. It's good for me, too. I like the little young'uns.

"Easy, easy!" I said when they clambered up the steps like stampeding cattle. They are rambunctious, just like all boys, but otherwise good and as cute as they can be.

First, while supper finished cooking, I got their measurements for the Halloween outfits I was going to make for them. Bundles of energy, both of them. With that done, I got them out of my hair for a few minutes by sending them to wash their hands good. All this time, Rowdy was right there with them, whatever they were doing.

"Now, you boys listen. Do not touch that dog any more until after supper. You've washed your hands, now I want you to eat without dog germs all over you."

I made sure they had good vegetables and not too much bread or sweets. If I hadn't, or if I kept Cokes in the house, they would be bouncing off the walls all night. That would not work. I needed them to settle down, not keep me up all night.

They helped me after we finished eating by clearing off the table and putting the dishes in the sink. I covered the leftovers and stuck them in the fridge.

"Now, y'all bring your pajamas while I run your bathwater down here." Rowdy watched me get the water going and then decided the boys must be doing something more fun, so he ran off up the stairs after them. I was glad. It is nerve-wracking to have little beady eyes on you.

I got the boys' towels out and ready, and poured in a little bit of bubble bath. I went over to the sink and opened the doors under it. I keep a basket of toys under there for whenever they come to stay with me.

As I stacked them on the bathtub ledge, the boys came stomping down the stairs. It is hard to believe two little boys could cause that much racket. Squealing and hollering came from the door as they roughhoused, panting out of breath and hitting and pushing each other.

"Beat you," Jason said to his little brother, while blocking the door with both arms. The younger one squirmed around and underneath. He took a run at the bathtub and jumped in, shoes and all, shooting up bubble bath foam like a torpedo had hit.

"Beat you," Mark said while Jason screeched like a monkey or some other wild jungle animal. Jason was about to jump in, too, but I caught him in time and said, "No, sir, you are not. Mark, get out of there and take those clothes off." He was just about to splash one foot out but I said, "Wait a minute. Second thought, stay in there and do it. I am not going to have you make an even bigger mess."

I turned to Jason. "You two are going to scrub down without tearing up this place. Now, I mean it. Don't let me hear you all ripping everything apart while I'm doing the dishes."

While I was at the sink, I looked out the window into my backyard. It was dark already, which would take a little getting used to, but after all, October was about over and fall was upon us. Before I knew it, Halloween would be here and gone, and it would be time to start thinking about Thanksgiving.

First things first. I thought about what I needed to do that night to stay on schedule. I would get the material for the boys' costumes, cut them out, and get them pinned where I could baste them together while we watched TV.

Speaking of the boys, I noticed it had gotten mighty quiet in the house. No battle cries or sounds of motorboats crashing and splashing. I rinsed off the last casserole dish quickly and stuck it in the drying rack. While I walked toward the bathroom, I dried my hands on the dish towel I had stuck in my apron waistband. I stood outside the door, which I'd left open a tad since Rowdy had gone in there with them. I listened but couldn't hear anything. I tapped on the door. "What's going on in there? Are you boys about done?"

I pushed the door open a few more inches and peeped inside. Three swooshes of water and foam shot up out of the tub. Water dripped down three plastered heads of hair. All three had guilty looks in their eyes. I put my hands on my hips.

Jason looked shamefaced. "Rowdy wanted to scuba dive, too," he said in their defense.

"Goodness gracious. Have you done any washing at all or has it been all playing so far?"

They didn't answer in words. The fact that they immediately grabbed their washcloths and started scrubbing told me I was right. "Well, finish up now and get dressed. And dry Lloyd Bridges off real good because I don't want wet paw prints all over my house. Hurry on up, now. We have some work to do before we can treat ourselves and watch that movie you want to see on TV tonight."

I left them to it. I straightened up everything in the

kitchen just right and stood back to see if I'd missed anything. I walked over to the back door and made sure it was locked and the chain was fixed. I twirled the miniblind rod to close the slats on the door's window and then lowered the one over the sink. I clicked on the light over the stovetop, gave the room one last look and cut off the overhead light.

As I passed the bathroom door, I hollered out, "Hurry up and come on in the living room when you finish." They didn't know it but that was a test. I've been training them to clean up after themselves, what little I can, only seeing them every week or two. Usually, I remind them to pick things up and put them away. This time, I was going to see if they did it without being told to.

I went on through to the small bedroom downstairs that I use as a sewing room. From the closet, where I keep all the fabric I pick up on sale or get for special projects, I took down the pieces I'd bought for the boys' costumes. On the way out, I grabbed my sewing box that has most everything I need in it.

The boys and Rowdy were just coming out as I passed. "Whoop. Wait right there," I said. I set down all the stuff in my arms on the dining room table. "Now, let's see how you did. Well, well. Not bad. Not bad at all." The towels had been hung up to dry. The toys were put away. The floor had a few spots of water near the bathmat, but nothing to fuss about.

"Good job, guys. Y'all go on in the living room. Don't cut on the TV yet. Get your Sunday school lessons out and settle down on the couch while I blow-dry Rowdy so he won't get a cold." I set the hair dryer on the lowest setting. I hate to say it, but his hair looked even worse than it had the last time I tried to fix it. I knew right then I needed some professional help.

Rowdy, all fluffy, dry, and proud of himself, led the way to the couch where Jason and Mark had their lesson books in their laps. I got the little one started first. His lessons mostly involved coloring pictures of Bible people. Jason, the eight-year-old, was the age to start looking up verses with his lessons. So once I got Mark settled with his colors at the coffee table and explained about Jonah and the whale, I helped Jason get started on finding his verses.

The time went by fast. I cut and sewed on their costumes while they worked. I have to admit, when the little munchkins aren't bouncing off the ceiling, it's like having angels in the house. Of all the good things in my life, this is the best, to sit and just be with them. I don't have any grandchildren of my own. My first baby was stillborn. I wanted to die myself and would have if Ronald hadn't been so good to me. I thought I'd never be happy again. But, a few years later, we had a beautiful daughter, Shannon, and she made everything all right. We had her for twenty-two wonderful years. She was killed in a car accident in Tuscaloosa where she was working after getting her degree at the university. Ronald never got over it. He started having heart problems right after that, and just kept getting worse. I sure miss them both. Not a day goes by that I don't send a special prayer up to them in heaven because I know they're there.

"Miz Phoebe." Jason put a finger down on a verse and held his Bible out to me so I could read it. "I don't get the last question. What does this mean?"

"Turning the other cheek? It means if somebody slaps you on one side of your face, rather than slapping them back, you turn where they can slap you again, except on the other side."

He looked confused. "Is that why Daddy tells us not to fight?"

"Yes, I imagine it is." Jason set the Bible down and began writing out his answer in his book. "Because it is not right to fight," I said. "It is always better to be nice and never hurt anybody. Okay, are you finished, too, Mark? That looks great. Let's put your books back in your satchels so we won't lose them."

Jason handed me his lesson and said, "Not even if they hurt you first?"

"That's right. Not even then. When you turn the other cheek, you stop the violence right then and there, see. Otherwise, it just keeps going on and on. So we never hurt anybody and we live in harmony and peace with all our brothers around the world who are also God's children. The Bible says so. Now," I said as I clapped my hands together, "I believe that good movie is fixing to start."

Mark hopped up onto the couch next to Jason and

both of them sang "Yay!" and bounced up and down on the cushions. I turned on the TV. "All right, then. Let's see who Mr. Schwarzenegger is going to blow to kingdom come for the good old U. S. of A. tonight."

fifteen
Jane Calls an Old Friend

*T*he coroner and Detective Waters had been quite sure the bones Phoebe and I found were not recent ones, and therefore not those of someone missing or perhaps killed and hidden in recent times. I tended to agree, given their brittle, stained look and the proximity of the carved symbols in the rock over-hang. Also, carefully placed rocks near the grave may have indicated an ancient burial.

I had seen many graves of all sorts imaginable in my day at archaeological digs, particularly in what I considered "my" part of the world, the border country of England and Wales. That's where I grew up. My father was a photographer in Bath, my mother's family came from a little village near Gwent in south-east Wales. It is an area full of cairns, which are rock burial mounds that dot the landscape. Many other rock monuments, smaller versions of Stonehenge and Avebury, are also scattered about, and had been my favorite place to play as a child when I would visit my grandparents. The stones, particularly the standing circles, fascinated me. I spent many a late evening among them, contemplating the sunset, in cold weather or warm, feeling their rough exteriors, wondering how many other children had done the same through the ages.

It had been quite a day. I walked out to my front yard where I could see the sun dipping behind the distant buildings of downtown Tullulah. Homer trotted toward me. He stopped, sat, looked up into my face as if to say, what shall we do now?

"Dear boy. How lucky I am to have such a willing accomplice, no matter the adventure." I sighed. "Well then, I have a small thought that seems to be taking the form of a plan."

We went inside for a cup of tea. I decided to re-house the contents of Cal's box #2 into more suitable, and cleaner, quarters. I took it into the kitchen. All Cal's paperwork I placed on the counter in two stacks, notes and maps. The two odd objects he'd seen fit to include, I lined up on the kitchen table alongside the tiny glass flower, the better to ponder them all under the circle of yellow light from the low-hanging ceiling lamp. The box was marginally fit for recycle. The objects were old, damaged by time and elements, their origins unknown, their possible importance inexplic-able.

They brought old times to mind and more thoughts of my old friend Michael. From among saved archae-ological magazines, I found an issue in which he was featured some years ago. I kept it for the photos of him, of course, though I never realized that was the reason before, not until now.

I kept it to remember his joyous look as he held up a find for the camera against a backdrop of lapis blue sky, and another as he bent upon his work with a delicate brush to gently sweep away dirt from something possibly unimportant, possibly a treasure. Either way, he smiled as if digging in the dirt was the happiest of jobs.

A glance at the magazine's date told me it had been over five years since we last talked. I could hardly believe it had been so long. I'd phoned him after the article came out. Much had happened in those five years as the Colonel's health declined, and I suppose I was so wrapped up in keeping him comfortable that all other things were pushed aside.

On a whim, I turned on my laptop and surfed the Web for mentions of Michael's work.

"Good heavens!" I hadn't expected anything so dramatic. In the third column, the article said, "Dr. Hay recently foiled thieves who attempted to steal a collection of precious relics from the university anthropology department. Dr. Hay suffered a mild concussion but returned to work immediately. The thieves are still at large. Thanks to his quick actions, the majority of artifacts remain on display. One item was taken, an eighteenth-century silver box from the bequest of Louis Welch, generous benefactor to the university for many years."

Poor dear. In the photo, only a small bandage above his left eye gave a hint of his bad experience. He had the same smile, the same twinkle of mischief in his eyes, with a good deal more wrinkles around them since I'd seen him last.

I rose from my chair to get my address book, with the hope that Michael's number hadn't changed. As it happened, I was in luck.

"Jane, my dear, how lovely to hear your voice," he said, his own voice perhaps a bit more gravelly than before, but otherwise with the same lightness of heart. We spent the first few minutes catching up with one another's lives. Among the chitchat, he told me his wife, Lillian, a brilliant researcher whom I had become quite fond of when we worked in Arizona, had succumbed to cancer two years earlier.

I didn't know what to say other than, "I'm sorry," the old standby that does nothing much to relieve either party. In any case, Michael, never one to dwell on what one cannot change nor sad events in the past, asked to hear of Tullulah's attraction. His astonishment when I told him where I moved didn't surprise me. But if I could convince him to assist me with the burial site, he would soon understand.

"Of course I want to come. Silly girl. Who needs rest when there are wonders to be unearthed? Interesting. I've never worked on a dig in the southeast. How could I pass up the chance? Particularly when no bureaucrats would be looking over my shoulder or fussing over budgets."

He phoned back within the hour with his travel arrangements. This pleased me no end. It made me feel he really did want to come, not just out of obligation or for a favor. I agreed to meet him at the airport in Huntsville the following day. Funny, but as soon as I hung up the phone, my first thought was not of cooking or cleaning in preparation but of Phoebe and her assuredly pointed interest in what might be the most handsome man she or I had ever known.

With that arranged, Homer and I rounded the side of the house, across the wide stretch of back lawn to the small shed that held my gardening supplies and other various tools. The door hinges creaked against the aged wood planks.

Though it was waning, there was enough daylight to see inside without aid of the flashlight I brought. I could have found what I wanted by feel, if need be. I took down my old leatherwork belt, hanging on a nail near the door. Once I coaxed Homer away from the many interesting smells around the shed floor, I latched the door behind us.

Rather than take the car, I felt like a night roam. We set off, crossing Anisidi Road and heading back toward the bones.

Once under the tree canopy, I reached into my belt for the flashlight. So long as I could see Homer blazing the trail, I had no worries usually, but with so many branches having fallen during the storm, I thought it best to play it safe. Homer knew these woods much better than I, having walked them all his life with Cal, his previous human. Homer, however, could see well enough to avoid tripping. The quiet enveloped us. I can't tell you the joy of complete freedom I felt, something few people experience these days it would seem, to be able to walk alone in the night, with no intrusive noises of loud humans, away from the fear of evil men whose only occupation is causing pain to others.

We came to the burial site easily. I removed the tarp and set it aside to gaze over the remains. Now that we were in the open on the high overlook, the last of the day's sunlight shone on the promontory and on the trees behind us in their autumn array, creating a moving yellow-orange glow around the clearing. It was as if a cinematographer had chosen a gel that perfectly accentuated the scenery's undulations, shrouding it with mystery. I glanced beyond the gravesite and to the right where the rock overhang's engravings were barely discernable.

They were covered for the most part by the brush that Cal had placed in front of the rock. He had done a good job, though certainly he was overly cautious. He had frightened off all locals who had attempted to enter his land. This particular spot would have been extremely difficult for anyone to happen upon, even if they had gotten past Cal and his partner, Homer, undetected.

Cal's respect for his ancestors would have made him be extra careful, however, and I understood that. I wondered for a moment if he would have wanted any sort of excavation, were he still alive and showing me this spot himself. It was hard to say. That was a subject of some debate between us. He had been adamantly against any sort of digging for scientific study. His people, he would say, deserved to rest in peace, not to be taken apart. I told him that respectful re-burial was part of the process. He seemed to waver at times, wanting, I think, to share the beauty of his land and also to contribute to knowledge of ancient times and ways.

I hadn't expected to come so quickly to such a decision myself. I'd thought I would have time to explore fully and then consider everything with much care. But here, with the storm's sudden intervention, I was presented with the first of what surely might be many such difficult situations. I moved to where Cal had stuck brush around the rock carvings. Only a few tugs and the brush camouflage pulled free. Once the entire area, approximately four feet across, was cleared, I flattened the leaves and branches into a makeshift pillow and sat upon it, facing the carvings, to meditate upon them.

At first, I concentrated on the textures of rock and crevice, imagined how a knife made of sharpened chert or limestone cut into the hard surface. Perhaps the writer tried many types of arrowhead edges before the one that cut best was used to finish the sentence. For it was, it appeared to me, something like a eulogy carved into a natural tombstone.

I let the figures run together as I scanned them left to right, over and over. It would be such a lovely adventure to hunt each down in Cal's books. I had barely scratched the surface in studying them. I gave a slow perusal of them once more and closed my eyes to see how many I could remember.

I managed four in the correct order, jumbled a few others. Once more, I slowly studied the lines in the dusk. Something about them struck a familiar chord. I didn't know why. With eyes shut, I imagined them again, lingering on each image rather than hurriedly trying to remember the next. I willed them to turn, as if three-dimensional, in the soft yellow-orange glow of the sunset against a backdrop of black.

One by one, the symbols paraded before me as I contemplated the wonder of their making, of the person buried here, of those who mourned. Again, a familiarity tugged at my memory. My thoughts drifted to the surrounding area, of forest and beyond to the low mountains in the east, to my dear little town. Yes, I realized, I thought of it as mine now, even after such a short time of living here. It had been in my heart, in my dreams for many years before I even knew it existed.

My mental movie traveled back from the town toward the forest again, with trees and plants moving past me as if I watched from a car window. The camera's eye stopped at me, slowing, examining, first myself as I sat, then Homer a few feet away, then sped up once again as it careened deeper into woods, circling and returning. It hovered just in front of me over the rock where a swirl of blue mist settled in a roughly cylindrical shape and slowly spread across the breadth of the rock.

It sparkled there with an indefinable movement in its center. It rose a few inches above the rock and, emulating my previous mental exercise with the symbols, it turned for me, slowly, as if it too were three-dimensional, as if it were showing off, smiling perhaps, joyful, beautiful, very old. Though I was aware this was merely a sort of hallucination or dream state, it felt as if I were witnessing a real object. No, not an object, a being. Not exactly that, either. A personality made of earth and rock.

While this fancy played, another train of thought moved along another path, like a soundtrack accompanying film. It didn't move through the forest, but through time, backward, passing swiftly to before my arrival, before my house was built, before the arrivals of tribe after tribe who passed, camped, and lived here. Such beautiful feelings swept over me as I watched each era pass by. Yet even as they warmed me, a growing sense of dread crept in.

Much goodness has been in this place, kind people filling the air and soil with their purity and goodwill. Even so, evil found its way here. I remembered reading about the death of a young child, found murdered over eighty years earlier near my property.

Suddenly, the blue swirling image stopped turning and I heard, felt, a great *whump,* a mixture of pressure and sound that reverberated through the forest as if a great bass drum had been struck.

With a jolt, I opened my eyes. I sat in complete darkness. The sound had not been only in my imagination. All night noises stopped abruptly as birds, insects, all living things within the forest listened, waited, to consider the intrusive and possibly dangerous sound. Something rustled to my left then Homer pressed his muzzle against my hand. I patted his head, let my hand drape over his solid back.

As my eyes adjusted to our surroundings again, I blinked, trying to understand what was in front of us. The sun was well set, but the carved symbols were visible through a light blue mist or aura that illuminated the entire rock surface, above and below to the ground. It stretched across to enclose the circle of ground where the bones lay exposed and a large area around them on the forest floor. Homer and I sat perhaps an hour or more longer, just watching the sky, the flood of light from an almost full moon, listening to the woods' night song.

That night I dreamt of black stars, burnt into a sky that was in relief, suggesting a great void rather than a universe full of wonders. Charred trunks of trees stuck up like the jagged edges of serrated knives, across an expanse of dead ashes that was once fertile land. All burned. No birds or animals moved about on the barren landscape, only a cold relentless wind.

sixteen
Jane Gets a Gift, a Call,
and a Visitor

*T*he next day, I donned my running clothes, tied on my shoes, and went downstairs to meet the new morning. I had much on my mind.

Phoebe had something planned for me. Her excitement over the library's annual Halloween haunted house seemed to be contagious. In spite of my disinterest in the holiday and my reluctance to participate in whatever silly schemes Phoebe had concocted, I found myself agreeing to help. Phoebe, I had learned, is a strong force. Once pulled into her orbit, the objects of her intent rarely escape whatever fate she has in mind for them.

She had not revealed my part, only that I was essential and that it would delight and horrify the little ones of Tullulah to such a degree they would be speaking of it for years, if not decades, to their own children.

"Jane, it's going to be big," she told me, waving her arms out like a movie director who was trying to convey the big picture.

"What, exactly, do you have in mind, as far as my part is concerned?"

"I'm not sure yet. I haven't figured it all out. I'm still cogitating."

So, with a shrug, I left it at that with the small hope

I would be written out of the script by the time she finished hatching the plot.

The sun was just a sliver behind the far hills when Homer and I returned from our morning run. My tai chi routine cooled me down and left me invigorated.

"Ready for breakfast, dear?" I asked Homer. He answered by licking his lips and quickly setting off for the kitchen.

Rather than follow me to the refrigerator and sit nearby, he turned away and sniffed the air. He went slowly and carefully away from me, in the other direction, straight to the center of the room, just as he had done when Boo left the little blue flower. His nose worked furiously as he neared something on the kitchen floor, something that had not been there the night before.

I stopped in place. After a moment of staring, I moved as well. I set the towel down from wiping my hands and walked toward Homer with a bit of a flutter in my chest.

He circled the object before he stopped and sat facing me. He gave me a meaningful look then returned his attention to the object, hard-looking and colored red and brown, about four inches long and a half-inch thick, with flat areas on both sides.

He dipped his face down until the very tip of his nose touched it ever so slightly before he jerked his head back with a start. He reached out a paw, gave it a test tap, then another with a bit more force. It skidded a few inches, whirling slowly to a stop.

I bent down beside Homer as we both considered it. The coat of green moss and mud on the alleged rock's uneven surface considered us in return and, like the two of us, remained mute.

After some moments of silence, Homer whispered a breathy woof, though never breaking his intense concentration on the rock until I spoke.

"What has he left us this time?"

He blinked. I tugged his ear. "Well then, it appears to mean us no harm. Once our breakfast is done, we shall contemplate it further."

Homer stayed with the rock at first, dividing his attention between it and my movements. The opening of the refrigerator door, however, proved to be too much of an enticement. He trotted over to me, and we resumed our usual morning routine.

Once the kettle was on, he followed me to the den, where I turned on my computer to listen to the BBC, usually Radio 4. I find it gets the day going properly. So, after I'd set our breakfasts down and taken my first sip of tea, Homer and I listened to the latest installment of an Agatha Raisin abridgement. We sat and thought, both of us staring at the rock that should not be there but most assuredly was.

Though the trek through the woods later that morning was still muddy on the paths and slippery on the leaf-strewn hillocks and clearings, my spirits lifted with each step as I neared the bones. The lightning tree, as I had come to think of it, had kept coming to my mind in flashes. Now, as I crested the edge of the last rise, I slowed and stopped there to look at the great felled tree.

It looked like a giant in repose. I took out my notebook to jot down a few questions and random observations that began to stir and surface.

First, why was this spot chosen for a burial? According to Cal's notebooks, most native burials have been discovered in the mounds found near rivers. Yet, Dr. Jenkins mentioned that he had seen native burials similar to this one, with nearby rock engravings. I made a note to research burial methods in Cal's book collection.

Was this place chosen for this particular tree perhaps? If so, why this one out of the hundreds of thousands that surround it? Or was it due to the cave overhang? Again, why? I suspected many more shelters similar to this one must dot the land here from what I had heard so far. Or was there some other reason, something more personal and simple, like this was where he lived? Were other family members also buried here?

That thought gave me a bit of a jolt. Until then, I hadn't seriously considered Phoebe's earlier suggestions, that this might be a cemetery. I reminded myself I must take great care in all I do here.

The tarp covering the bones looked undisturbed, the rocks I'd placed around its edges unmoved. Nevertheless, I moved them aside on one end and pulled back the bright blue sheet to satisfy myself that the skeleton was still there.

A bit of research the previous night reminded me to bring a few extra tools along this time. I reached into my work belt for a tape measure and set about recording data of what was visible. It took great willpower to keep myself from clawing into the earth to reveal the complete skull from which I might make a few preliminary determinations. Any disturbance must wait until after Dr. Norwood gave her approval.

All I could surmise from the small area that lay exposed was that it was the head of an adult of fairly advanced age, for the cranial fissures were almost completely gone. What little I could see of the hand and arm that protruded from the grave gave me no further information. But what wonders would be found below? I began feeling more anxious that the coroner would get back in touch soon. Another feeling came that surprised me, a certain giddiness at the prospect of seeing my old friend Michael very soon.

Now that I'd given the site another look, my earlier misgivings about the coincidences of box, storm, tree, and dreams had vanished. This was the site described by Cal in detail in his notes, of that I had no doubt. The drawings and maps, and the three odd articles in the box had been collected here.

Precisely how they would fit into the larger story of this place remained to be seen. However, I knew they would fit and that they would reveal their purposes in their own time. After living here hardly a month, already I'd learned that what might be considered spectacularly unlikely, wildly improbable, or even impossible in other places, might be considered an everyday occurrence here.

When Homer and I returned home, he went out for a prowl. The phone rang while I swept the front porch, trying to tidy up a bit before Michael arrived. I leaned my broom beside the door and stepped inside, expecting to hear Phoebe on the line.

Static greeted me instead. A tiny shiver ran up my neck before my caller spoke. "Miz Jane? This here is Dad Burn. You doing all right?"

"Yes, Mr. Burn. Quite well. And you?" I immediately chastised myself for it occurred to me that asking after one's health might be insensitive if the person in question is deceased. Dad, being the kind soul he is, allayed my concern.

"Oh, I'm doing very well, thank you. We have a better connection this time."

"Yes. I hear you much more clearly."

"Good, good. Listen, there's a couple of things I need to tell you. It's about that tree . . ."

Dad and I had spoken on only one other occasion, at which time it became clear he was privy to things related to another odd set of experiences. Dad Burn, you see, is on the other side. The other side of precisely what, I couldn't say. In our previous conversation, he called in order to pass on information he thought would be helpful. He was right. I wondered what he or his fellow dearly-departees wished to relay this time.

"Excellent! What can you tell me about it?" I asked.

"Ain't it a beauty? Or was. Actually, there's two things, but mainly the scar."

My first thought was of the bones, that he meant me to look for a scar on them, perhaps indicating foul play from a knife wound.

"No," he said, though I hadn't voiced my thoughts. "The scars on the tree. Where the lightning hit. Cal says to look in those Indian books about lightning."

"Cal is there with you? Could I speak to him?"

After a bout of loud static and a moment or two of silence, Dad said, "No, I reckon that's not going to work. Sorry. I don't rightly understand why."

"No apology necessary. It's lovely speaking with you."

"You, too, Miz Jane. You're sure enough a peach. And while I'm thinking of it, everybody over here wants to say thank you for what all you and that firecracker Phoebe did. Lord have mercy, what a sight that was."

While he laughed, I cringed at the thought that Phoebe and I inadvertently had an otherworldly audience during our grand adventure several weeks earlier. It made me feel a bit like a Roman slave at the Coliseum, there to provide entertainment that might or might not be fatal.

"But that scar," he continued. "Cal says it's important, so read in his books, and then he says to go see Ruby and tell her about it. She'll know what to do." The static increased in volume once again, as if the power that made Dad Burn's call possible were fading. "Anyway, it sounds like my time is about up. For some reason, I can't last very long on the phone, seems like. So, I'll let you go."

"Wait. You said you had two things to tell me."

"I did? Oh, right. I sure did. Sorry about that. I wish I'd died younger so I'd still have my memory. The second thing is that Reese has some things connected to that tree and that box Cal left you, so you need to go see him when you see Ruby."

His words suddenly sounded distant, as if he turned his head away from the phone receiver to talk to Cal, because he said, "All right, all right, I'm getting there. I'm a'fixin' to tell her right now. Keep your drawers on, for pete's sake.

"All right," he said in full voice to me. "He says when it's all over, go look in Reese's barn."

"But, Dad, who are Ruby and Reese? How do I go about finding them?"

"They live farther out the county road, past your place. Phoebe knows. Take her with you. For crying out loud, Cal, what is it, now?"

Another bout of static came over the line. Then silence. "We seem to be losing signal," I said. He didn't answer. "Dad, if you can hear me, I'll say good-bye then. Perhaps we can talk later. Thank you very much indeed for the call. Please call again. Anytime."

"He says . . ." The static was now even louder. "Can you hear me?"

"Yes," I said. "Faintly but I hear you."

After a pause, he said, "Cal says be sure and take . . ." His voice was progressively weaker.

"Take what?"

". . . be sure and keep your rifle with you. All the time." The line buzzed a moment longer, then went dead.

I headed straight away for the nearest chair to collapse. Even friendly encounters with the other side left me in need of a bit of rest. One thing was certain. I could have done without that last bit. However, the incident gave me an idea I should have thought of before. I made one more phone call.

"Riley? This is Jane Thistle."

Riley Gardner hunts ghosts. He and two of his friends, all young people in their twenties, come out to my place on occasional nights in the hopes of finding proof of spirits.

"I may have a hunting tip for you," I said. "The next time you and the girls are in the area, come into my backyard to the old shed, if you like. Homer and I heard noises there the other night. And I . . ." I caught myself before I told him I had actually seen a ghostly figure as well. That would not do. The less others knew about my affliction, the better.

"That is, Homer and I felt something, a presence, if you like."

"You got vaaahhbes?" he said with hushed fervor.

"Yes, vibes, I suppose you could say, or something like that. I thought I heard crying."

"Thank you, ma'am. We'll check that for you, sure thing. Thank you."

Such a nice boy. It made no difference to me if his team found anything or not. I was glad to have something to offer them, something they might enjoy doing since they were such lovely kids. For them, the thrill was in the hunt, in the hope of finding something magical. Not so very different from myself, I suppose.

Later that afternoon, I was well into a nice weight-lifting routine when Homer barked outside. He came into view on the other side of my Florida room's mostly glass wall. At first, my arms automatically continued their rhythm. He must have barked several times before it registered with me what an unusual occurrence this was, for he rarely made a sound.

He never barked, certainly not more and more loudly as he was then. I set the dumbbell in its stand. While I wiped my towel across my face, I walked through from the sunroom to the living room to look out the window.

A car had rolled to a stop in my drive. I didn't recognize it or its driver, a man in his forties, I thought, dressed in jeans and a long-sleeved Native American–print shirt. A string of terra cotta beads hung from his neck. He was a tall man with deep red hair that hung in strings around his ears.

"Mrs. Thistle? I'm Lyle Graybear. I'm with tribal affairs." His smile revealed unnaturally perfect teeth. His speech revealed an accent that was neither local nor Southern.

"How do you do?" I shook his hand and waited for him to continue.

"I hear bones of an Old One have been found on your property. I'm here to help the local tribe oversee the handling, to be sure proper respect is shown and that our people are re-buried with dignity."

"I see. Proper respect is certainly my intention."

"Good. Then we won't have any problems. I was hoping you would show me the site this afternoon." He looked at his watch. "I'd like to get an idea of what we're dealing with."

Something about his words disturbed me. Or perhaps the selfish side of me came forward, not wanting to share a part of my land with someone I'd only just met.

"Actually, this isn't a convenient time. I'm afraid I have guests visiting soon, and I'm unsure of my schedule for the next few days. Is there a number where I can call you?"

He hesitated, looking all around my property, both house and woods. "Sure." He pulled his wallet from a back pocket, found a scrap of paper, and wrote down a number. "This is my cell. You can call anytime. I'd like to have a look as soon as possible, though. If you don't mind."

I took the number but made no promises. Detective Waters planned to bring a few local tribe members over the following day. He hadn't mentioned that a tribal affairs representative would be here before then. I decided to ask him about this man first before I agreed to show him the site.

Later that evening, Riley Gardner stopped by the

house to have a look around the backyard shed. He and his ghost-hunting friends, Sarah and Callie, wore workmen's tool belts slung low on their hips and photographer's vests with many pockets. Small gadgets of unknown use filled them. They had come prepared to work.

Homer joined us and actually went ahead to wait at the shed's door as if he understood Riley and the girls' purpose here. Riley, tall and lanky, strode forward while readying a handheld device. His hair hung to his shoulders. His moustache looked similar, hanging in long strands past his chin. An out-of-date set of infrared binoculars sat on his head with the aid of a tight strap.

Sarah, a tall plump blonde with her hair cut in a short bob, carried a small digital video recorder, ready to shoot. "Is Mrs. Twigg here with you tonight?" she asked.

"No, dear. Not this time."

Her face relaxed a bit and she sighed. Phoebe, ever the skeptic, had given Sarah and the others a bit of a hard time when we first met.

"I'm getting a slightly elevated reading," Callie said as she looked down at a box with a glass meter, similar in looks to a voltmeter. Its hand bounced up and down the scale but not into the red. Callie wore farmer's overalls and a long-sleeved red shirt. Her pigtails were tied low at her neck and rested on her shoulders.

I opened the shed's door while the three of them

scanned their instruments around the area. With barely room for two at a time inside, they took turns, holding their instruments high and low over shelving, flower-pots and gardening tools, and quite a bit of dust. Standing outside, an air of disappointment hung about them. None of their gadgets registered any measurable phenomena.

We walked around the yard for a while, still with no results, when suddenly Homer stopped short and made a quiet *gruff* sound in his throat. He held per-fectly still, staring toward the creek.

I followed his gaze across the yard. The creek served as dividing line between the right side of my lawn and an adjoining meadow. It gurgled out of the woods and past my house, under the road and across to Cal's forest. At the section directly across from where we stood, I thought I saw a man kneeling and dipping his hand into the water for a drink.

Homer's body tensed but he made no further sound or movement. "Good boy," I said as I stooped near his ear. "Stay."

Callie noticed Homer's reaction. She was about to remark on it, I'm sure, when we heard a frightened cry. Though it was muffled, we all heard it. The others looked in the direction of the man at the creek but didn't appear to see him.

Riley pulled his binoculars down while Sarah and Callie moved out. The man cried again. This time, I could understand his words.

"They're coming! I see them on the road! Take

cover!" He ran toward us with an effort, with one leg stiff and a hand clutched at his side. As he approached, I could see he wore a double-breasted jacket. He had a bandage wrapped around his head and a terrified expression on his face.

Riley crouched as he moved his handheld gizmo side to side. When the man came closer, the gizmo beeped just as Riley grabbed one side of his binoculars. "Sarah! I'm getting a cold spot! It's coming toward us!"

Sarah clicked her camera on and followed Riley's body movements as he tracked the "cold spot." I knew what he meant. The binoculars could detect heat differences in objects. Many times, the presence of ghosts is reported to coincide with marked drops in temperature, so the theory is the special binoculars may help in detecting lack of or very low heat emissions in what might be ghosts.

The limping man breathed heavily as he came upon us. He looked about to speak but when he saw the set of binoculars strapped on Riley's head and the electronic devices Sarah and Callie were using, he shrieked and turned toward the house. Riley, Sarah, and Callie followed their readings and thereby followed the man, but not for long. His body glistened, winked out, and reappeared beside the back porch, sobbing throughout, then vanished into the basement wall.

"Gone," Riley said. His companions and their instruments agreed. They found no trace of him inside the house or out afterward, but promised to try again soon.

In the wee hours of morning, I heard him again. I crept downstairs to the kitchen and listened. He was still in the basement.

I had an idea. I kept a small recorder in my pocket on my daily forest walks. I used it for reminders and to note locations of special flowers or birds I happened upon. Once I retrieved it from the den, I moved down the basement steps as quietly as I could. The sobs continued. They still sounded muffled somehow, so I wasn't sure the recording would pick anything up. Still, I turned it on and left it running in hopes of catching something for Riley and his troops to hear.

seventeen
Jane's Old Friend Arrives

*W*hen I saw Michael making his way through the crowded airport, it was as if no time had passed. Time and age had hardly changed him. We embraced for a long while, happy, exchanging condolences and sorrows. The long ride home gave us plenty of time to catch up on each other's lives. Once we arrived, we hardly had time for a coffee.

"The police and forensic anthropologist will be here shortly," I said. "Perhaps you'd like to rest while I see to them."

"At the site?"

"Yes."

"Do I look so decrepit as that, love?" He put his arms around me for another lovely hug.

"Of course not. Very good. Get your things upstairs, then, and we can be on our way as soon as they arrive."

We heard the anthropologist's car first. Detective Waters drove up behind her. From the detective's unmarked police sedan, two other people got out and came to meet me.

"Grant McWhorter," the tall, well-built man said as he shook my hand. "It's nice to see you." His hair was short and chestnut brown with threads of silver. Beneath his denim shirt collar, he wore a bead-and-bone neck ornament that covered his throat, like the gorgets worn as neck protection during battles. Many had been found at native archaeological sites.

The lady with him reached out to shake my hand as well. "I'm Carol, Grant's wife," she said in a soft, pleasant voice.

She was a bit taller than I, and some years younger, perhaps in her forties. She wore a blue T-shirt, jeans, and a sweater. Her teeth shone like pearls in a lovely contrast to her light brown skin and eyes.

Both she and her husband had only a hint of native ancestry in their faces. If not for their clothing and accessories and that I knew their purpose here, I might not have noticed any hint at all. In fact, Carol's rounded features reminded me very much of a cousin in my father's family, all staunch denizens of Perthshire.

After Detective Waters introduced us to Dr. Norwood, the anthropologist, we hopped into the backseat of her car, which led the entourage slowly over the bumpy road, higher and higher into the woods, as far as the road allowed.

Michael, I had noticed, had become more and more fidgety on the drive. I smiled at his remarks on the beautiful fall foliage. It pleased me to see his reactions as we passed through the woods. He loved it as much as I do, I could tell. His appreciation of plants and trees pleased me so, but indeed it was no surprise. He had a great joy for natural wonders.

A breath caught in his throat. He reached for my arm without turning to look at me. "Look," he said. He pointed out the window. There, as if framed for a picture through a gap in the trees, in a sunlit clearing of white light, stood a doe and two young bucks. Four other small deer, just beyond them and more hidden by leaves, turned to watch the car lumber past, with curiosity rather than fear. No doubt they were confident of their own abilities to outrun such a slow and noisy beast.

Michael hardly knew I was there for the duration of the ride. He fixed his attention on the scenery, and it was only when the car came to a stop that he turned a glowing face toward mine. With a laugh, he embraced me, his gray curls brushing across my ear, his face scratching a bit across my cheek.

"Jane, my dear, you've found a paradise."

How well I knew. "I have indeed. I'm glad you like it."

He straightened his arms to hold me away from him. We sat there, looking at each other that way for some time, deeply, through years past and many memories.

A quick walk uphill brought us to the edge of the wide flat overlook where the fallen tree and its bones rested. Detective Waters led the way. "Not quite so muddy today," he said. "Yesterday I thought we were going to sink a time or two."

Michael walked past the site to stand at the crest of the mountain. He surveyed the lower peaks and the valley far below, where the river glinted in the sun. When he turned, he took in all that lay before us with a wide grin across his face.

"Ah," he said, as he rubbed his palms together then clapped them on his chest and took a deep breath. And then he did something that made my heart fill with joy. I had forgotten his habit of old. He began to hum. He always did this at the beginning of a project, when hopes were high. He stepped, or more accurately, bounced, closer to the blue tarp, taking note of what lay directly around him as he neared it.

So much like a little boy he was. I had to laugh. "Still fond of Gilbert and Sullivan, I see."

He smiled, turned, and with a theatrical stride, came toward me as he sang, "I am the monarch of the sea . . ." in a rich baritone.

I laughed at him. "No sea here, love, not for many miles."

He took another deep breath through his nostrils. "And yet I can smell the fresh tang of salt in the air.

The scent of adventure. We embark on our voyage to unknown lands, eh?"

He bowed low and waved his arm out for me to precede him before he resumed his jaunty humming. Quite so. His exhilaration at digs had always infected the crews and was the reason he never had too few colleagues with which to work. He had his choice of the best in their fields. His knowledge and his way of making work fun for everyone gained him as much respect as his strict adherence to detail on sites. Top drawer all the way, he was. I had missed my old friend.

When the tarp was removed, Michael's humming stopped and was replaced by soft moaning breaths with each feature he noted as he gazed at the large oval indention in the ground, left by the tree's giant upturned roots. In daylight, the blue aura I'd seen previously was barely discernible but still there, more as a vague blue film over the bones and perhaps a fifteen-foot square area around them.

Michael, Dr. Norwood, and Grant McWhorter settled on their haunches to study the partially exposed skeleton. Carol and I stood behind them, with Detective Waters opposite us, as a hush came over the group. Detective Waters looked at Grant and Carol. Grant nodded. He stood as he and his wife began a song, a low and sorrowful tune that caught in the cool fall breeze and twirled around us and down and around the inside of the burial indention to caress the bones with its ancient Indian words. At the end of the song, Grant and Carol chanted a short prayer, after which we paused in our own private meditations, mine on the unspeakable beauty of the world and of life.

We turned our attention once again to the exposed area. The skull was turned to the side, as if it tried to look out from the dirt that covered half its face in order to peer back at us.

"Photos first then?" Michael said. He, Dr. Norwood, and I all snapped pictures of every feature of the site. Once done, Michael took out a handheld recorder and spoke into it, noting observations and general thoughts.

I took out my notebook to jot down a few things, then as Michael and the forensic anthropologist began to speak, I moved closer. Their words might have sounded like code to anyone inexperienced in such finds. Fortunately, I had not been so long away from the world of digs that I couldn't decipher their meanings.

Dr. Norwood set her black kit bag down and opened it. She withdrew a small clear plastic container and unscrewed its top. Michael responded by taking out a short knife from the backpack of tools he'd brought. He reached in where the soil was more loosely packed, at the side of the gaping hole. Not a word passed between the two, yet they worked in concert like surgeons well acquainted with one another's methods.

With the soil samples procured, they moved on to

other spots of interest, sometimes snapping more photos, taking measurements of everything imaginable. I pitched in a bit myself as they directed me. Detective Waters stood aside, though the McWhorters watched and asked occasional questions. They had joined the detective, who had made himself comfortable by sitting on a waist-high rock part of the old wall.

We all became aware of twigs snapping and leaves crunching, not far away and coming toward us.

"You expecting someone?" Detective Waters said.

"No. No one knows this place."

He jumped off the rock, immediately running to his vehicle. We heard him opening his trunk. When he returned, he held a shotgun. From the edge of the ridge, he looked in the direction of the sound.

Along with the others, I stood still and listened. After a moment, I saw the detective's shoulders and arms relax. He transferred the shotgun under one arm and looked toward the sounds that could now be more clearly recognized as human footsteps. Since the first frightening thoughts I'd had were of black bears and bobcats, one would think I'd have been a bit more relieved.

I wasn't. I was furious. Only two other people knew of this place. The coroner would have driven here as we had. Phoebe would never have voluntarily walked through the woods and certainly not this far in over rough terrain. I expected to see the illegal hunter who had trespassed before.

As soon as he stepped into view, Detective Waters walked quickly to him. "You lost?" he said.

He attempted a smirk, but when he saw Detective Waters, he tried to run away. Obviously, the two had met before and were not the happier for seeing each other again. The detective was too fast and too close. He put his arm around the man's shoulders and held him there.

"Mr. Graybear!"

Graybear cast a glance at Grant McWhorter. "I have a right to be here."

"You're wrong about that," Grant said. "You're welcome at our camp as our brother. This place is only ours to visit by invitation."

"Mrs. Thistle, I take it you did not invite this man?"

I shook my head. Detective Waters leaned his shotgun against a tree. I looked over my shoulder. Michael was just getting up. Dr. Norwood, already up, watched, shifting her weight to one leg.

Carol had something else on her mind. She moved across the burial opening as if she were protecting something. At first, I thought she meant to block the view of the skeleton. However the angle looked wrong.

Detective Waters released Graybear. He relaxed his hands and rested them on top of his belt. "I'll say this, boy, you are one mighty fine Indian." Waters smiled and spoke in his fake country way. "You got that tracking through the woods down good, don't you, son? What did you do, hop on my bumper and ride in with us?" Detective Waters laughed. He gave our intruder a manly slap on the back and squeezed his shoulder. "You might want to work on that stealthy part though, huh? But you don't have to worry about crashing through the woods or jumping on my bumper on the way out."

He gave him another clap on the shoulder when suddenly he moved his free hand to the back of his belt. At the same time, he brought the hand on Graybear's shoulder down and clamped his wrist in a firm grip. He snapped on a pair of handcuffs, quick as a flash. The cuffs had clicked shut and Graybear's other arm brought to his back for the other side of the cuffs before the rest of us had hardly registered what happened.

"No, sir, you're going to ride out in comfort in the backseat of my car. You are under arrest for trespassing." He looked down at his captive's hands and spoke in a deceptively gentle voice. "You didn't fall and hurt yourself on the way here, did you?"

Graybear said nothing.

"Because your fingers sure are dirty. Oh, yeah, I was supposed to ask you if you had any dangerous objects in your pockets that might hurt me when I search them."

Graybear grimaced and closed his eyes.

"What is this we've got here?" Waters retrieved two small objects from one pocket. He held them up, each about three inches high, between his thumb and index finger. Arrowheads. "Where did you get these?" Graybear said nothing. "Because they've got the same kind of dirt that's on your hands. This does not look good for you, son."

The detective recited Miranda rights, then pulled his charge toward the car. Graybear jerked his body in the opposite direction but was no match in strength for the larger, taller policeman. Graybear did, however, gain a step or two to his right.

"You'll hear about this from my council."

"That I might," Waters said. "I heard from them last time, that they'd be happy for me to keep you. You just aren't very good at making friends at all, are you?"

Graybear yanked his arms once more in an attempt to twist out of the detective's grip. He didn't achieve that, but stumbled farther to the side. He gave me a look of distaste but only for an instant. His head moved so that he stared at a spot to my left and behind me. I turned to see what it was. He had moved too quickly for Carol to compensate before he saw what she hid.

It was the scar. His expression changed to one of awe and great interest for the few seconds of clear view he had before Carol blocked the scar once more. Detective Waters moved his gaze sharply to the tree for only a second then pulled Graybear around by the arms. Pointed in the opposite direction, he marched him to the police car.

"Y'all carry on. Never mind us. Take your time," the detective said. "I'll be right back."

Michael resumed his work, clearing away dirt with a careful hand around the skull. He assigned me a few tasks as he and Dr. Norwood worked steadily for the rest of the afternoon.

When I wasn't busy assisting the two doctors, I enjoyed talking with Grant and Carol, both of whom were quite knowledgeable about the plants that grew nearby. They pointed out a nice patch of ginseng as well as other healing herbs, some of which I'd seen mentioned in Cal's notebooks full of potions. They spent time at the rock overhang where the engraved markings were much easier to see in full daylight now that the storm clouds had cleared.

Grant put his hand on the slope of rock overhead and felt the markings. "Many other shelters like this one are scattered around. We've never been to this one, of course. It's a beauty."

We walked along the ridge together, away from the burial site, following the line of the low wall of rock built perhaps two yards from the edge of the mountaintop. I took more pictures, and when Michael took a break, we walked around it again and back to muse over the overhang engravings.

We heard Detective Waters's car returning through the woods. Michael and Dr. Norwood agreed that the day's work was done and began to repack their tools.

This struck me as odd. I didn't question them, but found it strange that they would stop while we still had a couple of hours of daylight left. With time short as far as re-burial regulations of native bones, it seemed to me that it would be better to do as much as possible as soon as possible. However, when the detective joined us again, Michael made everything clear.

"We've been able to make a few determinations," he said as he knelt beside the bones. "We will both check our measurements against profiles in our software programs to confirm our findings. But neither of us have doubts in a few key areas."

He ran a finger over the dome of the skull where the joints of bone interlocked. "Here you see the sutures are vague, almost completely grown together. I would say he was about forty years old at the time of death."

"He?" Detective Waters said.

"Yes." Michael moved slightly so as to reach the hip bones that they had exposed. "Here, the angle of this notch in males is narrow." He put his thumb on the notch and wiggled it. "Too tight. In females, the angle is wider." He moved back to the skull to point at other telling features. "Several things here, a retreating forehead, square chin, the occipital protuberance here at the back. The more rounded blunt superior orbital margins." He gently traced the eye sockets. "Most definitely male. But the things of most interest for all here today are these."

He moved his hand over the nose area, the cheeks, the chin, and the teeth. "A long nasal opening that is tall and narrow. The chin is projected. The anterior protrusion of the dental arch, the oval eye orbits. All these tell us that this person was not Native American. He was Caucasian."

A silence fell over the group. I hadn't even considered that this was anything but a native burial, yet surely I should have. Cal's ancestors who were white would also have been buried on this land for many generations. Most likely, it was one of them.

"This doesn't look much like a white graveyard," Detective Waters said.

"That's true," Dr. Norwood said. "Out here in the early days of white settlement, that tradition may not have been observed. Excavations might reveal other family members. Then again, they might not. It could have been a single man, a trapper down on his own who had no family here."

Detective Waters scratched his forehead. "The first trappers were here in the early 1700s. So the two of you would agree with the coroner's assessment, that these bones have been buried here at least a hundred years? Or more?"

Michael nodded. "Oh, yes, no question, at the very least one hundred in my view, though my guess would be older. The color and patina are quite telling. The rate of deterioration depends on a number of factors, so looks could be deceiving. Soil tests will tell us more. Dr. Norwood will take a DNA sample from one of the teeth we found loose. That will give us a much better picture."

As he spoke, I remembered another long-forgotten habit of my old friend. When he knew something from experience but didn't want to discuss the matter until testing proved him right, he always stood with his hands clasped behind his back, and would not make eye contact with anyone. Instead, he'd move his head side to side in a certain way. He was doing that now. I knew it meant he was holding something important back.

I suddenly thought of Cal's books. "I may be able to find out who this is in Cal's papers."

The small radio device on Detective Waters's belt screeched. He unclipped it and held it closer to hear the dispatcher's message in code. He hesitated, hung his head, then responded with, "Waters. I'm on my way."

On the return trip home, he didn't tell us what the call was about. It was only later that evening when I talked to Phoebe that I learned what happened. Search dogs had found Brody Reed, the old man and forest guide who had gone missing. The poor man was dead.

eighteen
Phoebe Comes Up with a Plan

*Y*ou would never guess that Jane, the sweetest thing in the world, was a sneak, just by looking at her. Her face is so innocent and she's so tiny, she could play Tinkerbell or one of those little fairies that giggles real high and hides behind a buttercup in the forest. She's a sneak because she never let on that

Michael, her friend she has known for years, was one studly hunk, even if he is older than she is.

She could have warned me. When she told me he would be coming to help her with the digging, she showed me his pictures. Honey. That boy should have been a movie star. Sure, he's kind of an old geezer, a little tweedy and moth-eaten around the edges, but big deal. All those college professors are like that. They're distracted by too many facts crammed into their brains so they forget normal stuff like haircuts and taking their jacket to the cleaners. Michael's up a notch or two from that because he does keep his moustache and beard trimmed. I'd say his only fault is he could stand to gain a few pounds. He needs a woman who knows how to cook.

He's not for me, though. I like a man with some meat on him. Even if he was my type, it only took one look at them together to see he was sweet on Jane. He wouldn't come all the way down here to help her if he wasn't, would he? She acts like she doesn't give a flip about him, other than being friends.

Jane told me once she didn't want to ever get married again. Goodness knows she could use a big strong man in that creepy house out by itself. That thing is surrounded by wild animals, I mean *wild* wild. Ones that could eat you alive if you're not careful and not armed. Thank goodness Jane is no dummy. She's sitting on that big stash of guns, the good kind, so she's not defenseless. The only thing better would be if she had a husband to do her shooting for her.

I guess I'm old-fashioned. There's nothing like a man around the house to make you feel safe. It gets lonely around here. Ronald was the best husband anyone could want. I sure do miss him. I wish I could find another one. Not that it's likely. There's about as much chance of that happening as for Elvis to come back from the dead and star on Broadway as Scarlett O'Hara in a musical version of *Gone with the Wind.*

Jane, on the other hand, has a single, handsome, potential husband dropped right on her doorstep. And that is why I came up with a plan to get those two more serious about each other. For their own good, naturally. Jane needs a man, and Michael needs to move out of whatever dirty, rat-infested, crime-ridden city up north he's in. I forget which one, but wherever it is, Tullulah is much better, no question. I mean, it's not like he's living anywhere exciting like New York City or Chicago or Portland or somewhere like that, where people are cultured.

Actually, it's probably a good thing he's not in Portland, because if he was, Jane might want to move up there with him because of all the trees. Instead of vice versa.

But back to Michael. See, Jane needs a certain kind of guy. Not "weird," but that's what comes to mind first. Maybe "eccentric" is what I mean. She needs somebody like her, who wants to mess around in the dirt and get all surprised and excited when he digs in it and finds a rock. It's beyond me. That's what I'd expect to find, wouldn't you? I just don't understand the appeal. It takes all kinds.

When Jane asked if I wanted to ride with her to pick up Michael at the airport, I said no. They needed to be alone to catch up on old times. I told her to bring him by the house on the way home if she wanted, so she did. I fixed them some homemade soup and chicken salad sandwiches. We sat at the kitchen table, getting acquainted. Michael wanted to hear about Tullulah, so Jane told him about the town and about how all the people were friendly. And then she snapped her finger, like she remembered something, and asked me a question that knocked me for a loop.

"Phoebe, I hear you know a couple of interesting people I'd like very much to meet. Ruby and Reese?"

If she had asked me what time the mothership from Jupiter usually lands on the square on the weekends, I wouldn't have been any more surprised.

I turned in my chair to face her straight on. "How in the world do you know about them?"

She hemmed and hawed around a minute, like she was trying to think up a lie. That's not like her. That made me even more curious.

"Oh, dear," she said, "it must have been someone in the grocery. Or the bookstore. I can't remember at the moment."

"Huh. You might've seen some of her special preserves at the bookstore." But I knew that wasn't it. I knew somebody had been gossiping about my crazy relatives. That's the only reason I could think of that

Jane wanted to meet them, because she heard they were bonkers. Plus, that would explain why she lied. She didn't want to finger the gossipers. She has too much manners and class, like I do. Remember how I said she enjoys talking to people who aren't all there? She sure couldn't have picked better examples than those two. Anyway, I told her we could drive out and see them tomorrow.

Now, before I tell you about them, I want you to understand that my family does not believe in superstitious mumbo-jumbo. We are all good church people. I say that so you'll understand when I tell you about Ruby. She's a fluke. Just remember that. The rest of us are normal. As normal people though, we have normal intelligence. So when things have kept happening around her over the years, things that couldn't be explained by science or common sense, our normal intelligence has verified that Aunt Woo-Woo, which is what we've always called her, was the one doing it.

She's not right. And it's not like she's one of those New Age people who were perfectly fine before they found Gandhi or whoever that is they make all the statues of over in the Far East. No, Aunt Woo-Woo has never been right.

As early as age four, according to her immediate family, she could read their minds. Granted, none of her brothers or sisters had much of a mind to read in the first place, but still. And the older she got, the more weird things would happen around her.

I don't hear about that sort of thing much anymore. She lives way out in the country by herself. Just about all her close kinfolks are dead now, so I never get any reports. These days, she is mainly known for her special preserves and her tea recipes and for one other thing, which will make me sound completely koo-koo myself just for saying it, but here it is.

She's got this rock. It sits off to the side of her house near her well. It isn't like a plain old hump on the ground, like a lot of the rocks Jane and I see out by her place. This one is taller, about six feet high, thinner, say about two or three inches thick, and it has a hole in it. It's a little over shoulder-high on me, so you stretch your arm up to touch the hole that is about as big around as a basketball. Two other big rocks lean on the ground up next to it, but they don't have any holes or anything, they're just regular.

For as long as I can remember, people have told stories about how they took their babies to Aunt Woo-Woo when they were sick. Sometimes she would make them a homemade salve, or give them herbs or weeds to brew into a drink. Other times, if it was a tiny baby, what they would do is hand the baby through the hole in the rock. Nothing else. Aunt Woo-Woo would put it through and the mother or daddy would take it on the other side. Within twenty-four hours, the baby would be well again.

I'm not saying I believe it completely. And I'm not like some people who think it must be the devil doing it. I wouldn't believe it at all if my own mama hadn't said she knew it worked and that the devil wasn't involved whatsoever. She put me through the hole one time when I was a baby and look how I turned out. Just as normal as could be. So I know for a fact it worked one time and, from what I hear, lots of others, too.

More people go out to Aunt Woo-Woo's house just to touch the rock rather than sling a baby through it. They say if you're having bad luck, or you have a special need or wish, you just have to touch the rock while you think about your wish and it will come true. Others take something that belongs to them or the person they have a wish for, and they throw it through the hole. I am not making this up. They throw it through the hole and before they know it, *sha-zam,* they get their wish.

Now, Reese is her nephew. He lives in the next house down the road. They say when his parents, Bill Evans and Lottie Evans, who was Aunt Woo-Woo's sister, saw that Reese wasn't like everybody else, they sent him to live up yonder with her. He's not as crazy as she is, but it's rumored that if you visit and you take them both a gift, your luck doubles from what the rock does for you by itself.

All of a sudden, a brilliant idea came to me. I got up from the table and got my scissors. "Michael," I said. "Sit still right like you are. You've got a clump of hair sticking out that the barber missed. It's bugging the fire out of me. Just one little snip and that will take care of it." I chose a curl that looked longer than the rest and clipped it before he could say anything. I went over to the trash can like I was throwing the hair away, but when I turned my back, I stuck it in my pocket.

I walked behind Jane. "Sit still," I said. Snip. "There. You had a little cowlick, too." The trash can routine worked again. Now, all I had to do was sew them in a square of fabric, which I have tons of, so they would stay together and be heavy enough to go through the rock without floating off.

Jane's stubborn. As much as I'd like to help out, the truth is that if she wants him, she wants him, and if she doesn't, nothing I say or do will make a difference. She's a grown woman, unlike my sister Corene who could use some real help.

I'd do one for me and one for Corene, too. Since we don't know specifically who our Mr. Right would be, I'd make a fabric square with something of ours in it, one for each of us. I'd use one of her hair combs at the rock. I found it on the floor after she left my house that last time. Then while Jane gets her fill of crazy talk with Aunt Woo-Woo, I'll slip out to the rock.

I already knew what I'd say. I'd wish that Corene would find somebody nice to settle down with, that Jane would wake up about Michael, and that I could catch a man myself.

nineteen
Jane Meets Phoebe's Relatives

*P*hoebe agreed to take me out to visit Ruby and Reese the next morning. All along the way, though she drove down a curving, narrow street, she turned her head toward me in the passenger seat, giving me more attention, I feared, than the road.

"Now, Jane," she said, "I need to prepare you a little for Aunt Woo-Woo. Because when people see her for the first time, sometimes they act a little odd, not meaning to or anything. So when we get there, I don't want you to stare at her. She's harmless. It's just she looks a little insane sometimes, in the eyes. So try not to stare."

"All right. I'll be careful. What exactly is it about her that makes one want to stare, if I may ask? Is it solely a difference in her eyes then?"

Phoebe hesitated. Her brow furrowed. "You'll like her. She's sweet as can be." She seemed to consider saying more but, after a moment's thought, returned her attention to the road. For that, I was thankful.

"How did she come by such an odd name?"

"Well, first of all, she's not really my aunt. She was my daddy's second cousin. By marriage. She got the name from one of her nephews. He couldn't say her real name, which is Ruby, when he was first learning to talk. Most people called her by her full name, Ruby Alice. Anyway, the nephew couldn't say Ruby, and he called her Aunt Woo-Woo. The name stuck because that bunch already had another aunt named Ruby. So they called one Aunt Ruby and Ruby Alice Aunt Woo-Woo."

"She must be quite old then. Has she not aged well, is that why people stare?"

"No, it's not that. She was a late child and not that much older than my husband. She must be in her late seventies now. She still gets around good, as well as we do. Doesn't hobble a bit. And she only started wearing eyeglasses within the last couple of years. Not even real glasses, like from the eye doctor, either. Just the cheap kind from the drugstore and she only needs them for reading. She is sharp as a tack upstairs, too." Phoebe tapped a finger on her head. "Sharp but a little off. You'll really like her. You never told me, but I'm guessing that's why you want to meet her and Reese. Because they're not normal." Phoebe emphasized the last word and gave me an odd look.

"I don't know what you mean. No, I was told I should ask her about lightning strikes. I read a bit about them in the new books I bought. Fascinating. Especially in relation to trees they strike and their burn marks."

"Like what?"

"Well, for instance, native custom says one must never touch a burn mark because it's very bad luck."

"What! I rubbed all over those things!" she said with a note of panic in her voice. It was true. I remembered how white her hands were, moving over the black wood. She tossed her head and sighed. "Not that it matters. I don't believe in superstition."

We drove past the outskirts of town, past the road I remembered from our last trek this far out into the county when we visited Pale Holler some weeks earlier. We kept going, down into a valley dotted with farms and cow pastures, then up again onto a sparsely populated hill. Sparsely populated with humans and houses, at any rate, but lavishly, abundantly blessed with trees of all types.

The road narrowed to a lane as we climbed. "It's just over this little ridge," Phoebe said as we bumped over fallen branches and took a right turn into a cleared parcel of land. At its center sat a house made of thick logs. Smoke rose from its chimney and gave the clean fresh air the scents of burning apple and cedar.

"Phoebe, you never said exactly what it was about your aunt that made others stare."

"I'm still thinking."

"Why is it so difficult?"

"Because it's not a thing, like a humongous mole or a hump or anything like that. It's like she takes on another personality. Not permanent, but like she's trying it on, like playing dress-up. Every time I've seen her, it was something else. Strange. And she reads too much, that's what her problem is."

"What an odd thing for a former librarian to say."

Phoebe blew one of her characteristic huffs out her nose. "It's the truth. Whatever she's reading, see, she kind of adopts it. Like a kid who is obsessed with Spiderman and wants his clothes and underwear and pajamas and bedspread and everything to have Spiderman on it."

"I see."

"So if she walks out of the house wearing a tinfoil dress and has curly-cue antennas made out of coat hangers stuck on her head, we'll know she has been reading about bug invaders or some foolishness like that. But don't stare or mention it. Just act normal."

"Right. I'll do my best."

Phoebe drove slowly around a circular path that surrounded a large oak, one with bright yellow plumage. The chatter of starlings came from within it as we got out of the car and walked toward the broad plank porch. The door creaked open, revealing a darker interior and soft lamplight. The shape of a figure appeared and stepped out into the afternoon light.

"Now remember what I said." Phoebe adjusted her skirt as she walked. She lowered her voice to a whisper. "Don't look straight at her or she will zap you."

"Zap?"

"Shhh! Keep your voice down. She has got ears like a bat. Yes, zap. Just do not look at her when she is looking at you. Look past her. And don't let her get between you and the car. She has been known to take a run at visitors and knock them out."

Phoebe put on a smile, waved and took the gift she brought Ruby Alice from the backseat. Together we watched a tiny lady step gingerly down three steps and wait there as we made our way over the driveway's covering of leaves.

I couldn't imagine what Phoebe meant. The harmless-looking woman before us didn't look as if she could lift a can of beans with her skinny arms that hung limply at her sides. Her cotton print dress was long and demure and came to midcalf over rolled-down hose. She wore house shoes with imitation sheepskin linings. A thin blue sweater lay upon her narrow shoulders, held together by an old-fashioned gold chain with latches on either end. I couldn't imagine her rushing a guest like a linebacker.

Phoebe talked nonstop, just pleasantries, I presumed, for I had not paid attention to her actual words, only the constant flow of them. Instead, I found myself studying this lady, wondering what on earth Phoebe had been on about. I saw nothing whatsoever unusual about her.

She had a kind face. It was a lovely brown color, the color of pecans. She combed her hair, thick gray with a good deal of black still underneath, back into a bun. The dark brown eyes held much delight, whether due to our visit or to the joy of being alive, healthy, and surrounded by such natural beauty, I couldn't say. It looked to me as if true happiness was her usual disposition. The wrinkles and laugh lines that covered her face had not become so deep through only occasional use.

The eyes. Why had Phoebe warned me not to look into them? She was being even more cryptic than usual. In the short time I've known her, I've learned that it is not necessarily essential to take Phoebe's words as gospel truth in every case. She has a pliant sense of reality at times. I suspected this was one of them.

I thought at the time that perhaps Phoebe feared her. Her voice changed a bit when she talked about Ruby Alice. Again, I couldn't imagine how this could be.

Ruby Alice reached out a slim bony hand to mine. "How nice to meet you, Jane," she said in a low melodious voice that was slightly scratched with time. "Come in, come in. There's tea ready."

"Here, I brought you something," Phoebe said. She handed Ruby Alice a plastic container and pulled the snap-on lid open to show her the contents.

Ruby Alice's face became animated with delight. "Sausage balls! Thank you, sweetheart. You always remember my favorites."

Phoebe gave her a hug and walked with one arm across Ruby Alice's shoulder, preceding me toward the house. Casting a look backward, Phoebe gave a little shake of her head. I had no idea what she was attempting to convey.

The cozy room we entered brought to mind illustrations from some of the British children's books I adored as a child. Rosy, that is how I would describe it, everything clean and neat, with an overlying glow that seemed to emanate from the furnishings and putty-colored walls. From the kitchen, a soothing aroma of cinnamon and cloves filled the air.

"I have special tea for you. Sit down, sit down," Ruby Alice said. She directed us to sit on the over-stuffed sofa, done in a soft velvety fabric of cream with a large rose print.

On the coffee table, a low one made of thick dark wood that gave it a primitive look, sat two small teapots. From underneath each, the edges of white crochet doilies peeked and curled.

Phoebe took a seat on the end of the sofa where several pillows leaned in the corner. She fluffed them, arranged them behind her back, and made herself at home. I sat nearer the other end by the window. The view of Ruby Alice's back lot made me smile. Bluebirds flew in and out of a copse of apple trees on the edge, between lawn and woods. Watching, it was as if the clock had turned backward and I glimpsed a scene of my own childhood.

I turned to glance at Ruby Alice who stood on the multicolored hook rug. She clasped her hands in front of her, her eyes magnified and dancing behind smudged eyeglasses. She returned my smile and I felt as if we floated, suspended in a golden moment of time, free of reality.

She stepped toward us. She wrapped her small fingers around the handles of each pot, lifted them, and switched their places, setting each one on the other's doily.

"Now then," she said. "I didn't know who would sit where."

Phoebe gave me a blank stare. I translated it as,

"Didn't I tell you she was off?" or something along that line.

Ruby Alice fussed with pouring our tea into the mismatched cups and saucers, lovely delicate china, already before us. She didn't ask how we took our tea. She splashed a bit of cream into the brown-tinged but clear liquid in my cup. Into Phoebe's a light green concoction with tiny floating bits of flower petals or herbs, she dropped a cube of sugar. Satisfied, she pulled an old rocking chair closer to the table and sat, watching us expectantly, looking from one to the other.

We drank. Phoebe's eyebrows rose high on her forehead as she took a long, loud sip. "Mmm. That's good, Aunt Woo-Woo," she said. "What's in it? Cinnamon?"

"Secret," her aunt answered with a wink.

I took a second sip. A hint of cinnamon in mine as well with the tastes of both herbal and traditional pekoe teas. Chamomile, perhaps. "Delicious," I said.

Ruby Alice clapped her hands together as she got out of the rocker and walked out of the room. "Be right back. Drink up."

She returned with a plate of warm teacakes, an old-fashioned recipe with only butter, flour, and a dash of sugar and vanilla. I remarked on how much I loved living in an isolated place in the woods, just as she did. She told us a number of stories about the mountain and its people. Phoebe, I could see, had heard most of these. She fidgeted for a while then finally set her cup down.

"I need to go to my car for a minute," she said as she stood. "I believe I'll walk around your yard while I'm out there. You all carry on and finish. I'll be right back."

"That's fine, hon," Ruby Alice said distractedly. "You go right ahead. You know where it's at."

Phoebe froze. She didn't look at either of us. After a second or two, she continued on her way and went out the front door.

At the time, I thought perhaps this was the type of "crazy" thing Phoebe referred to in regard to Ruby Alice's eccentricities. Stating the obvious, that Phoebe knew where her own car was parked, was a bit quirky. Outside, I heard a car door shut.

Ruby Alice smiled. "You have new visitors," she said. She sipped as she peered over the rim of her cup.

"Only one, actually. An old friend." I wondered how she knew about Michael.

She nodded. "One you know, two you don't know."

"You mean I have more coming? Surprise guests?" I couldn't imagine who that might be.

"Oh, no. These have been here for ages. Already here. Just arriving. It's that time, you know. When the spirits are freed."

Her perplexing words made no sense, yet they reminded me of an old legend my grandmother told me. At Halloween, which was the ancient holy day of Samhain, it is said that ghosts are no longer captive to their usual haunting places, but may roam freely

182

during this holiday's full moon. I hadn't a clue if that was what Ruby Alice was on about.

She talked nonstop on all sorts of topics after Phoebe's departure. I nodded politely and was about to take a sip of tea when a movement out of the corner of my eye caught my attention. Outside the window, I could just see Phoebe, creeping stealthily from the side of the house to a bed of yellow pansies. She stepped behind them where a garden ornament of some sort, a standing rock like a short monolith, stood.

I had no idea what she was up to, only that she behaved in a very strange manner. She looked about, as if to be sure no one watched her. Once satisfied, she quickly rubbed her hands and arms all over an opening in the rock, fronts and backs and each individual finger. She then took something from her pocket and closed her eyes. Her lips moved as if in prayer before tossing a small object through the hole. She did this twice more.

So as not to be rude to Ruby Alice, I turned more squarely toward her. However intriguing Phoebe's antics, I didn't want to be distracted from my hostess. I brought my attention back fully to her words. We talked about the lightning legends and also a little about medicinal herbs.

"How fascinating," I said. "You must come to my house for a visit sometime. Cal also used plants for medicines. Perhaps you could help me learn how to recognize them in the woods."

Her eyes googled about behind her thick glasses, quickly darting left and right. I supposed this was an expression of excitement. Surely this phenomenon was what Phoebe thought of as "zapping" me. I wanted to laugh. As she instructed, however, I did my best not to stare though it was out of respect, not because I believed I might be turned into stone.

"And you come out here anytime," she said as she got up from her rocker. She picked up Phoebe's teapot, cup, and saucer. I followed suit by gathering the rest of the tea things and trailing behind her to the kitchen. "Phoebe should be about done out there. Why don't you pick out a jar of preserves from the counter. Get one for her, too."

I set the teapot and china beside her sink. Across the room, the counter she indicated held dozens of Mason jars filled with jams and jellies. I chose two and thanked her.

"We can go out this way," she said and waved a hand toward the kitchen door at the back. When I pushed open the light screen without a sound and stepped into the yard, Phoebe's head jerked in my direction.

I had caught her with her hands up and inside the rock's opening again. After a moment of surprise, she adopted an air of nonchalance. She brought one arm down, set that hand on her hip, and left the other as it was, resting in the opening. She patted it a few times before swinging her arm down, whistling softly as she walked toward us. She brushed her palms together several times, then against the sides of her pants.

I handed her a jar. "A gift from Ruby Alice."

"Oh, boy. Peach. Thank you."

On leaving, we thanked Ruby Alice for the tea and our gifts. She closed Phoebe's door and leaned into the driver's side window. "Tell Reese to come up for supper if he wants to. You two take care. I'll see you before long," she said with an enigmatic smile, waving and then turning toward the house.

I almost laughed. I'd seen no sign of any mental illness, as Phoebe'd warned. She was perfectly lovely. As we eased down the driveway, however, I caught a glimpse of her in the door's rearview mirror. She reached behind a chair on her porch to retrieve a round object. I squinted. It was a football helmet. To my dismay, she put it on before walking slowly inside the house. I didn't think it was the sort of thing Phoebe would be interested in, so I neglected to mention it.

We did not turn right, the way we had come. Instead, Phoebe turned the wheel left so that we headed deeper into the mountain's woods.

Ahead I could see the long black roof of a house, and upon getting closer, could see the rest of it, a white clapboard ranch style that sat between two hills.

Along the way, we passed small hand-painted signs stuck on the side of the road. These appeared more frequently, in the manner of the old Burma Shave signs. "Welcome to Bible Gardens . . . ," "Jesus is just around the corner . . . ," "So please drive slow . . ."

The gravel track we followed curved between the front of the house and a side plot of land with tall hedges and an entrance. Beyond it, I could see many flowers in fall colors as well as a number of bushes that flowered in spring and summer. An arched gateway painted bright red opened directly into what looked like a maze of small hedges.

Between the house and the large garden area, a thin man wearing a baseball cap stood at a makeshift table made of an old door across two sawhorses. He worked with a small chisel and hammer, standing over a block of wood held between two clamps. He never looked up at Phoebe's car as we rode down into the little valley, but kept at his work, smiling gaily as he sang in a loud voice.

By the time we parked, he had finished his song, yet his lips still moved in speech, all the while smiling, apparently finding himself an amusing conversationalist. He set down his tools and came around his makeshift worktable to take note of his visitors.

"Hey there, Phoebe. Ma'am," he said to me with a tip of his cap. "Y'all out sightseeing today?" He held out his arms and walked toward the extra lot as if to herd us there.

"We sure are. Jane, this is Reese Evans. Jane here is new in town, Reese. I thought she might like to see your project . . . thing." Phoebe waved her hands toward the lot's hedge entrance.

This produced an even wider smile from Reese, who began nodding his head. "I'm so glad to meet you, Jane. Go right through that gap. It's all in there."

Phoebe had told me nothing about what lay beyond the hedge. However, I appreciated her control in not saying we were here because she thought I'd like to meet someone she considered strange.

To my discredit, I must admit I expected to see something along the line of old tires made into birdbaths or other amalgamations of cast-off items one frequently thinks of in relation to rural Southern yard ornaments. What was actually there couldn't have been more startling.

Once past the hedge gap, a lovely water garden of lily pads and willow trees filled the area between where we stood and a high stone wall. It was approximately fifty yards away and looked quite old. Stretched along the lot's entire length in front of the wall, an earthwork sloped gently down, upon which I beheld a familiar and beloved sight.

"Jerusalem," I said. My heart gave a little leap. It was a place of dreams, one I'd longed to visit and, once finally there, a walking dream every day I was privileged to be in its glorious streets. I'd dreamt of my future there, where the Colonel and I had been so happy. No sight in its alleyways was unremarkable, no vista on the surrounding countryside seen without its own dreams of the past. All of time came together there so that there was no division in then, now, or tomorrow.

"That was quick," Phoebe said.

"It could be nothing else." The buildings in the city

panorama, made with textured plasters of varying gray, yellow, and white tints, reflected light and cast shadows down winding streets and alleys. Their proportions looked so realistic, it was as if real buildings had been shrunk, not created in miniature. The sight of the rock of the dome, here made with a half-globe of gold, perhaps formerly a Christmas ornament but none the less majestic, sent a thrill through me. "I've been too long away. I must go back soon. What astonishing work, Mr. Evans." I walked slowly past the scale model of the entire city, memories flashing as I traced some of the familiar routes I'd once taken.

"You've been there?" Phoebe said with excitement. "To the Holy Land in person?"

"Oh, yes. Many times. The Colonel and I lived there a while. In fact, in this area here. In a small apartment."

"You never mentioned it. I'd have brought you here sooner."

Reese seemed pleased with my reaction. "It's a work in progress, of course. Always something new to do."

"Have you visited often?" I said. "The detail is quite good. You must have spent quite a lot of time there as well."

He shook his head. "No, ma'am. Never been. Always wanted to. I do everything from pictures, that's all."

I couldn't have been more astonished. There were market stalls, ones I'd visited, in such detail and in perfect relation to their neighborhoods that I could hardly believe Reese had never been in them himself. The entire city wasn't complete in every respect. In many sectors, he merely had whitewashed squares and rectangles to represent buildings, yet those he had worked on so far showed exquisite craftsmanship.

His smile grew wider. "I'm working on this part right now." He walked around to the end where a small table sat. Upon it were various implements and glass bottles filled with mixtures of what looked like paint. Spills of greens and white and black blotched the old metal tabletop. A wooden crate on the ground held small bits of glass, metals, and what appeared to be ceramic. Broken dishes, perhaps.

Reese walked along slowly in front of other displays, speaking in a rich, lilting tone about his other interest. We passed a miniature Rome, where he reached into the tiny Hippodrome to retrieve a fallen orange maple leaf from its center. "I do something little, usually, and then I get interested in what's around it. Or I do another place. Depends on what I find."

At each section, similar crates to the one I saw at the miniature Jerusalem sat nearby. I noticed the small pieces inside them were similar. China, broken plates or cups possibly, some looked like broken glass vases. Other bits of wire and metal, rope lengths, all sorts of sundries.

When Reese had walked farther on, Phoebe leaned into my ear and whispered, "People bring him all that junk there and he uses it to build stuff."

"So I see. He does a remarkable job."

"Yeah, pretty good, huh? Got the hands for fine work. His mama was the best seamstress around here in her time, so he gets his hands from her."

We approached a beautiful scene of sculpted hills and valleys that sloped down to a shore. Upon the water rested a wooden ship, meticulously made from tiny sticks and string.

"Look," I said to Phoebe, "its hull even sits a bit below the water. Very realistic."

"He does those ships in bottles, too, don't you, Reese? And makes toy boats that he sells at the flea market."

"I like to stay busy." He raised an arm to direct us around the end of the rock wall.

We strolled past other exhibits, most inspired by Biblical themes or particular prophets and other Biblical figures, but also a few battle scenes with Roman gladiators and English soldiers from various time periods.

Just as with Ruby Alice, Reese himself had exhibited no signs of "weirdness" as of yet. This appeared to be another example of Phoebe letting her imagination get the best of her.

"Oh. I almost forgot. I brought you a little gift," Phoebe said as she opened her purse. She took out a small brown paper bag and handed it to him. "I didn't have any use for these and I thought you might."

He turned the bag to pour its contents in his hand,

then looked at his palm, filled with glistening bits of glass, buttons, and other trinkets.

"Now be careful with that broken glass in there. That dark green. It was an old Avon bottle."

He thanked her profusely, as if she'd given him a sack of gold nuggets. A childlike glow came over his face. He chose a particular translucent bit of glass and turned it round and round. He gave a throaty laugh. "So you've found me, have you? Let's get you settled in your place then."

He turned but continued talking, so we followed him to an old barn. We didn't go inside, only watched as he moved boxes and searched the lower area. I craned my neck, not sure what I searched for as I remembered Dad's words. The barn's walls held farm utensils on hooks, many of which were unfamiliar. In the darkness at the rear of the barn, I could make out a sled and other recreational items hung on the wall, along with what looked like half a globe, only much larger, with tattered black material flapping in the breeze from the open doors.

"Good to see y'all," Reese said. "Stay as long as you like. There's a lot more to look at down yonder." He indicated the Bible Gardens displays on the other side of the pond. And then off he went, almost at a trot, clutching the bag Phoebe had given him in one hand and his new treasure of broken glass in the other.

Phoebe gave me an unblinking stare, an "I told you he was crazy" look, but I didn't comprehend it. I found him to be a lovely gentle soul. Phoebe, on the other hand, had already made her feelings about him clear.

"Let's go, Jane. He's gone." On the way to the car, we walked the length of his yard, passing a workshop that looked much newer than the barn.

"See? What did I tell you? Wacko."

"He was perfectly charming. Not 'wacko' at all."

"I knew you'd say that. He wasn't so bad today. When he shuts off like that, though, there's no telling what's going on in that mind of his. For all we know, he could be one of those serial killers. Going around chopping people's heads off and burying them in the woods."

"Really, Phoebe. He was a dear."

"Whatever. Just don't turn your back on him."

We rode in silence a while, Phoebe humming along with the radio. I watched the passing hilly scenery. "Phoebe, if your Aunt Woo-Woo and Reese disturb you, why do you visit them? I know you did this today for me, and thank you again, but from the conversations, it seems you come out often."

Phoebe sighed. She shrugged.

"Jane. You and I are real friends, right? Real friends who have been in the trenches together."

I raised my eyebrows and nodded while I tried not to laugh. Our trench service together lasted all of an hour, perhaps one one-hundredth of the time she had spent since then retelling the event to all she encountered.

"So, you know I wouldn't tell you stories."

"Of course not, dear. I trust you implicitly."

She sighed again. "Okay. I come out here for the same reason a lot of other folks around here do." She paused, weighing her words. "Because it makes things happen. Kind of. Good things happen, I mean." She turned her head toward me to see how I took this startling news from a confirmed skeptic.

"You're saying it brings you good luck."

"Yes. Like that. People who are sick or maybe there's somebody being mean to them, and they go see Aunt Woo-Woo and Reese, and the kids get well and the mean people go away. Which I know you're probably thinking is a load of bull hockey, and we're just a bunch of ignorant hicks who believe in superstitious things. But we're not ignorant hicks. At least, if we are, it's not because of that. But I'm telling you what is the truth. There's something about those two. It's a proven fact. You believe me?"

"Certainly." I did believe her. However, I wasn't sure I could confide in her as she did in me. I didn't know how to tell her I had my own confirmation. The line she draws between what constitutes the supernatural and what doesn't has been difficult for me to pinpoint.

I knew she was right about the luck. I knew it because I could see it. It shone over their houses and the trees on their property. I had witnessed the same sight in my own woods for the first time on the day Phoebe and I were in our "war." The same arcs of golden strands in the air around us then were here in great number and moved like comets over Ruby Alice's and Reese's land.

Perhaps these brought the good luck somehow, something Ruby Alice and Reese could direct to others. Maybe simply living in this place allowed the two of them to absorb some magical quality, akin to the manner that my own land apparently granted me my special new abilities.

Magic, however, was most definitely not part of Phoebe's belief system. I ventured a question on the subject. "Phoebe, are you ever afraid of this? Of something that happens that can't be explained?"

"Oh, I can explain it," she said with a confidence that left no room for doubt. "It's a small-scale version of those virgin miracles."

Her answer perplexed me. I thought a moment but couldn't make the connection. "I don't understand. Like the birth of Jesus?"

"No, I mean all those virgin statues crying and bleeding and their faces appearing to people. That kind of thing. The days of miracles are over, but we still have signs."

"I see," I said, though I didn't.

"You don't believe me."

"It's not that. I do believe you. It's just that you've shown a slight aversion to any sort of supernatural phenomenon before."

She shrugged. "Whatever this is, it works. So therefore it is real and not supernatural at all. Reese and

Aunt Woo-Woo might be nuts, but they're not doing actual magic stuff. Here's what I think. It's because the Lord gives them special blessings, you know, to make up for their low brain wattage. And then it's too much for what little brains they've got, so it spills over onto other people. Simple law of nature. They can't hold it all in and it seeps into anybody who comes in contact with them. So don't be surprised when something happens to us."

I gave her a mock incredulous look.

She winked at me and laughed and then said, "We'll see."

twenty
Phoebe and the Brain

*J*ane and I decided to ride over to the library. I had been telling her all about the haunted house. I wanted to check on the progress of the Trail of Terror props and make sure the kitchen had all the utensils I would need for the refreshments. I hoped seeing it all would get Jane excited about it. She was going to be perfect for the special part Grace and I had in mind for her.

The Trail of Terror is what everybody looks forward to every year. Grace comes up with some good gags for the kids. We both enjoy acting like fools in our spooky get-ups and they all seem to get a kick out of it.

Let me tell you, there's nothing more fun in this

world than scaring the living grape juice out of a little kid. Now, mind you, we don't get the little bitty ones upset. Well, not too much anyway. We save all the real good stuff for a select few who make upsetting other people, like their parents and teachers, into an art in real life. Yes sir, buddy, we get those young hellions good. Jane looked a little shocked when I told her this.

"I thought you loved children," she said.

"I do. Even the mean ones. They want to be scared, Jane, or they wouldn't beg their mamas and daddies to pay their way in. We don't hurt them, for goodness sake. We just play fun tricks on them. Then once they get their hearts out of their throats, they laugh about it."

Come to think of it, it's pretty fun to play tricks on little old ladies, too. One night the week before, I had a small trick ready for Jane. I got the coffeepot started and walked to the refrigerator.

"And now, for dessert, a rare delicacy," I said, all innocent. I had been careful to not let Jane see in the refrigerator since she got there. I couldn't wait to see her jump out of her skin.

I carefully pulled a plate off the top rack and said, "Okay, close your eyes." When she did, I set the plate in front of her. "Surprise!"

She opened her eyes and stared. She sat real still. She looked up at me with a deadpan expression on her face.

"It's a brain. How wonderful. I've never seen one so

appetizing." She picked up her fork and knife like she was about to dig in.

"You didn't even blink. You're one tough old broad, you know that?"

She couldn't hold back any longer and laughed out loud like she was a kid herself. "Why, thank you dear. You're quite the stalwart yourself. I take it this is for the haunted house."

I nodded. "I got the mold from the Archie McPhee catalog, the one where they sell all kinds of weird novelties. I got some big squishy eyeballs from them, too. When I turned the page and saw that plastic brain mold, I knew I had to have it. I've made several brains so far. I'm experimenting with the color. This one looks the most natural. I mixed lemon Jell-O and vanilla pudding this time."

"You've seen a good many before, eh?"

"No, of course not. Why? Does the color look wrong to you?"

"I thought they were closer to gray." She opened her mouth and took a breath, but then changed her mind and didn't say anything.

"Hmm. Well, I'll keep working on it. Maybe if I put some chocolate syrup in there it would look gray."

Jane turned the plate around and studied the jiggly concoction from other angles. "It's actually quite nice. Just as it is. Well done."

When we turned into my neighborhood, we talked about all the Halloween decorations we passed. It's about like Christmastime. A few people have those huge blow-up air balloons of things like Frankenstein or witches. Most have smaller things, like strings of orange lights in their bushes and carved pumpkins, but even those give the neighborhood a festive look.

"Isn't that funny," I said. "Look over there. What has Junie Reed got fixed in front of her door?"

Junie is one to go all out decorating, no matter what time of year it is. She's big on making something new for the different seasons. She had a Halloween-collage wreath hanging on her screen door and had little fake jack-o'-lanterns set a few feet apart inside the screened-in porch.

"The lighted sacks that line the walkway? I like those."

I slowed to a stop by Junie's driveway. "No. Right there in the middle of the air. How did she do that? I don't see any wires."

"Nor do I," Jane said. "Is it moving?"

We both stared. "It looks like it's floating," I said.

"Perhaps it's a reflection?"

"Maybe. I can't tell where it might be reflecting from though. I'll ask her the next time I see her. Right now, we've got to get to the house. I don't want to miss my show. Hey, you know what? I saw another funny thing there the other day. That candle is right where I saw that dog."

"What dog?"

"The big white one. It was standing in front of the door, big as a Shetland pony, and howling like the end of time."

Jane gasped. Her hand came up to cover her mouth. "What is it?" I said.

She didn't answer right away. She turned all the way around in her seat as we drove by, not taking her eyes off the candle. "Its flame is blue," she mumbled. Her voice sounded so weak, I almost didn't understand what she said. I sure didn't understand why the color mattered.

twenty - one
Phoebe Takes Rowdy
to Get His Hair Fixed

Even though I know how to fix hair just about as well as a beautician, my expertise did not extend to fixing the hairball's fur. Its texture is not easy to work with, let me tell you, because I tried everything I had in my bathroom pantry to make Rowdy look presentable. So, even though I hated to spend the money, Rowdy had to go to the doggie groomer.

Sissy Breedlove, who runs Smoochie Poochie on the town square, worked Rowdy in the very day I called. It kind of made me feel bad when she said I could come anytime since I've always thought it was a pretty foolish business. That wasn't right of me. Sissy is a good person and is just like everyone else, trying to make an honest living to take care of her family.

I figured her having an empty schedule must mean she doesn't get much call for dog pampering here in

Tullulah. We're not like those fancy big city people who treat their pets like children and sometimes better. A dog is a dog. The silliness of getting all kissy with a slobbering fuzz ball is for the birds, something people around here have better sense than to do. We just don't throw money away, like for painting dog's toenails or stupid antlers to put on their heads at Christmas.

Rowdy's hair needed help in a bad way, though. Since I couldn't get it to act right or look decent I decided to take him to an expert just this once. With any luck, Corene would be back before long to take the rug rat away so I wouldn't have to have him detangled again. I couldn't wait. I'll say this for Rowdy, he didn't whimper or act crazy a bit in the car.

When I pushed through the door, it surprised me that three other customers were in there. Ginger Taggart, who cleans my teeth over at Dr. Chandler's office, had a puppy under her arm at the cash register. Another customer was Betty from the drugstore. She stood by a table where a young fellow was holding up her dog's ears, discussing what kind of cut it needed.

"Hey, Betty," I said. "How are you and your Porkie-poo doing today?"

"Not Porkie-poo, silly. Yorkie-poo."

"Oh," I said but nothing else as I eyed that poor thing's fat belly. There's times when the facts aren't necessarily the same as the truth.

The third person was Delilah Newberry. Delilah stood on the other side of the room, twirling a rack of silly-looking dog clothes. She waved at me so I walked to her. She had her sunglasses on top of her head and two more pairs of glasses hanging on a long gold chain around her neck. She works for the newspaper, so she needs different strengths to read that tiny print.

"Phoebe, what are you doing here? I didn't think you were a dog person." She took one pair of glasses and held it up to her eyes to read the price of a leather biker vest.

"I'm not." Rowdy had his head stuck out the top of his wicker basket. He was doing his pitiful wet-eyed look. Delilah reached over and rubbed between his ears while making baby noises that had Rowdy blinking and licking his lips. Little spurts of whimpers, along with Delilah's *goo goo gaga schweetie bitty boo boo* nonsense, just about made me barf.

She straightened up, pushed her thick white hair behind her ears and said, "So what kind of trouble have you been getting up to? How's your new friend out at the Hardwick place?"

The Hardwicks were the old Tullulah family who built Jane's house and lived in it for several generations. "She's fine. We haven't been in any trouble lately, unless you count the mugging at the Pig or finding those old Indian bones at her place after the storm." I told Delilah all about both. She looked pretty interested, enough to stop that baby talk with Rowdy.

Sissy finished up with her customer and joined us. Delilah said, "I have to get back to work. I'm still thinking about what I want. I'll come back later, okay?" And off she went with her eyeglasses and chains rattling up and down as she trotted out the door.

Sissy turned her attention to Rowdy. She took one look at him and said, "Were you trying to make braids?"

"Well, it wouldn't stay down. It kept sticking up no matter how much I tried to comb it."

Her eyebrows wrinkled up as she studied Rowdy, lifting a knot of hair here and there while walking slowly around him. When she got to his face again, she took his jaw in her hand, looked him straight in the eye and said, "Don't you worry. You're going to look like a million bucks here in a minute."

She stroked the ratty hair on his head and touched the end of her nose to his, like the Eskimos kiss. I pulled back, thinking about Rowdy's wet little nostrils and how I'd hate to breathe in cooties like that on purpose. I guess that's one of the pitfalls of needing a silly pet around all the time. Luckily, I'm perfectly self-sufficient in that department.

"So, do you want any kind of special cut?"

"No. Just regular. Make him look as normal as possible. No frou-frou stuff since he's a boy. And nothing expensive since he'll be leaving soon."

I heard a screech outside. Delilah's car jerked at the curb but stopped quick to let a car go by. Her tires squealed again when she pulled out in the street. I wondered what she was in an all-fired hurry for, going from lolly-gagging to speeding like a stock car racer all of a sudden.

twenty-two
Jane Takes Michael
to the Corral

After our trip to see Phoebe's relatives, I spent the rest of the day at the bones site with Michael. He caught up on his sleep while I was out that morning. It didn't surprise me that he had found his way to the site and started working before I returned. With all his tools spread around him and several small areas cordoned off with string, he looked up as I walked toward him and grinned, happy in his element.

We decided to celebrate the end of our first official day in the field together by going out for dinner. Phoebe suggested several restaurants some miles away in a larger city, but I wanted Michael to experience Tullulah's special cuisine.

We settled on a little place on the edge of town, the Catfish Corral, Home of the World's Best Hushpuppies, as its neon sign proclaimed. They were certainly the best I had ever tasted, light and crisp and deliciously seasoned. We each ordered the house special, Cats and Dogs, catfish filets cut into planks then battered and fried with a special dipping sauce, and hushpuppies, with a side order of coleslaw and choice of fresh vegetables.

The meals arrived quickly. Michael and I were both ravenous from the excitement of the day's work, so we set into our dishes with hardly a word spoken between us for some time. The owner and chef, Jack Quick, made his rounds of the tables to make sure his customers were happy and full. "Fish and chips, Southern style," Mr. Quick told us in an exaggerated accent. "Dessert is included in the price. Homemade orange rolls. My grandmother's recipe." When we sat back to let things settle, coffee arrived, along with the dessert rolls from which emanated a most heavenly aroma.

Michael's face positively glowed. He tapped his lips with his napkin and sighed. "My dear Jane. What a day. And what a glorious end to it." He reached both hands across the table to hold mine.

"You must be exhausted," I said.

He laughed. "Yes. And much work to do tomorrow, as well. A bit of a rest is certainly in order for the old man."

"We'll make it an early night then. Unless you want another dessert."

"Heaven's no!" he said with a smile. "Not tonight. But I wouldn't object to visiting again while I'm in town."

Once home, Michael was anxious to look over the photos we took at the site, just for a few minutes before he turned in. He downloaded them from our cameras into his laptop computer in the den. We put it on my writing desk underneath the green shade of the banker's light there. Homer, who had come inside with us for a visit, took up his usual spot on the rug by the fireplace.

Michael set about highlighting photos on the computer screen with a bright yellow square around various areas of interest. He drew small rectangles around spots that lay several feet away from the skeletal remains. "The soil discolorations," I said as I looked over his shoulder.

"Yes," he said. "It pleases me to see you can still read my mind after so many years." He tapped away and quickly became absorbed in his work.

When we took the photos, he had snapped a shot and looked to me with one of his old meaningful looks. I knew he meant me to note it but not mention it.

Now he clicked through four pictures and reversed through them again slowly. They all showed different aspects of small darkened spots in the dirt. He brought a finger up to hover over a particular close-up. "This is the photo I hoped you wouldn't react to, Jane. I thought it best to wait. Until we were alone."

Just over his fingertip, two of the rectangular discolorations met to form a perfect right angle. "Some sort of structure once there, eh? Covering the body?"

He nodded thoughtfully. "And in these," he said as he clicked on photos that showed the other side of the small pit, "that are still partly covered by a root, it appears likely we have the opposite corner underneath. The size of it, you see. That's the worry. Too large to be a coffin. Too proportional to the body to likely be a preexisting structure." He shrugged. "Or not."

We looked at other photos of the darker spots and various angles of the skeleton for a while.

"It bothers you," I said.

"Yes. Something isn't right," he said softly.

I waited, watching him as he concentrated.

"The thing is, we have a man who, we presume for the moment, lived sometime in the 1800s, Dr. Norwood guesses, when Scottish and Irish settlers moved in numbers into the area. We know many natives still lived here as well for most of that time and certainly long before. Yet this idea of a structure, built expressly for burial, is not traditional for any of those peoples of that time to my knowledge. And I admit my knowledge here is quite limited. I could call someone about it."

"No," I said. "Please. I don't want anyone who is not directly involved to know about the site. Not yet. All right?"

"As you wish. It may be we will find exactly this sort of thing in limited cases when we research. Still, other smaller things, or I suppose rather the whole of it, to my eye at first glance, doesn't quite fit together properly." He rubbed his fingers over his chin, clearly puzzled.

"Michael, it's the first day. You're weary from travel and from work. Everything will come together, just as it always does, with a little time and a little digging. And a little well-deserved rest."

He smiled and gave me a hug before going upstairs to bed. Homer rose from his place by the fire and into a stretch. He trotted to the kitchen, took a few bites from his food bowl, and went to the kitchen door, where he sat, waiting for me to let him out for his evening rounds.

Before I turned in for the night, I wanted to look through the books I inherited from Cal. Specifically, I needed to find what information I could on tree "scars," as Dad Burn had called them on the phone. He told me Cal thought it important I read about them, and that I would find references among his book collection. Somewhere. I looked over the stuffed bookcase that contained Cal's books on native lore. Next to it, another stuffed bookcase held his many volumes on animal and plant life of the forest. Too many. This would call for tea.

First, I decided to look through the books I'd bought at McGaughey's. They were of no use whatsoever, whether they had a blue glow or not, as they covered such disparate subjects as building walls, the discovery of America, and the history of Wales. It was silly of me to buy them without even looking at the titles. None had anything about trees or lightning strikes.

About an hour into the search, I came across a booklet, cheaply made and without a hint of scholarly attention, which listed native superstitions that involved lightning. A couple of items looked promising. One legend said it was unlucky for a person to touch a tree where it had been struck. Another said only a medicine man could touch the lightning scars without causing an adverse effect to himself. He could say a blessing over the wood to take away any bad luck or potential harm should another person touch it.

In addition, a tradition among some Cherokee was that the medicine man could take splinters or strips of the burned bark and make paint from the blackened wood. With this, he would paint the faces of young men competing in sports, so the strength of the powerful lightning bolt might transfer to the athletes and give them an edge to win.

I spent awhile longer looking through books on legends, but found nothing more that might relate. Was the thought of this scar and the special qualities the paint might possess what captured Mr. Graybear's interest at the dig site? Did he think he could sneak in again and cut out the bark to sell for profit?

I looked at the clock. It was still early enough. I rummaged around my desk, pushing Michael's things aside. I found my notebook under a stack of his notes and found the McWhorters' phone number inside. I wanted to see if their tribe happened to have a medicine man I could borrow.

"We sure do," Grant said. "The best there is, if I do say so myself."

"Wonderful. I'd like to have him come out to the site, if that would be all right."

He chuckled. "Ours is a medicine woman. I'm sure she would be interested. Let me see when she can come and I'll be back in touch, okay?"

I thanked him and hung up the phone with a sigh. The excitement of the past few days was catching up with me. I turned the banker's lamp off and walked upstairs, more than ready for a good night's rest.

THE FOLLOWING MORNING, HOMER WAITED FOR ME OUT-side the back porch's screen door as he always does, precisely at the appointed time for our early run. I believe we returned more quickly than usual, due to the autumn chill in the air, rather than the presence of a guest in the house. Once I'd finished my tai chi routine, I walked around to the front of the house to retrieve the morning paper.

With care, I moved about in the kitchen, trying to be quiet as I made a pot of coffee. Homer, patient though he was, looked concerned as he wondered, I'm sure, why I wasn't cooking up his egg and ham treat on schedule.

"Not long, dear," I whispered. I poured a cup of coffee and set the newspaper on the table for a leisurely read before Michael came down for his breakfast. I suddenly became more fully awake on seeing that the story that took up the entire top fold of the paper stood out in bright yellow. I moaned and squinted my eyes shut. "It's a bit early in the morning for that, isn't it?" I said, though I wasn't sure whom I imagined I was addressing. With a sigh, I drank some coffee and read the article.

The headline read: "Brody Reed Found in Forest." A large photo showed crime scene workers marking off an area of woods with tape. A park ranger and Detective Waters stood among the crew, away from the center of the action where photographers worked.

How sad to read of the old guide's death. The article gave no details of how he died, only that his body was found in Bankhead Forest near a certain tree. Apparently, the reporter found it unnecessary to elaborate on what the yellow Bear Poplar was or its precise location. I would ask Phoebe.

This reminded me of the candle. When we drove by the Reeds' home and saw the floating candlestick with a blue flame, something stirred within me. The feeling was strange and familiar at the same time. A memory lurked there that didn't come out from hiding until Phoebe mentioned the white dog.

When I was a child of about six, while visiting my grandparents in Wales, my great-grandmother Annie was still alive. One night, after everyone had gone to bed, we heard her screaming. We rushed to her room to see what was the matter. She stood at the window, as white and ghostly in person as her reflection in the glass, pointing out into the night.

There near the road, we saw a white dog. We had no streetlamps there but could see the white shape easily under a bright moon. It moved slowly and steadily toward our door, occasionally stopping to sit and howl then moving again, closer and closer, until it sat before the front door.

Great-grandmother Annie wasn't the only one scared half to death. The looks on my grandparents' faces also disturbed me. I was sent back to bed while the three of them stayed awake the whole of the night. Much later I learned they saw it as a terrible omen that someone in the house was about to die. They thought the dog had come for Annie, and that if they stayed awake and alert, nothing would happen.

They were right. Annie survived the night and the dog disappeared. She laughed and sang through the house the next day. That night, I happened to look outside from my upstairs window. A small light I hadn't noticed before seemed to hover in the yard before the front door. When I asked Grandfather what it was, he had a look himself. He started and went rushing to Annie's bed. She lay there smiling, having passed away peacefully in her sleep. The corpse candle, one with a blue flame, was said to appear at the door of a house where death had come.

With a sigh, I turned the newspaper over below the fold. The photo took me by surprise, so much that I gave out a startled cry. Homer jerked his head up. He was on his feet and beside me in seconds.

"It's all right, love," I said to soothe him. "Just a bit shocked, that's all."

To my astonishment, the photo was of my house. I recognized it as one previously used by the paper when Phoebe and I had our bit of notoriety some weeks earlier. Its accompanying article's title read "Bones Found on Old Prewitt Land" in large bold print. Beneath it, the reporter, Delilah Newberry, told of the discovery occurring after the recent storm. She knew lightning hit the tree. She knew the resulting hole exposed the skeleton. It was a relief to see no mention whatsoever of where the skeleton might be on my land. She did say that the coroner and police department visited the scene. She also noted that a friend of the land's present owner, yours truly, was called in for his archaeological expertise.

I wondered why the reporter hadn't talked to me. Not that I wished to discuss the matter and might even have refused to do so had she called. Of course, my telephone isn't terribly reliable, so she may have tried. Her information must have come from the police department, through the ordinary report that would've been filed. Grant and Carol, the couple from the tribe, didn't seem the sort to talk with the media, though they may have made their call to the state historical commission. They, in turn, may have notified the Indian Affairs Council that the bones were most likely those of a Caucasian. Reports by the coroner and the forensic anthropologist would be done, certainly, but it seemed most unlikely to me that any of those offices would have received or filed reports available to the media so quickly.

That left only three others beside myself who had been to the site. Michael had hardly been out of my sight since his arrival. The young Mr. Graybear could possibly be the source if he wasn't presently detained in jail. No, if he were the informer, he would have given the reporter a more native activist slant and made himself the center of his story. As I read the article again, my feelings became stronger that all the above scenarios were unlikely to have been the case. In my heart, I knew the real culprit. As I said earlier, I would need to have a word with Phoebe.

twenty-three
Phoebe Goes to the Library

Early next morning, I saw the news that old Mr. Reed had been found. He was on up there in years, but still, it was a terrible thing. Since the newspaper didn't say how he died, I hoped it was some kind of natural cause. I knew that it must mean something else, something bad, or they would have said. I couldn't help but cry. He was a nice old guy and from a mighty fine family.

The rug rat trotted over to the side of my chair to see if I was all right.

"It's okay," I said. "I'm fine . . . uh . . . what am I going to call you now, huh?"

Sissy Breedlove had dropped a bomb on me when I went to pick Rowdy up at Smoochie Poochie. I took one look at him when the assistant brought him out for me to see his new hairdo and knew something was severely wrong.

He looked like a completely different dog. All the knots were cut out, and all the hair left on him was smooth and sleeked down. The coat was shiny. The big difference was I could see his face and the hair around it was either cut pretty or tied up on top of his head.

"Hey, Sissy," I said. "Now, granted, you've sure done a great job here. I'd even say it's close to miraculous. But remember, I told you I didn't want any of this frou-frou stuff like ribbons and toenail polish. I'm not sure I can afford it all, and besides, it's not right to embarrass the poor boy and make him look like a girl."

She laughed so hard she dropped her doggie comb. "Phoebe, darling, I don't know how to break this to you, but 'he' is a 'she.' She's supposed to look like a girl. Surprise!"

I was surprised, all right. Surprised at myself for being dumb enough to take my sister's word for anything when I know better.

"The bow and the toenail polish are freebies. Isn't she gorgeous? You ought to enter her in a dog show. I'm serious. She's beautiful. I want to show you some pictures in this magazine. Look at that. This one here, same breed, wins dog shows all over the country. And Rowdy, or Rowdy Anne, or whatever you're going to call her, is much prettier, don't you think?"

I thought I'd never get out of there. Sissy wouldn't let me go without giving me suggestions on what dog clothes would look good on Rowdy. She knew I wouldn't buy any, but that I might want to make some myself like the ones in her shop. Sheesh. When we got home, I tried to get work done around the house but couldn't quit looking at Rowdy. The sex change was going to take some getting used to.

You know, the little munchkin wasn't so bad after

all. She had started to get to me with the good manners and all. Never barked unless there was a good reason. Since Sissy Breedlove dolled her up and made her coat all shiny and smelling good, I didn't mind when she got lonely and wanted to get snuggly in my lap while I watched TV. Which was most of the time.

In fact, she was a right princess compared to the only other little-bitty dogs I've ever known. My brother Gerald's wife Lila has had two teacup Chihuahuas, and I mean both of them belonged in the doggie insane asylum with straitjackets and padded kennels.

The first one would bite anything that moved by it, like my ankles or shoes. Thank goodness its teeth weren't big enough to do any real damage because that little thing was flat out vicious. Its daughter, Lila's next Chihuahua that is fourteen years old and still alive, would go berserk anytime anybody came over to visit. She wouldn't attack their shoes like her mama. She'd make a beeline to the living room coffee table and run around and around it so fast she was nothing but a blur, yapping and squeaking at the top of her lungs. She wouldn't stop, either, until the person left. Sometimes Gerald or Lila could catch her but not often. That thing was as slippery as she was fast. She could wear out a braided rug in six months, no lie. I would not put up with that mess, let me tell you.

So I knew I was lucky that Rowdy had a completely different personality. She didn't seem to mind going places with me, either. She didn't fuss a bit when I took her with me to the library.

I had finished the last alterations on Grace's costume. She likes to be a witch every year. She has this wig of white hair that's thick and sticks out all over, so she never wears a pointy hat. We like it because it makes her look more like a half-witch, half-voodoo woman.

This year, I added some things to her dress to make it look different from last time. When I ordered the brain mold from McPhee's, I also got some stick-on blood drops and a bony, withered-up hand to hang out of a pocket. At the fabric store, we found rhinestone patches in the shapes of the moon and stars. I sewed those on the top of the shoulders along with a black cat with green glow-in-the-dark eyes.

"And who is this?" Grace said when I took Rowdy out of the wicker basket. Grace held out her arms to take her. She did the very same thing Sissy did, gave Rowdy an Eskimo kiss on the nose, then cuddled Rowdy up under her chin and started rocking her like a baby. "Aren't you the pwettiest wittle doll? Aren't you? Yes, you are."

"Oh, for heaven's sake, not you, too," I said, though it did make me proud that Grace liked her.

"You just missed your boyfriend." Grace took Rowdy over to the counter and set her on it so she could walk around.

"To what boyfriend are you referring, madam?"

Grace slapped my arm. "You know exactly who I

mean. That old white man I introduced you to in here the other day."

"The one from Ohio? He wasn't that old."

"Indiana," Grace said. "And he is old. Extremely. He's so old, he makes Colonel Sanders look like a spring chicken. Which makes him just right for you."

"Very funny. He didn't trip my triggers. Help yourself."

She threw her head back and laughed real loud. That made Lucy, who has always been a stickler about keeping the library quiet, give us dirty looks. "No way," Grace said. "He's much too long in the tooth for my young blood."

"Too long in the tooth, huh? Maybe he would agree to come be Dracula in the Trail of Terror."

"Ha ha!" Grace laughed even louder. Lucy set her mouth in a line and turned on her heels to go shelve some books. "He's sure white enough to be Dracula. He'd make a good one, as pale as he is. You know, when I mentioned it, he sounded like he might come to the haunted house. Probably wants to see a cute little redhead who happens to be in his age group. I don't think he has made any friends down here yet. He acts like he's lonely."

"Well, I'm sorry for him, but the last thing I need is a man up under my feet and in my way all the time. I'm too busy. See if Lucy wants him."

We both looked over at her, rolling a squeaky cart across the marble floor at approximately .00001 miles per hour. Otherwise, the whole library was dead silent.

"I imagine he'd rather have somebody more lively," Grace said.

"Don't let Lucy fool you. She's liable to jump into warp speed any second now."

We watched until she finally made it to her destination and gathered her strength. Her arm moved more slowly from the book cart to the shelf than her feet had moved across the room. Grace stared. "Her hyperdrive must be in the shop."

"Here," I said. I handed her the bag I was carrying. "Try this on to make sure I took it in enough. That way I'll still have time to fix it if it's not right. Otherwise, I'll see you on Halloween. I'll get here early to help get things set up, okay?"

twenty-four
Jane Talks to Detective Waters

Michael and I had finished our breakfast when he asked if he could borrow my car. "Just to get out for a while. You sure you don't mind?"

"No, of course not." I went to the den for my purse.

"I thought I'd drop into the drugstore for a few things, drive about town. We can still get to the dig site plenty early enough."

I tossed my key ring to him, then we walked out together and to the car. Homer passed us and set out across the road to attend to his own schedule. As I watched the car disappear around the bend, another car came into view, headed toward my house.

"Good morning," I said to Detective Waters when he stepped out of his car. "You're out early."

He shut his door and smiled as he walked toward me. "Morning. Yes, ma'am." His red eyes and tired-looking face told me he had been up for most of the night.

"Would you like to come in for coffee? Or could I make you some breakfast? It's no trouble, I assure you."

"No, thank you. I grabbed a bite on the way here. Was that your friend Mr. Hay I just passed?"

"Yes."

He nodded as he looked down the road, though Michael was long out of view. "Does he have some other friends here?"

"No. He's only going for a drive to see something of the town. Did you need to speak with him?"

"No. Just you. If you have a few minutes."

"Come. Have a seat." I motioned for him to join me on the porch, where we each took rockers. "I saw the newspaper this morning. I was sorry to hear about Mr. Reed."

Detective Waters rocked slowly and spoke in a low voice. "He was a fine man. The best hunter and tracker there ever was around here. He just had his eighty-seventh birthday." He rocked in silence for a while, deep in thought. "Never said a harsh word in his life."

"You were good friends?"

"Not really. He was good to everybody, though.

Took a lot of time with kids. Knew how to make them feel good about themselves. Always teaching them about the woods, how to survive, how to appreciate nature."

As Detective Waters talked, he looked out across the road over what was Cal Prewitt's land not so long ago. Without saying it, I could tell we both thought of Cal, another who had spent his life preserving the beauty of nature. His ancestors, white and native, had lived on this piece of land for many centuries.

The cool morning breeze swept across our faces and down the porch as I said, "You must have been up very late with the investigation."

"I was up late," he said, "but for another reason. I felt like I needed to let you know about it." The determined set of his jaw brought out Detective Waters's own native heritage. He gathered his thoughts and in a moment, he turned his dark eyes toward me. "There was another call. From Huntsville. A man was found dead in an alley, outside a rough night club known for fights."

"That's quite a distance outside your jurisdiction, I should think."

"It is. The detective in charge there called me after his team searched the deceased man's motel room. He had been living there for several weeks. Inside, they found a number of stolen goods. Including your credit cards and driver's license."

"My word! I never expected to hear about them again. And he lives, or rather lived so far away."

He nodded and began rocking again. "I'm afraid they won't be released to you for some time."

"That's quite all right. I understand. New ones are on the way. It's so kind of you to come all this way to tell me." I said the words, though I knew he surely had more on his mind. He could have telephoned to tell me about the cards.

"Mrs. Thistle, you're a tough lady. You're a direct person. I appreciate that. So I'll be direct with you and won't try to sugarcoat what I have to say."

I waited. He looked at his shoes a moment before he brought his head up to look me squarely in the eyes. "Your purse was found in the motel's dumpster. He had taken out the cash. All the other items, except for one, that you reported as being in your purse at the time of the theft, and the purse itself, were found intact. What I mean by that is, it looks as if the thief hardly gave anything in there a look. Nothing was disturbed. All still very neat. Usually, what I see with petty thieves is that they dump the contents to look for anything valuable. This guy didn't do that."

"How very odd. What was the missing item?"

"Your keys."

We stared at each other a while as he let the implications sink in.

"Mrs. Thistle, we didn't find them in the dumpster or anywhere in his room." He slowly shook his head left and right. "It could be that the thief dumped them somewhere else. Threw them out the window somewhere between here and Huntsville. It's a possibility." He didn't sound convinced.

"But if so," I said, "he would most likely also throw away the entire purse after taking the cash."

Detective Waters smiled and nodded. "That's right. At least, that's how I see it. Might not have happened like that. I thought you should know. Just in case you might want to change your locks."

"Detective, since he's dead, he won't be able to use the keys now. He didn't take them with him."

"You're right about that. No, he didn't." His smile faded. "But I left some things out. One thing is, this person had a record of small-time thefts and one charge of computer hacking that was dismissed. The second thing is, this person had a job. He had a custodian job on the night shift at Dr. Norwood's office building. Coincidentally, computer records show that, during that same shift, someone accessed Dr. Norwood's work files and printed out a few things."

I felt my breath catch in my chest. "Are you able to know specifically what things were printed?"

He nodded. "Her preliminary report of findings on your property. These pages included maps and directions to the site. None of those pages were found on the deceased or in his room. So we have missing keys to your house, and missing maps to your house and to the gravesite, and one very dead guy."

"You think he gave them to someone."

"Yes, ma'am, I do." He stared at me and confirmed that we both thought of the same thing. "It's likely that he was your burglar the other day, or he had already given the keys to someone else who used them to enter your house."

"You didn't mention anything about finding my statues among his belongings at the hotel."

"They weren't there."

We sat in silence, listening to the songs of morning birds, each alone in our thoughts. After a while, I said, "The thing is, my purse was taken before the storm, before anyone knew there would be a dig site with bones at all. Before Dr. Norwood became involved."

Detective Waters's broad smile relaxed his stone-like face. "I didn't say I had it all figured out. Too many coincidences. I don't like it. In your place, I'd change my locks, just in case he handed your keys off to someone. That someone might have been his killer and might have an interest in you and your house or your old bones in the woods."

A chill made me shiver. I did my best not to show the fear that was slowly taking hold and thanked him for his concern. It was only later, after the shock of it all had worn off somewhat, that it occurred to me he had slipped a few innocent-sounding questions past me. He had wanted to know when Michael arrived at the Huntsville airport, and if I'd picked him up there myself.

When Michael returned, we made the trek to the dig site and worked companionably the rest of the morning. I assisted him, mostly recording what he did by taking more photos and jotting down his thoughts as they came to him. When he was more settled, I began my own recordings of a feature we had discussed, a promising one that looked like the tip of a buried artifact, about four feet from the skeleton. Though I had all the opportunity in the world to bring up the subject of Detective Waters's visit, I didn't do so. I can't really say why.

I found that, wherever I happened to be at the site, my mind took particular notice of the surroundings. An old familiar feeling was getting stronger in my subconscious. It spurred the sort of thoughts I had in my previous life, when my government work involved evading—and sometimes constructing and implementing—security measures.

While I studied the site's access by road, places where traps might be concealed, areas from which a sniper might find cover, and other precautions to protect the dig site should I decide to take them, a heavy weight descended upon me. How was I to protect something so remote and so vulnerable? Was it time to buy a good tent from which I could stand guard at night? My one comforting thought, if it came to that, was Homer. There was no better alarm system.

I was brought out of my musings by a sudden chirping. It was not from one of the many bird species here in my woods, but from my cell phone.

It was Phoebe.

"Jane, may I come over and shoot out there at your rocks? You know where I mean. Where we found that poor dead boy last time."

"Of course. Would you like to come in the morning? I'll make breakfast. We can take a nice walk near there before Michael and I go out to the site."

"No, hon, I need to come right now. I mean, I appreciate the invitation to breakfast and all. But I'd really like to come on before long. If that's all right."

I noticed a faint huffing in her voice as she spoke, as well as a slight tightness in her words. "Is everything all right, dear?"

"Everything's fine. Smokahontas is a little restless. She needs to take care of a little business, that's all."

"Right, then. I'm at the site now. Meet you at the house?"

"I'll be right there." The phone clicked in my ear.

When she drove up, she saw me standing on the porch with a rifle, a canvas bag for my handguns, and a mesh tote filled with bottles and cans that I'd saved for targets. She waved with a half-flip of her hand out her window to indicate I should get in her car.

Without a word between us, we crossed the road and into the field that once belonged to my benefactor. We carried on down the road through the field to the place Cal had used as a practice range. He'd set small boulders, about waist-high or higher in a row several yards from the edge of the bluff.

Phoebe parked and got out of the car, taking long, quick strides to its trunk. From the trunk, she took her rifle bag, one made from sturdy canvas in a camouflage print, and unzipped it to reveal her pride and glory, Smokahontas, a smaller version of an AK-47 rifle. She put the AK's strap over her shoulder, reached in the trunk once more, and retrieved a small paper bag.

She gave the bag an odd look of distaste. Her lips pressed together in a tight line. I could see her jaw muscles twitch as if she ground her teeth. As preposterous as it seemed, it looked to me as if she were angry at the bag. She slammed the trunk lid down.

The slam reverberated in the air, bouncing and echoing in the stillness of the countryside. Birds, frogs, and crickets halted their songs momentarily in the wake of the loud noise before resuming, though with noticeable trepidation.

All this time, Phoebe hadn't looked to me again, so intent was she upon her task. I found myself walking softly and slowly. I said nothing, waiting, until Phoebe raised her head, her eyes closed. As they opened, she said, "I appreciate you letting me come on such short notice." Her voice was soft. Scarily so.

"Not at all. You know you're welcome here anytime."

"Well. You're sweet. And I do appreciate it. This won't take long."

Phoebe and I walked to the rocks first. I reached in my tote and took out the tins and bottles I'd brought and began setting them up in a line for our targets. Phoebe reached in her bag, as well. I'm not sure what I expected. More tins, I imagine.

Instead, I was quite surprised when she drew out a paperback book. She walked to the far rock at the end.

She took the book in both hands and, about every fifty pages or so, gripped each side of the book tightly with her fingers and cracked each section back to the spine, then proceeded to the next. Each crack was done with a quick and sure motion, as well as a certain tightening of her facial muscles that indicated a perverse pleasure. A story Phoebe told me once about watching her grandmother wring the necks of chickens came to mind.

Thus fanned, the book stood upright on top of the rock's flat surface without a quiver, though in its place, I had no doubt I'd be shaking down to my shoes, considering Phoebe's poorly concealed anger. She walked past the line we used for handgun practice, going farther out and turning where we usually stood to shoot the larger guns.

"Isn't that the book you were raving about just yesterday?" I took out my handgun. I'd only brought the one this time, a Walther PPK. Phoebe had mentioned she might like to try it since it was associated with James Bond.

"That's the one," she said.

"I thought you said you were enjoying it immensely." I popped the magazine in the PPK and racked the slide.

"I was."

I was perplexed. "You said the beginning was the most exciting you had ever read."

"It is." She snapped the fully loaded cartridge up into her rifle and gave it another hard smack for good measure. "That boy can write up a storm. There's no doubt about it. The first four pages of him describing how awful the villain is—and I'm not talking about a weenie villain, I'm talking about the most disgusting, godforsaken, lawless, heathen subhuman ever known—blew me away."

She stared at me the way she always did when loading the AK. She loved the sound of it, more than actually shooting the rifle, I suspect. The distinctive clicks of the loading mechanism gave her a thrill and her face always reflected it as now, like a naughty cherub smiling with the macho pride of being cool.

"Unfortunately," she said, "I had a little problem with page five." She gave me the look as she pulled the bolt back and let it go to snap into place with a *slick slock*. Her grin widened. She took aim, squinting, with her cheek against the gun's body, and fired.

The barrel roared as she fired three successive shots. Pages fluttered in the wake of them, but the book did not take a direct hit.

"Because on page five, when the disgusting, heathen subhuman spoke for the first time . . . ," She adjusted her aim and squeezed the trigger again. *Boom. Boom.*

". . . that boy had a Southern accent." Her hands went white as she gripped the gun's body even tighter against her. She stepped closer and closer to the target, firing once with each step. "Which would've been fine, except the story is set . . . ,"

Boom.

". . . in North . . ."

Boom.

". . . dad gone . . ."

Boom.

". . . Dakota."

BoomBoomBoomBoomBoomBoomBoomBoomBoom-Boom.

The trigger clicked but it didn't matter that she'd run out of ammo. The paperback had lifted straight up perhaps six inches with the first of the last three shots and twirled in midair with the second. The third didn't hit. Nevertheless, the book fell down again on the top of the rock, flat on its face, its pages sprawled out like lifeless limbs. It moved no more.

Phoebe let out a sigh. "But that's okay. It's a free country. And I'm used to that kind of garbage." She examined her handiwork, one single hole just below the title on the cover and the top right corners singed, as she picked the book up. She held it away from her with two fingers by one end of the spine, as if she had bagged a squirrel or possum and held it upside down by the tail, as far away from her body as she could in case it might be diseased.

"I learned something though," she said. "I learned never to buy another book that won four awards. You'd think using such a worn-out cliché in the first five pages would've disqualified it. Nope. Not in this world. Those judges were nothing but a bunch of cheese-eaters. Now I know. Now I ain't so ignert." She said the last word with an exaggerated accent. "And yes, that is a proper word. Ignorant, Ignernt, Ig

Nert. It's the superlative. It means 'the most ignorant' and is therefore better than that plain white stuff in hoity-toity grammar books." Her face blazed with color as she turned to me. Her eyes watered with a mix of anger and hurt feelings. "Everybody wants us to be ignert, Jane. That's all that matters. That's what everybody thinks, don't they?"

Slowly, I took the book from her fingers and set it upright again on the rock's ledge. I placed my left hand gently on her shoulder and spoke in a soft voice.

"No, dear. Not everybody." In one motion, I brought my right arm up straight, shoulder height and at its full length, and fired three successive shots at close range. They roared, hitting so soon one after another that the book looked stunned, jostled but unable to move until the final hit, and fell straight on its back like a domino with a firm *splat*. Smoke misted from its new holes.

"Dang, Jane. What do you think this is, open season?"

I smiled as I held it up for her inspection. "Yes. On cheese. Swiss, anyone?"

We laughed as we walked back to the line to finish up our ammo. I knocked off a few bottles I'd brought. Phoebe hit her book more consistently. In fact, she didn't try to hit any of the other targets, only the book, emptying three more magazines of bullets in the effort, though only a couple made contact.

After we had taken thorough care of the deceased paperback, she underwent a change. Her body relaxed, her face emitted a glow of calm and joy, reminiscent of small children and Buddhist monks. With our guns emptied, we sat on two low rocks for a rest.

"Jane, you're a true friend. I'm sorry I lost my temper. I really do want to be more calm and mindful of the universe, like they say, and all that. It's the right way to be. It's just that no-account book was the last straw. A lady can only take so many pushes on her hot buttons before she blows up."

She reached down to a clump of tall spindly grass, broke off a green blade, and began using it as if it were a toothpick on her bottom teeth. "Yeah, Jane, I sure am lucky to have a good gun therapist like you when I need one. Now if only I could get you to show me some of those fancy moves, I believe I'd be a lot calmer all the time."

She amazed me. Perhaps, I thought, she was finally interested in the meditative qualities I'd gone on about when talking of my daily tai chi and meditation practice.

"Wonderful. Would you like to learn a couple of steps here? We can go through the moves together, a few at a time until you learn them all. Anytime you like."

"Hot dog. You're the best. Show me one."

We walked a few feet away from the rocks where the grass was soft and the ground flat. "Now," I said. "The first thing about practicing tai chi is . . ."

"Whoa. Stop right there," she said, holding up a hand. "That's not the moves I'm talking about. Swinging my arms around like a windmill or standing like a flamingo on one leg while pretending my hand is a little Chinese basket doesn't interest me in the least. Jujitsu is what I'm talking about. Karate. Things to defend yourself. Fighting off bad guys. Stuff that makes you want to go 'Hee-yah!' Maybe if I already knew any of it, that boy who mugged us wouldn't have gotten away."

I sighed. It was also true that he might not have been killed if I'd been able to hold him until the police arrived.

"Sorry," Phoebe said. "I didn't mean it to sound like I could have done a better job than you did. Only that, if there had been two of us karate chopping him at once, he might not have gotten away."

"You're quite right. Don't apologize. You made me think of something else that has been weighing on my mind." I told her about the visit from Detective Waters and all that we talked about, except for one thing, his questions regarding Michael. Those had no bearing on the situation whatsoever. Just thinking of the detective's suggestions gave me a feeling of disloyalty. I trusted Michael with no reserves and would have been uncomfortable in relaying what amounted to gossip to Phoebe.

"Goodness, Jane. You poor thing. It is beyond me why somebody would have any interest in a bunch of old bones, no offense, much less steal or kill somebody over them."

"It's not quite clear whether that's actually the case. We don't know anything for certain as yet."

"Get real, Jane. You know as well as I do that the whole thing sounds like somebody is after you or wanting to find that grave. That crazy Graybear boy, for one. I'm sure Dan Waters is already on the stick as far as that kid is concerned. If he's the one, Dan will put an end to that foolishness right quick. It's the chance that it's somebody else that is so worrisome."

She was right. As always, Phoebe got straight to the heart of the matter. It was precisely my fear. Someone unknown to me wanted access to the bones site, a person who most likely thought they could find native artifacts to sell on the black market. But was that enough to lead them to murder?

"I think we would both feel better if you taught me a self-defense lesson or two," Phoebe said. "It would get me ready in case we get into any more trouble, and it would be good for you since you might be getting a little rusty. Right now, you need to be on your toes."

"Good point. All right, then. Let's start with a few simple pressure point techniques. Kyusho Jitsu."

"Bless you." Phoebe bowed low from the waist, her palms together.

She did remarkably well. We practiced grabbing each other by the wrists and arms, using the proper twists to bring an opponent to the floor. Phoebe particularly enjoyed learning the vulnerable points on the body that could be struck or merely pressed, just so, in order to immobilize an attacker.

We rode back to my house in a good mood, both feeling better after the rigors of the workout. Phoebe didn't have time to come in for lunch as she had last-minute things to do related to her Halloween party at the library. We set a time to meet the following afternoon. I would go to her house, then to the library to help entertain the children.

twenty-five
Jane Takes a Closer Look

*L*ater that afternoon, the movie crew's trailer parked once again at the Piggly Wiggly. I wondered if they had filmed anything in town yet. Their gear always seemed to be here, in the grocery lot.

"It takes a long time to get prepared, they say," the cashier told me. "They're working somewhere around here. They must not need all the fancy equipment yet."

She could be right. Interviews and the like would take time. I returned with my groceries to my car, right next to the trailer. Through one of its windows, I couldn't help overhearing a conversation inside between two men.

"We'll do it tonight."

"But if we're not using the regular stuff, what do I bring?"

"Just shovels and those bags. I want to get it all in one trip and then split. Don't forget to pick up more batteries for the lamps."

Shovels? To make movies? A familiar twitch in my stomach told me something was wrong. That same feeling served me well on many a dangerous mission in my younger days.

I quietly opened my car door. When I sat behind the wheel, I heard the trailer's door open. In my rearview mirror, I saw two men walk from the trailer toward the Pig. One was young, a bodybuilder, not very tall. The other man was taller and had gray hair. Neither turned around.

When they entered the building, I got out of my car and walked behind the trailer. I tried to see inside the small windows. The trailer looked mostly empty. What I saw beside the small dining table shocked me. There was no doubt in my mind that it had belonged to me. The green metal box stolen from the antique trunk in my den had unmistakable scratches and paint marks I would recognize anywhere.

Immediately, I thought of calling Detective Waters. I paused. How would I explain the illegal devices inside? I decided I wasn't ready to do that. I peeked around the trailer and waited until the parking lot was clear. I took my ring of keys from my pocket. By feel, I found the one I would need.

One never knows when the tools and skills required in a former job will come in handy again. In my part-time work for the government, it was necessary to know how to get inside places that others wanted kept locked. I was a spy, you see. I worked in cities all over the world, wherever my military husband was assigned. I became proficient in shooting and fighting, skills I already possessed that my husband, the

Colonel, helped me advance. And now, only a special aptitude with a skeleton key was called for. Easy.

Stepping up to the trailer's front door, I slid my special key in the lock, opened the door quickly, and closed it behind me to take a closer look.

What struck me first was the absence of film equipment. No lights or stands. No cameras. I did find a couple of boxes that, upon inspection, contained what looked like smuggled goods from Central America. I saw no sign of my missing statues, though my search was hurried. I took my own box and left.

Another surprise waited for me on my own doorstep. As I unlocked the door, I happened to look down. A round piece of mud lay on the threshold. Imprinted on it, I saw tread marks from a shoe.

I stopped cold. It was true that Michael might have tracked this here, after playing about in the woods for the last few days. Yet I didn't think so. We each made a habit of leaving our dirty work boots on the porch on a small mat I'd set to the side of the doorway, precisely for that purpose. The soil bits on our mat had a dark brown hue. This divot of mud was brick red.

I eased the door open, though I felt a bit silly for doing so. We were the likely culprits. However, as soon as I entered the living room, I knew someone had been here in our absence. A smell of sweat with the faint odor of onions greeted me.

Quickly, I set down my gun bag, retrieved the PPK, snapped in a new magazine, racked the slide, and systematically searched the house for intruders. In the kitchen, I noted the back door's dead bolt had been unlocked. Not as I'd left it. A brief glance out the door's window and onto the screened back porch made me reasonably sure my visitor or visitors had left the premises this way. A few tiny clumps of the dirt speckled the porch's wooden slats. Still, I continued through the house, looking in every conceivable hiding place from basement to roof.

When searching the den, a terrible thought hit me when I saw my trunks. My guns. Thank goodness I'd moved them and stashed them all over the house. Even so, the trunks' locks had not been tampered with. That was a small relief. Other guns about the house were hidden, some not so well, I realized, given the present circumstances. Most all were under lock and key, but a determined thief could easily take off with some of them, case and all. Luckily, I accounted for all of them during my search.

With a great exhalation of relief, I returned downstairs. No one was in the house now, and only a few papers and notebooks on the desk looked disturbed. So far as I could tell, nothing was missing.

I took a few minutes of rest in my easy chair, as well as a nice shot of brandy. With an effort, I shook off the troublesome events and packed a lunch for Michael and myself. He would be hungry and ready for a break.

On the way through the forest, my mind worked on problems of security once again. Several plans formed, ones I dearly hoped would never be necessary. Before I left the house, I called the police station. Detective Waters was out. It was just as well. As I calmed down, I realized I had nothing but suspicion to report since I couldn't tell him about the metal weapons box and had seen no sign of my statues in the trailer. How would I explain my presence in the trailer at all? No, it was better to think it all out for a bit. On my walk to the bones site, my head cleared. I came to the conclusion that my imagination was getting the better of me, an old woman with old thoughts of intrigue still rattling about in her head. I would buy better locks and take more precautions at the house.

When I arrived at the site, Michael and Homer were not at the dig pit. They approached from the west on a trail that followed the curve of the stone wall's remains. We met under the rock overhang to eat our lunch in its shade.

Michael didn't take the news of our intruders well. His voice shook a little after I told him it was clear someone had been searching through our notes and paperwork. I imagined he was thinking about his own recent experience with thieves, when he was attacked at his former university. We ate in silence for a while.

I tried to lighten the mood by talking about Phoebe's shooting session. He laughed when I described the book. I asked how his work went after I left. He said he had become distracted from the skeleton but refused to say more. A twinkle in his eye told me he had found something.

"It must be extraordinary," I said.

"What?"

"Whatever you're not telling me."

"I don't know what you mean." He munched on his sandwich, observing it as if its contents fascinated him.

"You've found something. You're humming again."

He stopped tapping his foot. His head stopped the barely perceptible movements it made in time with his song. With a throaty laugh, he wrapped his sandwich again in its foil, grabbed my hand, and led me to his discovery.

He had not worked on the areas where it appeared corners had been constructed, as I suspected. Instead, he had painstakingly brushed away the dirt surrounding the protrusion we noted, midway between the imagined rectangle of the burial container's edges. I sat back on my haunches. Michael followed suit.

It was then I suddenly saw a deep blue aura where Michael had been digging. Other than seeing this phenomenon immediately surrounding the bones, what I saw thus far at the site had been subtle, like a fine pale mist. Here before me, however, the same dark blue, almost like a shield, covered what Michael had exposed. The color distracted me at first, to the point that I couldn't differentiate clearly between the dirt and the object.

"Well? What do you think?"

As my vision adjusted, I could see the upper part of a large curved object about three inches thick, its arc above the dirt about one foot wide. A space, perhaps an inch wide, separated the object from something else Michael had exposed.

"Definitely a wall of some sort," he said happily.

"What's this then?" I gently traced the curve.

When he didn't answer, I looked up to find his eyes sparkling with delight. He hid his smile behind a hand, the fingers tapping above his upper lip. When he spoke, his voice was low and dreamy. "Many years ago, a former professor called me to a site. This was in the south of England."

"Is this going to be one of your longer stories?"

"Yes. It was a gravesite found when the railroad was going through. One of the railway workers was digging, he struck what sounded like metal, and when he looked in his shovel, it held a shiny cup made of gold. My professor eventually identified the site as an Anglo-Saxon burial room, an entire room as big as your den, in which the bones of an old soldier and all he might need in the afterlife had lain untouched for almost fourteen hundred years. Fourteen hundred years!"

"Amazing. How did you know he was a soldier?"

"By the great sword at his side, among other things. But the thing here that makes me remember that particular site is this." He indicated the space with the tip of a small paintbrush. "You see?"

"Heavens!" I leaned closer. Behind the curve, a smaller curve of something thin lay atop what was surely a type of nail, still imbedded in the wall.

"This is what I was getting at with the story. The

Anglo-Saxon site had a number of items still on the wall, just as they had been buried. I think this is a bowl. And it is hanging by a handle, perhaps one of two on either side." He shrugged. "Perhaps not. We'll have to see. But my first guess is that our fellow died in his kitchen."

We hugged each other and laughed. Michael pulled me to my feet and we danced upon the bright yellow and orange leaves that covered the flat area around us. I had forgotten the joy of discovery, even such a small thing as a nail, and of being with a man as full of life as Michael. We embraced again, ending in an unexpected kiss. Laughing it off after a moment's hesitation, we returned to gaze and consider the new find.

As we worked, we continued to speculate. Michael suggested we hire another worker or two, as it was slow going with just the two of us. I responded in a vague way. More people meant more chance of word spreading. I didn't want that. Even with no publicity in any national archaeological journals and newspapers, we already had a possible threat.

He asked me to clear away dirt from around another site of a suspected artifact. He'd made a small beginning already near where the feet of the skeleton had been. What looked like the corner of something solid protruded, just barely, above the soil. Though I'd been over this area numerous times already, I hadn't noticed it. Michael's experienced eyes missed very little. Now that he had pointed it out, I could see the pit's blue aura was a bit darker there, exactly where the object stuck out.

I worked to uncover it, bit by bit, seeing that it was rock, flat and rectangular, about ten by four, and increasingly blue the more I uncovered. I selected a different brush to delicately sweep away dirt from what I thought were thin fissures in the rock. I stopped.

"Oh, heavens," I said. Michael looked over at me. I couldn't keep the excitement out of my voice. "Michael, dear. I believe it's engraved."

We took many photos of it, working steadily and almost silently, other than directions from Michael, until the daylight waned. The engravings were not in English, but were instead about ten symbols. Whether two or three of them ran together or were separate, we couldn't tell as yet.

"Remember," I said. "Don't breathe a word of this to anyone. I don't want to attract attention." He promised and stuck his camera in his bag.

Bone tired but elated, we closed up shop for the night. "Another most excellent day," he said. "I think we should celebrate with a bottle."

"Oh? Wine or champagne?"

"Neither. A bottle of rubbing alcohol for my old sore muscles might do better. It would hit the spot just now, with perhaps a few aspirin."

When we drove out of the property and onto Anisidi Road, we saw Phoebe's car parked in front of my house again. Once out of my car, Phoebe called to us to help her carry sacks and boxes inside. She had returned home after our shooting extravaganza and made our supper.

"My dear, you shouldn't have," I said. Wonderful aromas escaped from the containers and reminded me how hungry I was.

Phoebe handed off everything to the two of us, except one package, Rowdy's wicker basket. In the kitchen, with the covered dishes and plates set on the table, she lifted the little dog out of his carrier to scamper about on the floor.

"My, how pretty Rowdy looks today," I said. His coat of white, brownish gray, and red no longer stood out on end but now lay flat and sleek. With it all combed down, that which hadn't been cut off almost reached the floor. His face looked positively gorgeous with the hair cut and styled around it.

"He's not Rowdy anymore," Phoebe said. "And he's not a 'he' anymore, either. Are you ready for this? Sissy Breedlove over at Smoochie Poochie told me Rowdy is a girl. Can you believe that? I don't know what is wrong with my sister. Anyway, so that's why I renamed him. Or her. Michael and Jane, I'd like you to meet Jenette."

The "he" who was now a "she" looked up at us and blinked.

"Won't that confuse her when she goes home to Corene?" I said.

Phoebe snorted. "What, are you crazy? Corene can't take care of herself, much less a dog. Why, it would be inhumane for me to send this poor animal home with her."

Homer, who had come inside the house with us but retreated to the den so as to avoid disturbing Phoebe, ventured slowly into the kitchen to greet Jenette. When Jenette saw him, she barked. Her long silky hair undulated with each yap.

Phoebe scooped her up in her arms and held her close to her own face. At that moment, I realized why the little dog had always looked so familiar to me. Now, I could see it was not another dog she reminded me of, but a person. She reminded me of Phoebe.

The resemblance was remarkable. Both wore red bows in the center of their hairdos. Jenette's eyes were darker, and she had only a patch of red hair at the top of her head as opposed to Phoebe's full head of it, but both girls possessed a certain facial expression that conveyed an ebullient spirit, a bit of impatience, and a dash of mischief. Both looked down at Homer, then up again to me, then directly into one another's eyes. Phoebe turned to me.

"Jenette don't like dogs," she said. She sniffed at the idea and exhaled a quiet huff. "Do you, hon?"

They looked at one another, face-to-face. Jenette sniffed and also exhaled a small ladylike huff out of her tiny nostrils. Nevertheless, she wagged her tail when she looked at Homer again and wiggled as if she wanted to be let down in order to get to know him.

"Nonsense," I said. "Give her a chance and she will love him as I do. I'll set out a bowl for her as well."

Phoebe did so with reluctance, but all went well with their introductions. We washed up and set into our meals.

"What a feast," Michael said when we sat at the table loaded with the goodies Phoebe provided.

"I just threw together leftovers. Fried chicken, mashed potatoes, broccoli casserole, some yeast rolls, and chocolate pie. It's not much. I just hope it will be worth eating."

We assured her it was. Michael praised her with almost every bite.

"So, Jane," Phoebe said. "What are we going to do to keep lowlifes off your property over yonder?"

"I have a few things in mind. I thought when we finished eating, you and I could set up a simple roadblock, just across at the entrance, while Michael takes his shower."

"Okay," she said. She put her napkin in her lap. "But that won't help much if they're hiking types."

"That's true. It's the best we can do tonight, I'm afraid. Maybe tomorrow I can secure the area around the dig somewhat."

Michael, I noticed, couldn't conceal his amusement at our conversation.

"What is it, dear? Did we say something funny?"

"Not at all. Your desire is commendable. I question whether a roadblock will be much deterrent. I don't mean to criticize but, frankly, if the two of you are able to move blocks in place, a motivated thief could move them out of the way just as easily. And the idea of protecting the site. Jane, dear, be reasonable. You couldn't possibly guard such a large area as the forest. A night guard at the pit itself, perhaps, yes. But to keep trespassers out of the surrounding woods you would need to be in possession of an arsenal of military-grade weapons and an army of expert marksmen."

Phoebe got up from the table. On her way to the sink, she raised her eyebrows in an "Oh, yeah?" gesture. She mouthed, "An army of two," while alternately pointing to herself then to me. I wanted to laugh but didn't for Michael's sake. He didn't know about my former government work or about the Colonel's obsession with collecting guns. Rather, I sipped my coffee and listened to him more intently in a way I hoped he interpreted as rapt attention.

The roadblock we used didn't consist of blocks but of trash cans and wire. After Michael went upstairs, I brought up an old trip wire alarm system from the basement, one the Colonel and I used on our doors and windows in Florida. Phoebe helped me string it across the entrance to what used to be Cal Prewitt's place and was the only access to his forest from the main road.

"What if a deer happens to walk through?" Phoebe said.

"The wire might keep deer away. I think they would go around it. Now that you mention it, I haven't seen any deer this close to the house." Once finished, I tested the wire and was rewarded with a shrill siren.

"Phase one. Operational," Phoebe said.

"If you have any free time tomorrow," I said, "I'll be working on phase two, until it's time for the Halloween party."

"I'm not sure I can with so much to do. But I do know this. I want to be in on any kind of business that involves running thieves or trespassers out of here. I don't want you doing it by yourself."

"Don't be daft. That's too dangerous. If anything happens, I call the police. Simple as that. We were very lucky before."

Phoebe grunted. "In this world, Jane, luck isn't what matters. Things like hand grenades and smoke bombs matter. You have some in one of those trunks full of goodies, don't you?"

I hesitated. "I do, but remember, you mustn't tell anyone. Besides, we couldn't use anything that might start a fire, for the sake of the forest or the dig site."

I didn't mention that, considering our last adventure in the woods, there might be more than just we two in attendance. Once more, Phoebe's unpredictable reactions to the idea of ghosts and the supernatural made me hesitant to bring up the subject.

I'd tried to tell her the truth about what I saw that night, during our last adventure, but before I could do so, she insisted it was angels who had helped us. Maybe angels were there, only invisible to me. The pertinent question at the moment was whether or not we would have such assistance again, were it needed. That was something else altogether.

Phoebe and Jenette returned home not long after we

finished. Michael was already hard at work on his computer when I returned to the house. He was busy checking the rock inscriptions against native engravings found across the southeast.

Later, I got a phone call from Riley Gardner. He asked if he and his ghost hunter friends could prowl about on my land the following night. I smiled. It would be Halloween.

"Certainly. Please stop in for a chat if you have time."

"Thank you, ma'am," he said in his slow drawl. "We might just do that. You seen the moon? It'll be completely full for Halloween. Can't pass that up. Good hunting weather."

I was happy to give him permission. "One more thing, Riley. Do you ever hunt during the day? I wondered if perhaps you might have seen a car here or around the refuge, or anything out of the ordinary?"

No, he and the girls worked during the day and had not been on a hunting expedition near me at night since their last visit, Riley said. So much for possible witnesses of our house intruders.

twenty-six
Jane and Phoebe Return
to the Bookstore

*P*hoebe and I met early the next morning at McGaughey's Books on the square. I wanted to get some special blank journals to record my new findings. I would need several, a large one for more sketches with plenty of room for notes on random subjects, and one for follow-up notes on Cal's boxes. Mainly, I needed one to devote entirely to the bones site. I wanted to note everything from the very beginning, from looking through Cal's box, writing summaries of my first thoughts as well as all other subsequent thoughts and actions taken by myself and the authorities.

While I browsed, Phoebe scanned the shelves for more of her thriller action books. We met at the counter with our arms full.

Cathy looked pleased. "Phoebe, how did you like the books you bought last time?"

"I loved some. Especially the pastry sniper. I hated a few. One in particular. That one you raved on and on about." She gave me a sideways glance. "It had a bad smell," she said.

"Oh," the bookseller said, looking aghast. "I'm so sorry. I'll be happy to replace it if it was defective."

Phoebe smoothed her hair. "No, it wasn't defective, per se. What I meant was, it stank. As in P-U."

"Oh. I'm sorry you didn't like it."

"That's okay. I aired it out real good. I couldn't return it anyway."

I braced myself. Even though I'd only known Phoebe a short time, I could already tell when she was about to launch into one of her wild "stories." Her mouth had a way of turning up slightly at the corners and her eyes opened wider, all while trying to maintain a completely straight face. She gave me a quick wink as Cathy bent to retrieve a paper bag from under the counter.

"It was the strangest thing," Phoebe began in her storyteller voice. "I'd thrown the book into the garbage, and a raccoon took it right out of the bin that very night. I saw him do it myself. He woke me up rattling around in there.

"I looked out the kitchen window and saw him jump up on the top of the fence with the book in his hands. He flipped a page or two, read a minute, and rubbed his little bandit eyes." This, she demonstrated. "And then he started ripping pages out." This, as well, with great feeling.

"I reckon he didn't like that part about the bad guy being Southern any better than I did. So, see, I couldn't return it anyway. I believe that raccoon wanted the pages he'd torn out for toilet paper." A short silence followed her words, delivered in complete seriousness, after which the three of us had a good laugh.

"Phoebe," Cathy said, "you're a mess. I can't understand why that book offended you. I don't even remember the villain being Southern. It didn't bother me a bit. I loved it. It's one of my all-time favorites. In fact, I love the whole series."

"You mean there's more?"

"Sure is. Here, I've found another book for you that you might like better." She turned her back to us and perused a shelf.

Phoebe said, "To each his own, hon. I'm glad you were able to enjoy it." Behind Cathy's back, Phoebe's face contorted for my benefit. She bared her upper teeth and stuck them out slightly. She brought her hands up to her mouth and pretended to make quick bites with her front teeth, as if she were a small rodent with something to eat in her tiny fingers.

My face was a mask when Cathy turned to us once again. I thanked her and promised to come back soon as Phoebe and I walked out and onto the sidewalk. With the door safely shut behind us, I turned to Phoebe.

She put on her sunglasses and shouldered her purse. "Cheese eaters. They're everywhere, Jane."

twenty-seven
Jane Takes Extreme Measures

I spent the rest of the day at the site, scheming and setting up equipment that might keep the dig safe, in case our mysterious thief should find it. Michael kept me busy as well. I did my usual recording and photographing chores as he progressed with the object attached to the wall, and I with the engraved rock.

This section of the pit held more soil than that on the other side where the bones lay. As he filled discarded dirt into a sturdy plastic bucket, I periodically sifted the dirt through the screen frame.

I was thankful the soil had such a nice texture, loose and almost sandy, which made the sifting process easy. On many other digs in my past, the dirt wasn't so cooperative when its content was a clay mixture. Very messy and harder to sift for the smaller objects, like arrowheads or other implements we expected to find in this area. I'd seen a number of sandy locations like this one around this section of the woods, particularly the outcroppings. In many places, wild cacti grew amidst the flat rocks that commonly paved rock overlooks. Here, about twenty feet of exposed rock stretched from the edge of the trees to the bluff.

When I had a break in my duties, I took a few devices out of a large carryall I'd brought. Michael didn't laugh, but his voice couldn't hide the fact that he thought I'd lost my mind.

"Those aren't going to be any help, I'm afraid." He referred to the motion-detector cameras that I placed on the trunks of several trees.

"Perhaps not. I have to do something. Surely you understand."

"You may get some nice photographs of birds swooping past or a curious deer."

That day, I had a difficult time as I tried to concentrate on the tasks at hand. Though I had become accustomed to the strange light blue cast that hung like a veil over the pit, I had noticed as the day wore on that the blue became a little darker. I thought of the large moon on the previous two nights and wondered if my odd new ability to see colors that others did not increased in relation to the lunar phases. Tonight, Halloween night, the moon would be at its fullest. And there in the pit, as I tried to focus on Michael's work and on the installation of security measures, it appeared as if last night's moon had brought out yet another new spot of interest in the dig area.

"What is it?" Michael said without turning away from his task. "Found something?"

"Nothing, really." A small circle of deep blue, about three inches across, pulsed slightly beneath the aura that stretched over the pit. "I thought I might explore opposite you."

He continued brushing, hardly taking notice of me as he went about his delicate work.

On the other side, nearer the feet of the skeleton where the engraving was found, the roots had torn out most of the dirt around the bones. Farther along where the circle of blue lay, the top half of the pit had become exposed in the storm, so the circle itself sat on a ledge of sorts, halfway between ground level and the bottom of the pit. I reached for my leather tool belt and extracted a pick. Little by little, using various implements, I shaved the layers of soil away. With each inch, the circle glowed a darker, brighter blue.

"Ah!" A startled cry escaped when the first edge appeared in the dirt.

"Are you all right?" Michael saw I was struck momentarily speechless and motionless. He smiled, stood for a long stretch, and walked around to have a look.

"Oh, lovely," he said.

A circular ridge had risen from the dirt. Another hour or so revealed the object as a short tumbler made of light blue glass.

Michael positively beamed. "Yes. Very nice." It wasn't a new piece of glass. Age and the soil caused some warping, almost the look of melting, but still quite lovely, sparkling there, half in the earth, half in the light. "More corroboration for a kitchen."

"A kitchen with a body on the floor?"

"Why not? An old man living in a cabin dies a natural death."

"We've seen no evidence of an actual cabin."

"In such a remote place, it may have been little more than a lean-to, one that didn't survive the years and the weather. It would explain the odd size of the burial area indicated by the corners. The soil makeup has preserved the bones fairly well. This lower layer, too. All above has rotted or perhaps was taken away for further use by another settler or huntsman."

I couldn't argue. Yet, the explanation didn't ring true to me. I can't say why. I stared at the glass, trying to take in its meaning. Other than what its place here might mean, as far as the excavation, it was another aspect that mesmerized me, caught me completely by surprise and stalled all logical brain function momentarily.

"You disagree?" he said. "Jane?"

"Sorry. No. It makes perfect sense."

Michael looked at his watch. "Did you want to call it a day? To get ready for your party?"

We agreed to stop. We finished jotting down our notes and tidied up. He assisted me in a final security measure but not without a good bit of ribbing for possibly going overboard.

"It's quite elaborate, my dear," he said with a laugh.

"No harm done if it isn't needed," I said.

He could scoff if he liked, but I could think of nothing else to keep our dig site from being destroyed, should the conversation I overheard in the trailer concern my land. Michael laughed at me because I'd dug a hole to look something like that of the burial site, only I situated it several yards away from the real thing. My plan was to throw a blue tarp over it, so the new hole would look like the dig site, and to cover the real dig site with black plastic and an overlayer of dirt and rock.

"Right," he said. "You worry too much. I'm sure we'll find everything just as it is now. Perhaps we'll find the missing flower tomorrow a bit farther down, eh?"

I said nothing. No, it would not be there.

Michael was referring to a decorative ring around

the glass tumbler we found, a raised line resembling greenery with crude glass flowers spaced just so, where all save one flower remained.

I knew it wasn't anywhere in the dig site. I knew precisely where it was. It was sitting in a row with the other mysterious artifacts, on the lip of a bookcase shelf in my den. Whether Boo had found it elsewhere, or dug it up, somehow, days before I dug out the rest of the glass tumbler, I had no idea.

twenty-eight
Phoebe Works the Halloween Party

I loaded my car to the gills. I stuffed that thing top to bottom and front to back. Had to. With all the food and decorations and whatnot that needed to go to the Halloween party, I barely fit inside myself. There was no room for any of it in the trunk, either, because I filled it up with fighting paraphernalia, in case Jane's murdering thief decided to pay a visit that night.

I figured he would. He wouldn't wait around when he had a map showing how to get there. Besides that, it was going to be a full moon. Where those bones were, way up on that bluff where there aren't any trees overhead, it would be like a searchlight shining down. A good night for stealing.

Jane knew it as well as I did. As much as I despise traipsing around in the woods, I wasn't about to let her stay all night out there by herself. I tried to think of it as playing Rambo in the jungle.

At the haunted house, high school kids volunteered every year to set things up. They already had the props up that made a hallway from the library's front lobby, around to the right, along the wall, and all the way back to the kitchen and hospitality area. They hammered two-by-fours into big frames to make the hall that the little ones would walk through. Black plastic sheets hung over the frames to make the hallway dark. Then Grace's son, Billy, who is an electrician, set different-colored lights all through it in strategic places to make it look spooky. The kids strung fake cobwebs everywhere and we had a record in the library of spooky Halloween sounds to play.

This Halloween, Grace made me dress up like a lunchroom lady. I don't do any of the acting on the Trail of Terror anymore. I have too much to do with getting the food together, and then I work in the back serving refreshments that are included in the price of the ticket. Several restaurants donate food, and a few other businesses furnish things like soft drinks, but I always make the special dishes for the kids.

I grabbed three volunteers to help unload my car. One took the stack of tablecloths in, the other two helped carry covered Tupperware containers. I carried my lunchroom lady outfit and a tote bag. We got everything put in the refrigerator, but not before Grace had a peek. She lifted the lid of a casserole dish and yelled at the sight.

"Spaghetti and eyeballs," I said. One of those women's magazines at the Pig's checkout lane had them on the cover. I couldn't resist. All you do is stick olives in the meatballs. The kids would love them. "I'm later than I meant to be. By the time I get changed, kids will be lining up out there."

"No problem. Everything's done. All that's left is for you to make the punch. And then it's showtime."

Grace looked scarier than ever in her voodoo getup. Thank goodness the little boys and girls already knew how sweet she really is, or one look and they would be running and screaming out the door. She stooped and cackled like a witch and off she went to get the Trail of Terror started.

Every now and then, we heard high-pitched screeching followed by high-pitched giggling as the children made their ways toward the hospitality room. One look at Jason and Mark, the little boys who stay with me sometimes, made me grin from ear to ear. It does me good to see them happy. Their daddy looked like he was having a good time, too, the poor thing. I hoped he could find a nice lady to settle down with before long. The boys came straight to me for a hug, talking and laughing up a storm, telling me all about the scary parts they liked. My brain Jell-O got high marks for looking real.

When it was all over, Jane came in, still wearing her nutty professor costume—a lab coat, some nerd glasses, and some crazy buck teeth stuck in her mouth. I laughed so hard I had to hold my side. Jane's outfit was also Grace's idea. She thought Jane's accent would make her the perfect mad scientist. Jane did it to the hilt, too, from all the reports I heard, pointing at a chalkboard full of equations and holding up jars with fake organs in them.

We don't do the Trail of Terror late. The last group comes through at seven o'clock. Kids want to start their trick-or-treating by that time. My sister-in-law, Amanda Jean, who lives in Pensacola, says nobody down there goes trick-or-treating anymore. Says it's too dangerous. Tullulah's not like that, thank goodness.

Jane took her buck teeth out so she could have a snack. I went into cafeteria lady mode. "Could I interest you in some bug juice, ma'am?"

Jane looked at it. "Is that a hand in the punch bowl?"

"Yeah. Looks good, doesn't it? You put water and food coloring in a rubber glove and freeze it." I ladled some of the green punch in a paper cup for her to try.

"All right then. But without the gummy worms and bugs, if you don't mind."

"Raisins."

"Yes. Straight up, if you please," she said. I fished out the bugs and handed her the cup.

"Mmm. Delicious."

I introduced Jane to everyone she hadn't already met. She helped me with the cleanup, and Grace came over to pitch in, too. We laughed and had the best time. While I washed the last dishes in the sink, I looked over at Grace and said, "Your old decrepit white boyfriend didn't show up, after all."

"And he missed seeing you in that sexy hairnet." She elbowed me. I splashed soapy water on her. "You know," Grace said, "I've been thinking about him. You remember how you got confused over which state he was from? You said he was from Ohio, and I said Indiana? Well, this morning I needed to check something on the list of new cardholders and saw his name. Next to it, he gave his previous address as Ohio. I would swear he told me he was from Indiana because we talked about my brother who lives near there. Oh, goodness. That reminds me. Wasn't that terrible about Brody Reed?"

"Lord, yes," I said. "Poor guy. Always helping folks out. And he raised a fine family. He put on some fun shows for the kids at the library over the years, didn't he?"

Grace nodded. "Yes, he sure did. Everybody in this town loved him and is going to miss him."

"Excuse me," Jane said, "but what reminded you?"

"What about?" Grace said.

"You were saying Phoebe's boyfriend was from Ohio, then said, 'that reminds me.'"

I held up a finger and said, "Please. Let's get this straight. He is not my boyfriend. He's too old for me."

"Oh," Grace said, tilting her head as if trying to remember. "It made me think of Brody because the last time I saw him, he came in to meet the old guy from Ohio or wherever he's from. Back in the county history room."

"What day was this, do you remember?" Jane said.

"A few days ago. Monday, I think."

Grace's voice trailed off as she realized what her words might imply. I was concerned, too. "That wouldn't have been the day he disappeared. Would it?"

twenty - nine
Jane Meets her
Medicine Woman

I heard soft footsteps coming up behind me. Both Grace and Phoebe stared beyond me, having lost their train of thought.

"For goodness sake," Phoebe said with surprise in her voice. "Aunt Woo-Woo, what are you doing out tonight? We've done finished our party, hon. You've missed it."

I expected to see the diminutive Ruby Alice in a simple cotton dress and a sweater again. Yet when I turned, I was surprised to see her wearing tight-fitting black leggings, a black turtleneck, and a black beret set on her head at a jaunty angle. Her hair was pulled back in a ponytail. She stood in an altered ballet pose, her shoulders and head thrown back, her arms clasped behind her. She pointed one black sneaker's toe forward and the other sneaker she moved behind, flat and squared off at the other's heel.

The most striking part of her clothing, however, was a black sash across one shoulder that draped to tie at the opposite side's waist. Small external pouches were sewn on the sash, reminiscent of a runway fashion designer's idea of a bandolier.

Phoebe moved her head up and down as she inspected her aunt. "You look like one of those Frenchie artistes. Are you fixing to go trick-or-treating?"

Ruby Alice's perpetually happy expression became even happier. After a few befuddled mutterings, she said, "Treats, ha ha, yes. But first, a few tricks."

Grace, Phoebe, and I chuckled along with the old girl. I tried to think of an acceptable response but she saved me the trouble.

"Now, I think." Her head bobbed in quick nods. "Yes. I think we should be going now. Shall we?"

"Where, Aunt Woo-Woo?"

"To the tree, of course. Grant said you asked." She looked at me. "He said you called."

Realization came at last. "You're the medicine woman? I wasn't expecting you. That is, he didn't give me a name."

"Yes, oh yes. Ha ha. I suppose I am. 'Healer' is what they call me most of the time." Her head bobbed quickly again. "Time, you see, yes, it's the time that is so very important." As she turned, she motioned that we should follow.

"Ruby Alice," I said, "wouldn't you rather wait until tomorrow? The tree is a bit of a distance into the woods. I didn't mean for you to think there was an emergency. We can go there anytime you like, some-time during daylight hours, if you prefer."

The laugh wrinkles around her high cheeks and eyes moved into their accustomed positions as she uttered bemused sounds that weren't quite words and ended in chuckling. "With this moon, we'll see about as well as in the day."

She rode with Phoebe to my house, where Phoebe parked beside my car in the driveway. Homer bounded off the porch to greet us. He soon found a new friend in Ruby Alice. Neither she nor Phoebe came inside. I told them I'd only be a minute.

Phoebe walked a little way with me and spoke in a hushed voice. "Hey, look here. I've brought a few choice items for when we go out there by ourselves later tonight. After I take Aunt Woo-Woo home."

She amazed me. I began to protest but she stopped me by putting her hand up.

"Don't argue with me, Jane. Forget it. I'm going. I've already planned on it. Now, give me your keys so I can pop the trunk and put those things in there. While you go talk to Mr. Honey Buns." She winked.

I handed the keys over while doing my best to give her a dirty look. It had no effect. I hurried inside while Phoebe made smacking kissing sounds behind my back.

"Michael," I called as I walked through. He stepped out of the den where he'd been working on his laptop. I explained that Ruby Alice had come to see the tree scar.

"Did you want me to come as well?"

"Only if you like. We shouldn't be long."

He hesitated and rubbed his chin. "I'm expecting a call, but if you would rather I come . . ."

"It's quite all right. We won't be long. I only wanted to let you know what we were about."

He leaned down and gave me a peck on the cheek before returning to his work at the desk.

When I reached the car, Ruby Alice already was sitting in the backseat. Homer looked quite happy and comfortable in the seat next to her. Phoebe, standing at the open trunk, jerked her head backward, indicating she wanted a private word.

"Humor her," Phoebe said quietly. "She's old and dotty but she's all right."

"Of course she is. She's perfectly delightful."

Phoebe grinned. Suddenly, she hugged me and said, "You're all right, too. Come on, let's get going." She helped me remove the trash cans and tape at the entrance across the road, then we made our way into the woods slowly over the bumps.

Ruby Alice was right. Much of the woods was pitch black at first. The higher we climbed, however, the brighter the patches of moonlight shone around us, even brighter than when Homer and I had made our late-night trek. At the summit, we parked in the lay-by and though we had our flashlights, we didn't need them once we walked up and over the little crest.

There, on the flat overlook, the moon filled the sky, huge and directly above us so that it resembled a spotlight. Its rich yellow-gold face cast a warm honeyed light across the mountaintop as if over a stage, awaiting a maestro's cue to begin the overture.

Ruby Alice admired the view, smiling and talking quietly to herself. She looked left over the blue tarp and over the clearing, gave as hearty a laugh as was possible with her tiny raspy voice, and moved across the plateau and to the right, directly for the fallen tree.

"She's going to fall and break her neck in the dark," Phoebe said as she passed me, keeping her flashlight beam just in front of her.

Ruby Alice showed no sign of doing either thing. Her high-tech sneakers made easy work of walking uphill and over uneven terrain. However weak her odd eye movements made her appear, she showed fewer signs of night blindness than Phoebe. She stood before the great tree's large scar, threw out her arms, then drew her hands over her heart.

I set my backpack and flashlight down. Homer lay beside her. Ruby Alice took two short candle stubs out of one of her pouches and centered them on a rock nearby.

Ruby Alice sang a short chant. Her eerie soprano moanings stretched across the open space. I recognized no words and was glad of it. Words would have ruined the timeless quality that sent me back in time, as if flying low over oceans and countries, kingdoms and ancient days.

When her song ended, she stepped to the tree to put her hands over the center of the blackened scar. She mumbled a prayer there as she reached into the hole made by the lightning. She seemed to be making a choice and finally broke off a long splinter about the size of a pencil.

"Good. Good," she said. "Very good." She opened a pocket on her sash and withdrew a small pot that she sat next to the candles. "Come," she said to me with a wave of her hand. I obeyed.

Another pocket produced a short makeup brush. She instructed me to sit on the rock while she stirred the burned splinter of bark in the pot. When satisfied, she dipped the makeup brush inside and showed me the tip. A gooey black mixture covered it. She touched it to my cheek and began to draw.

"You know," Phoebe said, "you never struck me as the face-painting type, Jane."

Ruby Alice concentrated on her work but laughed and spoke softly as she carefully drew. "Tonight, I am an artiste," she said. The more intense attention she gave to her drawing, the farther her tongue stuck out between her teeth.

In the soft yellow moonlight, the years vanished from her face. What lines and symbols she drew on mine, I couldn't see, only Phoebe's awestruck reaction. Ruby Alice stepped back to have a look at her handiwork.

"For strength," she said. She turned to a delighted Phoebe, happy to be included in the rite. If my own paint job looked anything like hers, we were both well covered in the strength department. Ruby Alice even drew a bit on Homer who, surprisingly, allowed it, though it wasn't visible against his black coat. Last, she handed the brush to me and directed me in the proper method to make the symbols on her own face.

Phoebe clapped her hands together. "Fun! I like this kind of Halloween. This is the real thing. Now, are we done? Because we need to get Aunt Woo-Woo home. That way, we make it back before midnight when the gremlins come out and all the wolves start howling." She gave me a theatrical wink.

Ruby Alice gently blew out the candles and returned her paint supplies to their appropriate pockets on her sash. Suddenly a gust of cool wind swooshed across our faces, fluttering our hair up and producing ghostly noises in the rocks and hollows. Another sound, barely audible under the rattling of a hundred thousand leaves in the wind, grew louder. And closer.

"What's that noise?" Phoebe said.

Ruby Alice gazed into the forest. "The gremlins," she said, her lips forming a goofy grin. "Right on time."

thirty
Phoebe Gears Up for War

*W*hen Jane realized the noise in the woods was a car coming toward us, she grabbed Aunt Woo-Woo and ran her to where the old rock wall was highest. Those rocks were directly on the other side of a small wooded strip that separated the rock wall and the big tree that the lightning hit.

"Homer!" Jane called. She helped Aunt Woo-Woo sit down and asked her to stay there and hide behind the rocks until Jane came back for her. When Homer ran up, she said, "Stay here, boy. Keep Ruby Alice safe." Jane put a hand on his back. He must have understood because he sat right there, stretched his paws out on the ground toward her and looked at Aunt Woo-Woo.

Jane jumped up. I followed her as she set off at a trot for the bluff. "Careful!" I said.

She set her bag on the dirt, rummaged through it, and found her cell phone. "Pray for luck. And good reception."

Thank goodness we were on top of the mountain where she could get any reception at all. Jane went as far to the edge as she could without falling over. A few seconds later, somebody answered because she said, "Yes. I need help." While she told the police dispatcher to get Detective Waters, I looked through my bag of supplies for my cap. For a second, I wished I'd left on my black wig that I'd worn at the haunted house. It's hard to be stealthy when your hair is so red it looks like your head is on fire.

I found the cap. What a relief. Then I was glad I'd taken the wig off. A black stocking cap matches war paint and an AK-46 and a half a whole lot better than a wig with a lunchroom hairnet stuck on it.

Jane clicked her cell phone shut. She looked relieved. "The police are on their way," she said and then she grabbed me. We fast-walked across and down the slope to her car.

"I'm sorry," she said. "I thought they would come later. I didn't want you to be involved in another dangerous situation. Sometimes you're too stubborn for your own good, you know." She opened her car trunk, took out a big gun case, and unzipped it. She hauled one of her monster assault rifles out of it. "This is merely a precaution. There's no need to worry," she said. "I'll take care of everything."

From the other side of the trunk where I'd put my things, I pulled my camouflage bag out, unzipped it, and took out my own big honking gun. I grabbed a magazine and loaded it underneath with a good hard slap. "I'm not worried," I said. "Because tonight I'm a gangsta. With protective face tatts." I smiled as I loaded the chamber with a loud *chock-chock.*

My gun bag is nice because it has all these compartments for your paraphernalia. I grabbed my double shoulder holster and put my arms through it. Then I took my CZ 75 out of one compartment, got a magazine for it out of another one, and smacked it up in the gun. I holstered it on my left so I could draw with my shooting hand. Jane looked at me funny when I took an extra thirty-round magazine out and holstered it on my right. I winked. "Just a precaution." From her look, I don't think I eased her mind.

She hesitated, and then she pulled a metal box toward her and opened it. "Now, Phoebe, I want you to listen carefully. This may be useful, but you must promise me not to use it unless absolutely necessary. In fact, don't, unless I give you the word."

She reached in the box and brought out a tiny green fire extinguisher. Or that's what it looked like to me.

"This can disable an enemy momentarily. It allows you to take advantage or get out of a bad situation." Jane said it was a flash-bang, sort of like a hand grenade but it doesn't destroy anything. When it goes off, it temporarily blinds and deafens the bad guy. I clipped it on my belt.

"So how do I work it? If there's an emergency?"

"You pull the pin out and toss the canister. Quickly. Before it explodes. Toss it, turn away, and cover your ears if possible."

"Can I bite it?" I said. "Bite the pin and yank it out with my teeth like they do in movies?"

"Let's hope that won't be necessary."

The car kept coming and was louder, but we knew it wouldn't be in sight for a while. Jane handed me a canvas bag to carry. She took one herself, plus her rifle. We ran to the top of the ridge and stopped. Jane looked in both directions. She pointed to a slightly open area in the trees. She set her bag down and took something out.

"Hold this," she said. She gave me the end of a spool of fishing line. "Hold it low, like so, only about two inches high."

She walked backward, bent at the waist, to run the thin line across to a tree trunk. She cut the line and tied her end around the trunk. From her bag, she took out what looked like a compact, then stuck her fingers in where the makeup or powder would be and rubbed the blackish contents over the length of the wire.

"Camo paint," she said. "To make it more invisible. If our visitors are the thieves and they try to get away, herd them in this direction."

"Why don't we put a line across where they'll come up the ridge and trip them before they even get up here?"

A sly little smile curled on her lips but there was a hard, serious glint in her eyes. She looked kind of scary, especially with all that war paint on her face. She spoke in a low, quiet voice that made her even scarier.

"Because I want them to come in," she said. "I want them to be caught red-handed when the police arrive. If we don't catch them, they go free and will no doubt continue to rob and perhaps kill again. Tripping them at the start would alert them to our presence. We don't want that. Besides, it would take the sport out of it. What fun would that be, eh?"

Sheesh. You think you know a person and then *wham.*

"Remind me never to cross you," I said. "But look, they'll know we're here because they'll see your car parked out there."

She shook her head. "Not if we don't show ourselves. Let them wonder. Now." She put her hand on my shoulder. "Don't be concerned. I have a plan."

While she talked, she pulled two headsets from her

bag. She gave me one, then clipped a small black box to my waistband. "I didn't get through to Michael. The line is busy." A microphone folded down from the headset. "We only need to whisper to hear each other. I prefer no talking, only when absolutely necessary, understand? Our goal is to stay hidden and safe until the police arrive. We do not want to give away our locations. Got it?"

"Gotcha. Testing, one, two."

"I checked them last night. Do you read me?"

"Roger that, Gray Fox. I read you loud and clear. Red Bird Tango, over and out."

We heard the vehicle as it came around the nearest bend, just about to us. Jane turned to me with a serious expression. "Tango?"

I shrugged. "I've always liked that word."

"Mm. It suits you. Now, go to Ruby Alice. You are not to fire a single shot, understood? Only in emergency and only a warning shot. I'm going to take cover behind the tree roots here to keep watch over the dig site. I'll be almost directly behind the three of you, just on the other side of these trees. Only come out of cover if I call for you. You alone. Ruby Alice and Homer stay where they are. In that instance, work your way away from the bluff around the length of the wall. Wait there for instructions. You'll be near the trip wire, so if you see me running our quarry toward it, you do so from your side as well. Understood?"

"Understood. Ten-four."

The vehicle was almost to us. Its lights bounced

around in the trees as it came down the last stretch and stopped. We heard it sit and idle a while. I figured they had seen Jane's car and were wondering what to do next. Jane pushed me in Aunt Woo-Woo's direction and took off for the big tree. A minute later, I heard the car move again. It parked and its engine cut off.

Would they hunt for us since her car was there? Or would they just start digging? I wondered if Jane would let them dig, to keep them busy until the cops got here. Or, if not, how she planned on stopping them herself. Part of me worried about Jane. The other part reminded me she acts mighty comfortable in this kind of situation. That sneak has done more of this kind of ambush and cowboy stuff than she lets on, I believe.

I heard a soft metal *clunk* as I rounded the strip of trees behind Jane. Now she was cocked and locked. She might talk big about not shooting unless absolutely necessary, but that didn't mean she wouldn't go ahead and get ready. That's my girl.

I slowed down so I could walk without making so much noise. All was as quiet as could be until car doors opened and slammed shut and then footsteps crunched up the hill.

here were three of them. Two heads came into view slowly above the ridge first, approximately ten feet apart, both young men. One was vaguely familiar. Neither wore hats or caps or dark clothing to blend into the night. They held no weapons.

They had expected no one to challenge them. Still, on seeing my car, their vehicle slowed. I pictured them sitting, considering a retreat. Why had they not done so?

Artifact thieves usually looted sites when they could be sure no one might interfere. Nonconfrontational this lot, not keen on assault. And yet, if my suspicions were correct, they may have assaulted Michael and perhaps others in order to bring loot to their buyers.

This site was unknown. Who would be interested and why? No great finds had ever been reported in this part of the state. Yet the young man who took my purse had accessed the forensic anthropologist's records and was killed. Was that a coincidence or was it because of those records? Someone thought Dr. Norwood's reports were important enough to kill for and now had planned to steal again. Yet other than the police, Dr. Norwood, and myself, no one else knew of those reports. Except for Michael.

Suddenly, his words came back to me. He had been

expecting a call. From whom? Someone he contacted in regard to our findings? My heart felt as if it sank into my stomach. He had promised to tell no one. And now, maps to the site had brought trespassers, ones who most likely had killed before. I hoped with all my heart that the call was personal and had nothing to do with our work.

The thieves were unusually early. They came at a time when I wasn't supposed to be here, when I still should have been at the Halloween party or at Phoebe's house as I had planned. Michael knew this. He knew I meant to come home some hours later on, have a short rest, and then go to the dig site with Homer for the night.

Michael had volunteered to sit with me, but I refused the offer. If no one came, he would have been uncomfortable all night for no reason. If anyone did come, he would have complicated things.

After all this time, I still thought in terms of casualties to civilians. I began to worry what Phoebe must think, now that she had even more evidence that I knew about the guns and other fancies of the Colonel's a bit too much. She suspected that I hadn't told her the complete truth about my past. I wasn't keen on telling her.

The thieves risked being seen on the main road and going through the entrance at a time that passing traffic, or I, looking out a window or sitting on my porch, might see them. Without Ruby Alice's unwitting intervention, the site would have been unprotected until much later in the evening. The thieves would have come, done their dirty work, and gone before Homer and I arrived for our evening vigil.

The tree-rimmed clearing glowed in the moonlight, a peaceful work of nature with only the incongruous plastic tarp marring its beauty. The two young men looked out from the ridge over the flat expanse and seemed satisfied. They looked behind them toward the car and nodded their heads as if giving the all clear.

I'd brought my AR-15, a large, dependable, and fairly common assault rifle. It's quite handy. I gently set its barrel on a tuft of moss on the tree trunk. I put an eye to the scope for a clearer look at the approaching figure, the one the two men had signaled.

I knew him. We had never met, but his photograph frequently appeared in archaeological periodicals in the nineties at the height of his career. I would have recognized the short man with a white beard and moustache anywhere. Dr. Edward Draughn. Once respected but now brought low by his shady dealings.

I heard him give a lecture once in Frankfurt, Germany, when I was between jobs. His status plummeted some years later when he was accused of smuggling rare Incan artifacts into this country. The charges were dropped on a technicality, as I recall, but he lost his professorship at a prestigious New England university. Reputable archaeological teams found other experts to head their projects. And now, it seemed, his new job was thievery.

He had a battered leather satchel over one shoulder

and carried an oversized battery-powered lantern. He meant to work.

"Hello?" he called, putting a spin of friendly English on the word. He stepped to the ridge, surveyed it left and right while his assistants moved forward with him, also continuing to scan the moonlit crest. The older man nodded, a curt signal that sent his companions back to their vehicle. They returned with two shovels, two more lanterns, and large empty duffels.

"Hello? Anyone here?" Draughn called again as the three of them moved forward slowly to the blue tarp.

The tallest of the three, a young skinny man who continued to look about the edge of the woods, set the tip of his shovel on the ground. "Nobody's here," he said, though he did so quietly as if he didn't quite believe his own words. "Probably had car trouble and left it here for the night. Walked back."

Draughn also scanned the perimeter of trees once more, slowly and carefully, in the quiet. He seemed satisfied they were alone, let the leather bag fall with a thud at the edge of the plastic covering, and set his lantern beside the bag. He turned the light on and squatted to adjust the bright beam that illuminated the dig area.

Then he stood and called out, "Michael? Are you here?"

I stopped breathing. I trembled at the words. My stomach felt queasy as I shut my eyes to get a grip on my emotions. I would not, could not, allow them to affect my judgment now.

I considered this new wrinkle and my options. I looked beyond the men into the trees. I cleared my mind, allowing it to dwell on the serenity of the woods. I submersed myself in it as a brief meditation until a calm, clear resolve took hold. Slowly, I adjusted the AR-15's position. I found my target in the scope and took aim with steady hands.

Though I'm not sure I heard a noise, I became aware of a presence to my left and slightly behind me. First I studied the three men's faces to see if they, too, had gone on alert. They had not. I turned my head only slightly, ready to swing my rifle if a fourth visitor had somehow outflanked us.

It was Phoebe. If her AK had not been painted an apricot orange, I might not have seen her right away in her present location behind the old wall's nearest standing rock. Her clothing blended into the rock's shadow and left little white skin to glow in the moon-light. The whites of her eyes stood out against Ruby Alice's remarkable artwork of black lines and symbols on her face.

With her AK held against her chest, she crouched in a near-seated position. Her body jolted when she peered from behind the rock to see the men. She jig-gled her head a bit as if she couldn't believe her eyes, shook her head harder side to side, and looked again.

She turned to me. The exasperation on her face probably reflected my own. I eased my left hand down and put it out toward her as a signal to stay put. I had told her to wait. Yet there she was, returning my signal with a few indecipherable ones of her own. She mouthed "O," then waved to me, wiggling the ends of her fingers while mouthing "Hi," then repeated "O," and ended by pointing with quick jabs at the men. My expression must have reflected my ignorance. She ended by mouthing the words "That's him," in an exaggerated fashion.

I gave her a stern look. I yanked my head sharply in the direction of Ruby Alice and Homer, hoping she would understand my silent order. Phoebe pursed her lips but obeyed and was soon out of sight. Apparently, her Mr. Gould from Ohio was really my Edward Draughn, once-prominent archaeologist.

He took more digging implements out of his leather bag. "All right. Let's see what we have here."

The younger of his assistants, a stocky man whom I felt certain I had seen somewhere before, looked as if he might be in his early twenties. He did the honors of removing the rocks that held the tarp in place. The other, skinnier assistant, whom I decided must be in his late twenties or early thirties, switched on the remaining two lanterns, setting them opposite one another on either side of the pit at its furthest points.

The younger man grasped the plastic corner closest him in order to pull the tarp off the pit. I moved the AR-15's barrel slightly, steadied myself, and acquired a new target.

Suddenly, Phoebe's voice whispered in my ears from her walkie-talkie. I listened, then silently swore.

thirty-two
Phoebe Takes the Initiative

*J*ane didn't like what I had to tell her.

I pushed the talk button on my two-way radio and barely whispered into the microphone. "Jane. Don't talk, just listen. Aunt Woo-Woo and Homer are gone. I can't see them anywhere. So don't shoot them by mistake. I'm going to circle behind you to the woods on your right. If you change your mind and want me to shoot after all, I will be in position shortly. Just say 'now,' and I'll come out and commence firing. Over and out."

That Jane is so stubborn. I'm sure in her mind she thought getting me out of the line of fire was for my own good. It was her own good I was worried about. She's the boss though, so I left like she wanted me to. I scooted back the way I came without a sound. When I got to the spot and saw that Aunt Woo-Woo and Homer were gone, I gasped. I covered my mouth quick and prayed nobody heard me.

I headed out along the long row of fallen rocks. I looked and looked the whole way but didn't see hide nor hair of the escapees. At the last of the rock wall, I slowed and edged forward as quietly as I could so I could see what Jane and those boys were up to.

I peeped out between two juniper branches and found Jane, now about thirty feet away on my left, with the sorry bad guys maybe another twenty feet down and farther out in the open. I knew one thing. As soon as this was all over, I was going to grab the tall one by the ear and walk him all the way into Tullulah to his worthless parents' house and make them tell me how they could've raised such a lowdown skunk. He and his parents both had some answering to do.

The head honcho giving orders was that sorry old white man from the library. I didn't recognize the young guy, the one who looked like a bulldog pup. He moved the tarp out of the way and then all three of those guys stood there and studied the dirt. Bunch of nuts. It beat all I've ever seen. There Jane and I were, guarding a hole in the ground from a guy who came all the way from Ohio to sneak out here and stare at it in the middle of the night. That lying white-headed so-and-so studied a little longer, then stood up.

"Byrd, you do this one. Quickly. You do the other," he said as he pointed out two bumps in the dirt. He was a bird, all right. Jeff Byrd was high on my to-be-plucked-and-fried list.

With Byrd and Bulldog working, Ohio boy nodded and moved farther down and beyond the tree trunk. He stopped at the symbols carved in the rock overhead and ran his hand over them. His teeth gleamed like a wolf's as he smiled and patted the rock.

"Next time," he said. "Too bad we left the chisels."

Ha. Too bad I was going to send him flying over the skies of Indianapolis with one mighty kick here in a minute. He snickered and went back to supervise his boys.

Meanwhile, Jeff Byrd set the shovel blade in a groove Jane or Michael had made around one of the bumps. Inside the middle of the square trench, I could see something blue. I couldn't tell what it was, as far away as I was. Not much stuck out of the ground. He chopped deeper around the trench until he made a square out of the dirt with the blue thing inside. Bulldog did the same around the rock.

I looked sideways to Jane. Why was she letting them do it? She looked ready to shoot any second. All I could figure was she wanted the police to catch them in the act or running away with the goods so they couldn't weasel out of it in court.

Jane finally looked in my direction and found me. She pointed at me, moved her finger around and to the right, like she wanted me to circle the guys. I started to sneak that way but she put her palm out quick with a stopping motion. She held up a finger. Wait. She tapped her mike, which meant wait until she signaled. I gave her the thumbs-up.

The slimeballs worked with not a word between them until both blocks were shoveled out, dirt and all, wrapped up, and put in the duffel bags they brought. I'll say this for them, they were careful with those precious dirt blocks. The world has gone insane.

All this time, I glanced around looking for Aunt Woo-Woo. Not a sign. Ohio zipped one duffel bag up and then the other one. Once they bagged all their tools, they stood. Where were the cops? It was high time they showed up. Not a sound had come through the woods yet that would tell us they were anywhere close. I looked to Jane, lit up by moonlight behind the tree trunk, and saw her hand move slowly down to the trigger.

All of a sudden, the big, square, heavy-duty lantern head exploded at the far end of the pit. It wasn't just shot with one little hole in it, either. Son, that thing was completely gone. Lights out and nothing but little glass and metal pellets chinking like hail out of the sky on the plastic tarp.

I watched Jane sweep her rifle across in a straight line a few inches and shoot again, blowing the lantern head on the far right to smithereens like she did the other one. Bulldog jumped backward like he had been shot himself. Jeff grabbed the duffels. Ohio was about to pick up his lantern right next to him when Jane blew away the lamp head in that sucker, too, with his fingers barely an inch from it.

The three men turned to cut and run. Jane jumped up and around the fallen tree. "Go!" she whispered into the mike. I froze at first. I don't know what came over me. All I could do was watch what she did.

She ran after them and to the left, enough to shoot past them. The blast made bark splinter and spray from a tree they were headed toward. Like sheep, the men herded themselves to the right, but only a step or two because right then Homer leaped out of the woods like a charging grizzly bear, barking and baring his teeth like he was about to eat them alive.

They decided to stop. All three put their hands in the air.

Finally, I jumped up and ran out into the open toward them. They didn't see me. I came from behind and ran toward them from the right. Jane had her rifle trained on them, standing a few feet behind them and to my left.

She signaled me to stay behind the men. I nodded. I would've rather thrown Smokahontas down and gone over to box Jeff Byrd's ears. But Jane had other ideas. I'd have my time with that boy sooner or later. She signaled again. Now, she stuck her arm out like she wanted me to back up more and move closer to her. I did.

Homer kept snarling. He paced in front of the men, giving each thief a bark as he passed and letting saliva drip out of his mouth like he was a drill sergeant, like he dared them to be his next snack. Bulldog boy chanced a look over his shoulder. I knew what he was thinking. He saw we were just two little old ladies. He smirked and decided we were no problem.

thirty - three
Jane Takes Care of Business

How foolish of me. I should have done something about the stocky assistant first. Of the three, only he had the physique of a man who works out regularly.

I saw him look over his shoulder and turn for me. I had just enough time to swing toward him and deliver an upper blow with the AR-15's body. It hit him across the clavicle and neck, making him stagger backward.

A black blur lunged through the air and Homer's front legs rammed the stocky man in the chest with such force as to knock him to the ground. I caught my breath. "Good boy. Stay with him."

I fired a shot in the air to halt the young man carrying the duffel bags in his tracks. I walked briskly to him. Of course, I couldn't be sure, but from the look on his face, he looked quite surprised when he turned to see two older ladies with large guns. Or perhaps, I thought, it was our face paint that gave him pause.

"Mrs. Twigg?" he said incredulously. "From the library?"

Phoebe took a tough-guy stance and gave him a long, cold stare. "I'm not your average librarian," she said in a low-pitched voice.

I used the young man's present stunned state to my advantage. When I reached him, I grabbed one of the bags he held by its handles with both my hands. I jerked the bag, and his arm along with it, down smartly, bringing his head to the level of mine, and slammed a left elbow strike into the side of it. He dropped to the ground, out cold, and would not be getting up soon.

I turned quickly to find Phoebe had already moved forward. The end of her rifle barrel nudged Edward's back. "Hold it right there, lover boy," she said.

A quick look told me Homer had his assignment well under his control, for he snarled and snapped if the stocky man tried to move in the least. I turned to take charge of Edward.

Phoebe still held her AK in his back. Not a comforting sight, even if I didn't care for the man. "By the way," she said to him, "how's that movie stuff coming along?"

He chuckled under his breath as he turned slowly, hands still in the air, to face her. He grinned from behind his white beard and moustache. "Very well. Thank you for asking."

"Did I tell you to turn around?" she said with a sassy tone.

His answer was a right punch to her jaw. I hurried to break her fall and was just able to keep her head from hitting the ground. I scrambled to my feet, brought the AR-15 into position as I stood, fully intending to shoot him as he ran.

I ran to the side and fired ahead of him into the bottom of a tree trunk before him at the forest's edge. I kept running forward. He stopped momentarily when I fired into the tree but clearly was about to run again. When I circled from the left and faced him with the rifle aimed, he raised his hands. I didn't understand why he smiled.

He stepped backward a few feet while holding up a small metal object high in his hand. I knew what it was.

"Drop your weapon," he said. He continued walking backward around the edge of the clearing. The small object in his hand had come from the metal box he'd stolen. It was the miniature flamethrower. I had forgotten about it.

I continued walking forward. "Close it," I said, forcing my voice to show no emotion in spite of the fear clutching my heart.

"I'll torch this place, I swear," he said.

"I'll shoot you, then put the fire out while you bleed to death. Close it."

Edward walked more slowly. He stopped at a low branch covered in yellow leaves. My heart lurched. He could reach it without fully extending his arm. "I'll trade you," he said. "For the artifacts." He smiled wider. "It's a good bargain. I get a few trinkets and you get to keep your precious woods. Now drop your weapon."

I had no choice. I'd heard no sign of the police as yet, but had to trust that they would intercept Draughn at some point on his escape route. I couldn't risk the damage one of these could do. With reluctance, I pulled the strap over my head and lay the gun down, never looking away from the flame. My voice shook as I watched. "Please. Take them." The words cracked. I steeled myself and tried again. "Close it."

"Very well." He snapped the flame shut. I breathed again. "Bring the bags closer."

I set them where he instructed, close to him but not too close for his comfort. I stepped back and held out my hand for the torch. He palmed it, as if he were about to throw it toward me. Instead he stopped. He flicked the flame on once again. The horrible smile returned.

A wave of panic flooded my body and mind. No more chances. I hurled myself at him. With both hands, I grasped his wrist and closed the flame thrower. I kicked his legs and attempted a knee to the groin but could not connect. He struck my face with the back of his hand then twisted me down to my knees. I watched in horror as he flicked the steel casing open once more, clicked on the flame, and tossed it several yards away into the clearing.

It landed on top of a small mound of leaves. Fire instantly curled and browned the edges of those it touched, creating wisps of smoke that roiled prettily before rising in thin white lines and disappearing into nothing.

thirty-four
Phoebe Gets Her Wish

Ohio's punch to my jaw knocked me down but not out. Well, maybe I did rest for a little while. All I know is, I raised up on my elbows to see Jane setting those duffel bags down in front of that white boy lowlife.

I smelled something funny. That was when I realized Aunt Woo-Woo was sitting cross-legged next to me. The tiny burlap bag she had held up to my face smelled like a skunk's dirty socks. I waved my hand in front of my face to get some breathable air. Aunt Woo-Woo stood and brushed herself off.

"Get up now," she said. "It's just about that time." She offered her arm and helped me stand. It surprised me how strong she was. I touched my jaw where it was tender but otherwise I felt fine. She closed the drawstring on the bag and stuffed it in one of her sash pockets.

Right about then, I heard a car coming and could see the light from its headlights out in the woods. Thank goodness. It was about time for the police to show up. At least, I sure hoped it was them and not bad guy reinforcements.

I heard a howl like a bobcat but realized it must have been Jane. I saw her rush at Ohio and attack him. When she did, that stocky bulldog boy that Homer was guarding made a dash for the woods in the direction of the cars. Homer went after him.

I knew I had to do something. All of a sudden, I felt dirt flying into my face and all around me. It made me sneeze. Then I saw it wasn't dirt, but something Aunt Woo-Woo was throwing in the air. She had another one of her tiny pouches in one hand. First, she slung the powder side to side like she was a flower girl at a wedding. Then she sprinkled some in her palm and blew it out of her hand like a kid blowing bubbles. I didn't have time for that silly stuff. I adjusted my rifle strap, said a prayer, and hugged Smokahontas.

I looked around for Jane. I saw her lunge sideways on top of a pile of leaves. Ohio watched her a second then turned and took off running. She flailed around, beating the ground and rolling in the leaves. It was like she didn't know or care that he was getting away.

It was up to me. I ran but there was no way I could catch him. He was close to the ridge and could be in his car and gone by the time I got there.

That was when the miracle happened. The wind blew in. Not just a nice little evening breeze. I'm talking about big strong gusts that just about knocked me down. They came in over the bluff and moved across the clearing like a typhoon hitting the beach. I halfway expected to see a funnel cloud because it took all I had just to keep standing up straight. Tree limbs that had been calm suddenly whipped around like they weighed nothing.

I staggered to take a step when all of a sudden the wind got even stronger and gusted and picked me up off the ground. Not just a little hop, up an inch or two and back down again, either. I mean way up high and I stayed there. I felt like one of those cows you see on TV swirling around in a tornado. Only I didn't swirl. I shot straight up like a missile. Leaves were flying around in my face like there was a helicopter landing and then that wind picked me up and slung me in a straight line from the middle of the clearing right and straight toward that no-account thief. My stomach flipped when I whooshed up but once I was high in the air, I felt like I was floating, like I was on a hang glider.

When I was closing in on Ohio's backside, I held Smokahontas tight and leaned back. I brought my legs straight out in front of me. As he stepped up the ridge, I reached back for my grenade flash-bang doo-hickey, bit the pin out like John Wayne, and threw that thing at him while floating in midair. A white light flashed and boomed right then below the ridge top. Another light flashed just as I yelled "Eeee-Yaaaah!" and karate-kicked that boy slap between the shoulder blades.

He should have gone down. Unfortunately, another gust of wind picked him up in the air and he flew straight ahead while I started falling. About that time, I wondered how I was supposed to put on the brakes.

The ground came up fast. I didn't actually make it all the way to the ground at first, though, because my foot touched down right next to the fishing line Jane had strung between the two trees. My right shoe caught on the line, and by the time my other foot came down, there was nothing but air to step on.

I tried to turn myself sideways for what I figured might be an easier landing. In between twisting and hitting the ground, I looked up to see Ohio boy doing the same thing, tripping and then flying off the ridge. And about to fall right on top of me. I held my arms out to catch him but wish now that I hadn't. They hurt for days. I doubt it softened the fall for him much, but it could've been worse. I could've let him fall straight onto Smokahontas and then he'd have a permanent imprint of an AK-46 and a half across his belly.

He hollered. I would have, too, but he knocked the breath out of me for a second. I pushed him off. He didn't stay down on the ground. He rolled and immediately began to get up. The police car was a lot closer now, but I'm not sure he even heard it. He got up on one knee, then winced as he grabbed a tree trunk to help him get back up over the ridge again.

"I don't think so," I said, but wasn't sure how I could follow through on it. I hurt all over. When I moved, nothing seemed to be broken. I wished Jane would be up there waiting to kick his sorry carcass, but I couldn't be sure she was able. I might be the one who needed to get up and go help her.

Ohio had a head start. No telling what he was thinking or was capable of doing. I groaned, got to my feet, and went up the ridge the same way he did, by holding onto trees.

The wind still gusted but not so strong as before. It blew steady across the clearing, swirling the fall leaves around in dust devils and scooting them into heaps. Ohio walked toward the two duffel bags. He bent to pick them up and put both in one hand. My heart about squeezed shut when I saw why. He had a gun in the other hand. It looked mighty familiar.

I slapped my hand across to my shoulder holster. Empty. That dog. What I would've given for another one of those flash things. I took a deep breath and tried to get a grip. I prayed for angels. And, would you believe, right after I thought it, I heard one singing. Ohio boy heard it, too, and looked up.

He shouldn't have done that. It distracted him and, unfortunately for him, trouble was bearing down on him from the other direction.

Jane, hardly five feet tall on her tiptoes and about as

big around as a straw, did not look like herself. She strode through the leaves straight for him like she was ten feet and two hundred pounds of meanness. She looked like a WWF professional wrestler on steroids, or Godzilla on a particularly bad day and mad as all Hades. I've seen her determined before, but this was way beyond that. Fire blazed in her eyes. Her head was slightly tucked under, purposeful, her arms were loose, and her legs moved steadily forward. She wasn't in a hurry, but sure of herself like a hungry lioness closing in on supper. Leaves and black spots covered the front of her clothes. I might have felt sorry for Ohio boy if he hadn't stolen my CZ.

Jane's assault rifle lay on the ground. She glanced at it and kept on going, right past it, clenching and unclenching her fists, zeroing her eyes on him again. That was when I knew he was in big trouble.

He didn't know what hit him. I believe Jane was past the point of gentleman's honor and a fair fight. She moved so fast I hardly saw what happened. She wound up her leg, spun it around, and delivered a roundhouse kick into his stomach that doubled him over and knocked him back about a yard before he fell and skidded on his backside another foot or two.

She walked very slowly. She stood over him and waited. When he caught his breath and remembered he had my gun, Jane pounced on him, knocking him on his back. She smashed his hand on the ground once, twice, and the third time his fingers let go. She picked up the gun as his other arm came up to grab her.

She grabbed around him, instead, and rolled him all the way over until she was on top again. This time, she got on her knees, cocked the hand that held the gun, and backhanded him across his cheek. She jumped up, racked the CZ's slide, and then pointed it at him as she took a few steps backward.

"Get up," she said in a low gravelly voice.

Blood ran down into his white beard. He put a hand to his nose as he struggled to stand. Just then, car headlights bounced over the clearing and a short blast of a siren came from over the ridge.

He looked at her, knowing it was all over. Unfortunately for him, it wasn't over for Jane.

She threw the CZ way across the clearing and walked forward, her eyes never leaving his face. Ohio tried to back up but didn't get far. A growl started low but got louder like a volcano erupting. She smacked both hands on his chest and grabbed his shirt in her fists, moving until he was right where she wanted him and then *boom,* sent a right hook into his jaw. I knew exactly what that was all about. That was for me, for the way he'd hit me earlier. Only Jane wasn't a sissy like he was. Compared to the hammering Jane gave him, he hit like a little girl.

We heard car doors opening and feet running through the underbrush on the other side of the ridge. We also heard that weird voice again and I realized that, in all the excitement, I had forgotten about the angel. I turned around to see it.

In all my days, I have never seen such a sight. It was

Aunt Woo-Woo doing a ballet dance and singing like a fairy queen, like she was on stage, oblivious to the siren and running and fisticuffs going on around her. She kept lifting up and down on the balls of her feet, and she could even walk on her toes like a ballerina in those fancy tennis shoes she had on. The headlights from the police car shone just below the ridge and gave Aunt Woo-Woo and the clearing an even weirder look than the moonlight already did.

When I turned back, Ohio had somehow made a small comeback. He growled and grabbed Jane's throat and started shaking her.

I ran to him, grabbed him by the shoulders, and yanked him off balance. I raised both arms up and hollered, "Yaaaah!" as I brought a double karate chop down on either side of his neck, real sharp, down and back up quick. I did it good, too, because that boy flopped to the ground like a puppet with its strings cut.

"This party's over, Junior," I said. "Get used to it."

Jane coughed as she looked at me. When she caught her breath, she rubbed her throat and said, "Phoebe! My word, who taught you to do that?"

I slapped my palms together to brush that sorry dog's evil cooties off me. "The best there is. Jackie Chan."

Jane inclined her head sideways. "Bravo. I must send him a thank-you note."

We heard Aunt Woo-Woo across the clearing. She ran laughing and singing with her arms out wide to a mound of dirt and leaves and sticks piled up on the opposite end from where the blue tarp and the hole in the ground were.

Detective Waters came over the ridge with his handgun straight out in front of him. He lowered it slowly when he saw Jane holding her throat, me rubbing my jaw that was still hurting, Aunt Woo-Woo dancing on the mound and wiggling her fingers at the detective, and two bad guys knocked out on the ground.

Once Detective Waters and his officers hauled off Ohio and his cohorts, Aunt Woo-Woo skipped over to the fallen tree where we left Jane's candles. Aunt Woo-Woo set the candles on a rock next to the dirt mound and lit them with a match she took out of a sash pocket.

She stood still on the mound, her arms out to the side again and her face turned up toward the moon that was even bigger than when we first got there. It filled her thick eyeglasses with a milky light. She didn't burst into song or start doing *Swan Lake* or anything, she just turned real slow until she could look straight at Jane.

All of a sudden, a fog moved in from the overlook and hung around the clearing with Aunt Woo-Woo right in the middle of it. I couldn't see her so well then until she smiled, showing all her teeth, and said, "Trick or treat!"

Well, she has always been loony, so nothing she says ever surprises me. I tell you what did surprise the corn squeezings out of me. Aunt Woo-Woo clapped her hands and giggled, and then she reached down to the edge of the mound and started digging like a dog uncovering a bone. Technically, I guess she was. In a few seconds, she had uncovered the edge of another bright blue tarp made even bluer in the moonlight.

Jane laughed and cried at the same time. She got down on her knees, mostly crying, and bent forward with her head down and her arms stretched out on the ground, like she was hugging it, crying like a baby.

thirty-five
Jane Wraps it Up

*P*hoebe raised her coffee cup to her lips. She blew across the top and batted her eyelashes at Detective Waters. "So, you think you can keep those mean thieves in jail for a while?"

We three sat together a week later, at my kitchen table.

"Yes, ma'am, I do," Detective Waters said. "We found plenty of evidence, for what they did here and a good many other places. Dr. Draughn has been busy. We think he will be a big help in busting up a few thief rings."

The detective told us they'd found plenty of evidence in the garage of Edward's rented house. His smuggling activities apparently included taking artifacts from South America and Italy, as well as stolen items from several Native American sites.

"You two sure pulled a good one on him," he said to Michael and me.

Michael protested. "I had little part in the deception," he said. "Jane thought of it. She dug the fake site and supplied it with a few buried treasures. Most realistically, I might add. I might have been fooled myself."

"I had to do something," I said. "My only worry was the thieves might notice the dig wasn't precisely in the right place, according to the maps they had stolen. I counted on their desire to hurry."

Detective Waters laughed. "It may be awhile before I can return your 'artifacts.'"

"Please feel free to keep them if you like," I said. He referred to a flat stone I inscribed myself to look like the one we found in the actual burial pit and a brand new blue tumbler I found at the dollar store. I knew how these thieves worked. They don't want to risk excavating properly when they steal. They're in too big of a hurry. They cut the earth away from around an object, if it is buried, and clean away the dirt at their leisure, well away from the site. I made the fakes appear to be easy to shovel out so they would take the easy bait. Still, they had to be covered well enough so Edward wouldn't spot right away that they were fakes.

It helped that he already knew what we had found. He expected to see a stone tablet and blue glass. Two of his accomplices had hacked into our computers you see. One had been our mugger at the Pig who had been killed earlier. The other was the stocky fellow Phoebe calls "Bulldog."

Between the two hackers, they retrieved information from Dr. Norwood's office computer, including her bone analysis and the location maps and records. Bulldog later tapped into Michael's e-mail program, where he found details about the artifacts. Michael had e-mailed that information to a colleague, an expert in ogham writings. This news was most unwelcome after Michael promised me he would not share any information about our dig or my land.

Edward Draughn originally hired his associates to look for Native American sites to plunder. Jeff Byrd, a Tullulah native, alerted him to Cal's land and its potential. When Draughn's hackers showed him our findings, he had too much experience to ignore the implications. He knew they might add up to an exceedingly profitable venture, more than an endeavor where only native artifacts might be found.

Michael wasn't involved. It was such a relief. He and Draughn knew one another, of course, from earlier years. Draughn knew Michael was here after he read Dr. Norwood's report. That was why he called out his name at the site.

Phoebe set her cup down. "Will he get a reduced sentence, after squealing on the other thief rings?"

Detective Waters shrugged. "Some. Maybe. He's under suspicion in two murder investigations, Brody Reed and another man in West Virginia. If those go the way I think they will, he may be behind bars for the rest of his life."

"You know what I don't get?" Phoebe said. "He met up with and killed Brody Reed before Jane and Michael even found anything. It wasn't in a computer yet. How come? How did he know to be here ahead of time?"

"Jeff Byrd," Detective Waters said. "He worked for Dr. Draughn ever since college where Draughn was one of his professors. Jeff knew about Cal's land, of course, since he grew up in Tullulah. He told Draughn about Cal's place a long time ago, how it must have all kinds of native artifacts since every generation of the Prewitt family always kept their place off limits. When Cal died, Jeff contacted Draughn. That's why Jeff moved back to town. They've been planning to come for a while. Your mugger took your keys so they could search your house for any pointers on where to start."

"He must have hired Brody Reed for that reason also, to get information and perhaps lead him to locally known native sites," I said.

"Yes, ma'am. That's what we think. We believe when they heard about the movie production company filming not far away, they got the idea to pretend to be part of that crew. They could park their trailer in any remote location without creating suspicion. People would think they looked for possible shooting locations, when they were really looking for artifacts to sell. When they heard about Brody and how he knew the forest like nobody else, they thought they'd found a gold mine."

"Only he found out their true intentions," I said.

"And it got him killed," the detective said. "Grant McWhorter from the tribe went with me to the spot where we believe Brody was killed. He showed us a cave nearby from which we have good reason to believe Dr. Draughn took artifacts, ones that have been there for hundreds of years. Brody probably saw him do it, tried to stop him."

Before Detective Waters left, we showed him the photos captured by the motion detector cameras I had installed on trees at the dig site. They had worked quite well. Ruby Alice looked striking on top of the dig site mound. I cringed at my own pictures. They were rather silly, with my arms akimbo in most, and my facial expression much too serious. The detective was particularly impressed by the one of Phoebe, flying through the air, holding her AK, and kicking her legs out while she screamed.

Phoebe was quite proud of it. "I'm having an eight-by-ten made," she said.

Later on, after Detective Waters left, we relaxed in the den by the fire. Michael's colleague, the ogham expert, e-mailed more photos of the ancient writing system for our use in comparing our tablet and the inscriptions on the shelter overhang. We saw nothing conclusive, but a few carvings in Ireland and Wales, dating to the thirteenth century, had similarities to our alleged native carvings, some of them quite strong.

Phoebe sat on the couch with Jenette in her lap and Homer at her feet. After she witnessed Homer's heroic actions at the dig site, her attitude changed toward him. Jenette, however, certainly is due the most credit for converting Phoebe to a dog lover. She snuggled in Phoebe's arms like a child, behind the book Phoebe was reading aloud to Jenette and Homer.

"See the picture of the little puppy?" she said. Jenette touched it with her nose and sniffed. "It says here that in ancient times, Lhasa Apsos guarded monasteries, way up in the snowy mountains of Tibet. They let their masters know when strangers were coming, and if there was any trouble, they barked first and then stepped aside for the big dogs to do the fighting. Now that is smart."

She continued to read. I enjoyed the lilt of her voice in the house and seeing her as the children of Tullulah saw her, the funny lady who reads to them at the library.

While Phoebe read, I noticed that Homer, who had been watching Phoebe's face all along, looked away as if something else caught his attention. His ears pricked up. They relaxed a moment later and his tail began a loud thumping on the rug. His eyes closed with contentment, over and over again. He got up to look at Jenette and away again, then back to her with a friendly nudge of his nose on her leg. It wasn't until Jenette repeated Homer's odd behavior of lazy contented eyes and wagging tail that I realized what was happening.

Boo was petting them. A gentle soul when in his earthly body and still a gentle one now that he is free of it, my resident ghost loved children and animals. He and Homer were old friends, and now Homer introduced him to a new one. It gave me an idea. I should have a tea party for children. The two little boys who stay with Phoebe could invite friends and we would have a grand time. It would be a small thing I could do for Boo, something that would give him such joy.

A certain measure of happiness, if not complete joy, has come to my visiting ghost in the basement through reading as well. Actually, as he has roamed my property much longer than I've been here, he might view me as the visitor.

The audio recording I made of him in the basement verified Riley's group's own conclusions from data they obtained on Halloween night. Their digital camera's sound and the separate recorder that Callie used on their Halloween excursion captured similar words and phrases as mine.

The one that made Riley happiest was the most clear, leaving no doubt in any of our minds that the ghost soldier said, "They're coming! The Yankees are coming!" With that, he had a new mission. He no longer saw himself as a mere ghost hunter, but also a ghost counselor. He proposed a strange therapy that seems to be working. He comes out regularly, sweeps his ghost detecting devices over the toolshed and around the basement, and once satisfied as to where the ghost is, proceeds to read from Civil War diaries or selections from a large volume of the Official Records of the war that contains officers' reports. This seems to console our young soldier. I no longer hear him cry in the night.

I walked to the bookshelf where I left the arrowhead and the ogham stick from Cal's box, and also the red-orange rock and the tiny blue flower Boo had given me. I set the four in a row on the coffee table, with the rock on one end. Had I not done so, I might never have discovered its significance.

Phoebe's purse had spilled earlier that day when Jenette and Homer, in a rambunctious mood, knocked it over while playing chase in the den. We thought we put everything back, but as I stood there that evening, I saw a glint of something shiny in the rug. It was a safety pin.

"Phoebe, this must belong to you," I said.

"Just put it on the table. I'll get it when Jenette gets up."

I did so, and it moved. It slid as pretty as you please about an inch over the tabletop and adhered itself to the rock. Why had I not realized it before? I knew very well, somewhere in the recesses of my brain, that the red color would be from iron oxidation. This was magnetite. A lodestone.

I stared at it for some time. Cal's voice, through the notes he left in box #2, sounded as if he were standing there next to me, speaking into my ear. His father found the arrowhead and the stick with writing on it in an old bowl. In the bottom, something metal, a few inches long, had rusted to nothing. If my theories ran in the right directions, the rusted metal could have been a needle of some sort, one used with a lodestone or on a leaf floating in a bowl of water to find true North. From another dusty corner of my mind, as I remembered the view into Reese's old barn and the dirty blackened half-globe that hung on the wall, large enough for a man to fit in, several cogs clicked together to form an idea that wasn't possible. It couldn't be proven. Other explanations would be said to be more likely. I agreed wholeheartedly. Yet with each small bit of discovery, an unlikely explanation might be the one that is eventually found to be true.

Michael stayed on for several more weeks. It had not been easy at first. We kept up a jolly front as we readjusted to our work following Edward Draughn's arrest. We only spoke of the e-mails he sent to his colleague once. He apologized for acting against my wishes. I understood how he justified doing so, because his colleague was one hundred percent trustworthy. Not in his wildest imaginations did he consider the possibility of e-mail theft, or that the information obtained would be used to violate our work and my home.

But you see, I must consider every wild imagination. I had already determined that no one should be told until I was satisfied it was absolutely essential and the person trustworthy. I must keep one step ahead of those who might destroy, for their own gain, what has been given to my trust. Michael betrayed me, however unwittingly. Though all the villains' information did not come solely from his e-mails, Michael's disregard for my wishes did contribute to the endangerment of what I hold most dear, something irreplaceable and priceless that must be preserved. Through his trusted contact, word could still spread to another who might yet endanger the forest due to Michael's dismissal of my request.

I miss my husband. When Michael was here, the loneliness that creeps over me and into my bones at times evaporated completely. Our common interests gave us much to talk about. The excavation certainly provided a special bond. His sense of humor and his intelligence made each day a pleasure.

In the clearing, at the moment Edward tossed the flame into the leaves, the danger made me realize how deeply my love for this land runs through me. As I watched the leaves burn, in those few horrible moments, it was as if I burned, curling and withering with the thought it might all be lost due to the cruelty of one man.

Michael had not been cruel. He is a wonderful companion. But when I fell upon the burning leaves, all else became trivial, everything narrowed. In relationships, men often dismiss the requests of their women and go against their wishes because they think they understand the big picture and the little wife does not. This is something I understand very well after so many years with the Colonel. It is something I have been willing to accept in the past. I cannot accept it now, not when it involves the forest and the treasures, such as the current dig, that it holds. I cannot allow this thinking, even from a man I care for very much, to jeopardize it again.

The DNA results from the tooth found at the site came back the day Michael went home. They confirmed the bones belonged to a Caucasian male of approximately forty-five years at the time of death. Though we were somewhat prepared by the corroborating finds, the true age of the bones still stunned us. They were found to be more than eight hundred years old, more than two hundred years before Columbus came to North America, a time when no known Caucasians were here.

Michael already suspected it, from the time he took the first skull measurements. His years of experience told him at first glance that the skull looked too small for the man's apparent age. Medieval skulls, however, fit his measurements perfectly, due to the proportions of the smaller cranial vault and jaws that are a good bit larger in modern man.

The blue glass tumbler is older than the bones. It matches others made in Wales in the 1100s exactly, down to the maker's imprint, made by a family of artisans in Gwynedd. Perhaps it had been an heirloom, handed down through a family of mariners, just as their seafaring ways had been learned from craftsmen of Viking and Irish descent, and then passed down through generations.

The tablet inscription and those on the stick found in Cal's box of notes and sundries have a less definite history. A small number of these sticks have been found in North America. Some historians believe they are records of lost native tribal histories, recorded in a type of shorthand. The shorthand is taught to each successive chief, with each symbol a reminder of a particular event in the tribe's history that is learned and then related orally to the people generation after generation. The faint carvings on the sticks are much worn, and therefore difficult to make a definite match.

Those that are clearer do match the smaller symbols inscribed at the bottom of the rock shelter overhang. And here's the curious part: Those symbols closely match ancient ogham engravings on stone, such as on the tablet found in our burial pit.

The practice of symbolic shorthand using ogham can be found in use as early as the fourth century in Ireland, a country that in medieval times had strong connections with Welsh mariners, and was still found in use into the medieval period. If the inscriptions on the sticks were, in fact, ogham symbols, it meant that system might have been brought to America in medieval times by Europeans, quite some time before Columbus.

When we read these results and their implications, we sat without speaking for a time. At last, Michael said, "There's no need to ask. I promise you I will never make this information public without your consent. We both know it is unlikely we'll ever have conclusive results. And that even with the compelling DNA evidence we have, and with the corroborating artifacts, no self-respecting scientist will buy into the theory. Welshmen in pre-Columbian America have never been accepted as an actual possibility, or anything other than a complete fraud. Perhaps, in time, we'll find more to substantiate. Or better, someone elsewhere does."

He plans to return periodically. A thorough study may take years. It would not be so if we had only found old bones. The problem, and the wonder of it, is that we have discovered this was a burial room, not a kitchen as Michael first suspected. It is something neither Michael nor I can find a precedent for in recent history. The Anglo-Saxon site Michael remembered, in which bowls were found still hanging on the burial room walls, is in England and dates from the 600s. Like it, our burial room has remained covered and intact for many centuries. We continue to dig and research.

A FEW DAYS AFTER OUR ADVENTURE ON HALLOWEEN, Phoebe and I each made casseroles for Ruby Alice and Reese. Ruby Alice, dressed that day in a maroon flapper dress and a cloche hat with a rhinestone pin set in the middle of the forehead, insisted I take a few of her tea concoctions. Phoebe led me round to the garden rock and instructed me on how to place my hand just so in order to get a wish.

"Maybe I shouldn't be the one telling you how to do

it," she said. "My three wishes when we were here the last time haven't exactly panned out."

"Would it spoil the wishes to tell me what they were?"

"Don't think so. If they were going to come true, they would have already happened by now. I wished that you, Corene, and I would each catch a man."

"Your wish did come true," I said.

She looked puzzled until she remembered how Draughn fell on her. She put her hands on her hips. "That's not the kind of catching I had in mind. Corene's didn't work, either, but I know why. She called last night and I told her I'd used her hair comb. She said that wasn't hers. It was Jenette's. Yours should have worked. You certainly didn't wake up about Michael like I asked for. Or you two would be man and wife right now. Honestly, Jane. He's perfect. What more could you want?"

Man and wife. Ruby Alice watched us from the kitchen door and smiled. The sadness I felt an instant before vanished on seeing small, gold, comet-like ribbons swirl above Ruby Alice's head. If this was the sensation of having one's mind read, I didn't care at all.

Down the road, we could hear Reese singing when we got out of Phoebe's car. He was nowhere in sight. As we walked toward his house, he called to us from his backyard workshop. "Over here, y'all," he said. "I'm just about done." White paint or plaster covered his hands. From the doorway, we saw that he worked at a table on a new building for one of his Bible Gardens displays. I stared at the interior scene.

"What?" Phoebe said to me. "You see a ghost or something?"

"No," I said and laughed. "A painting."

Reese, working his model into the right shape with his hands, looked up and beamed. With that movement, the scene clicked into perfection. I wondered if he could read my mind, too.

It was a Vermeer. Not an actual painting on the wall, you understand, but the real-life scene before me. On the left wall, the afternoon sun shone through a window, casting rays of white light over tables and hand tools. The right wall's main features were two large maps, not new ones, but replicas of the very early maps showing oceans and crudely formed continents. Beneath them, an astrolabe sat on a long workbench amid bottles and models of ships. But it was the centerpiece, the image of Reese concentrating on his craft, highlighted by the declining sun and its shadows, which gave the scene its heart.

He moved to a sink and began washing the white mixture from his hands. "Something smells good," he said.

"Chicken and rice casserole," Phoebe said. "I hope I remembered right, that you like it."

"I sure do. Thank you."

"Oh," I said as I reached in my pocket. "I brought you something also. I thought you might have a use for it."

He dried his hands as he walked toward the door. I held out the gift in my palm.

"Oh, ho!" His face lit up with childlike delight. He laughed from the belly and motioned us to follow him.

He led us to one of the displays that were not related to a Bible story. This one had no people and no story written on a display card as at other miniature scenes, only a shoreline and a boat in the water. "Still working on this one, as you can see," he said. "And look, isn't it a coincidence that I brought this box out of the barn just today."

He referred to a wooden box that sat on a small TV tray from the fifties. Compared to the other boxes of trinkets and glass pieces we had seen on our first visit, this one was quite small and had very little in it. The bits hardly covered the bottom. Yet what was there made me gasp.

From the shallow layer, Reese brought up an identical blue flower, tiny, exactly like the one I'd brought. He held them up in the light and admired them. "Now that I have two, I believe I'll use them here, maybe on the ship." He put one on either side of the hull to try them out. "Maybe. We'll see. I'll find a use for them somewhere."

I looked into the box more closely. Perhaps he had more of the detached flowers in there. I didn't find any, but did see something just as astonishing. "Reese, where did you get the flowers, and these?" I asked with a shaky voice. From out of the box, I showed him two sticks, wooden ones that were planed square where symbols were carved on the sides.

He shrugged. "From Mama, I guess. Or her family. Don't rightly know. We've had them a long, long time."

My mind reeled as I considered the stories from the books with a blue glow. The building of walls. The history of Wales. They didn't sound so preposterous to me now.

"Reese," I said. "I wonder. Might I have a look inside your barn? I saw something interesting there the other day."

He walked with me and opened the big doors. The darkness inside made it impossible to see anything clearly. Reese leaned inside the door and brought out a flashlight. He clicked it on and handed it to me. "What are you looking for?" he said.

I shone the light on the large half-globe that hung on the wall near the back. It's black paper-looking flaps moved as a light wind blew into the barn. "That. What is it?"

He laughed. "That thing is so old, it's falling apart. I'd have broken it up and used its parts for something useful, but it's the last one, so I reckon I'll keep it. Worthless as it is."

"It's the last one? The last what?"

"Boat. Ah, really more of a canoe. We had several passed down in the family. The rest rotted. That one seems to like where it is. It's holding together, so I just keep it."

The scenery we passed on the ride home went by unnoticed. I hoped Dad Burn would call again soon so I could thank him, and Cal, for the tip.

Back in Cal's woods, I have taken to sitting on the rock wall, at the corner overlooking the valley and, more importantly, the river below. I think of it as the watchtower, something it may have been when it was built long ago.

As with our other finds, the wall's history is uncertain. Other similar walls in Alabama, Tennessee, and Georgia have a legend attached. When Governor John Sevier of Tennessee asked Oconostoga, the chief of the Cherokee Nation in 1782, who had built the walls, he said the forefathers taught that the "moon-eyed people" who had come from across the great water made them. They were described as having white skin and blue eyes.

Another story is told of an expedition through Tennessee in the 1700s, in which the crew's interpreters, who spoke many native tongues, couldn't understand the language of a small band of light-skinned natives. Another member of the expedition stepped forth and was able to communicate with the natives. He was a trader from Wales who said they spoke an archaic dialect of Welsh. Similar stories, all debunked by scholars, involve different tribes but have the same themes of Welsh-speaking natives with light skin.

Many false claims of pre-Columbian discoverers have been made and debunked. Among them are the legends of Prince Madoc of Gwynedd, a Welshman who supposedly sailed to the Gulf of Mexico in 1170, returned to Wales, and brought ten more boats of settlers to the New World. The settlers, it is supposed, then traveled from Mobile Bay up the waterways through Alabama.

A stone fort in Desoto Falls, Alabama, is alleged to be identical in layout to the Madoc family castle in Dolwyddelan, which dates from the early medieval period. Other theorists say the Welsh explorers ended up near Chattanooga where they built the Old Stone Fort.

But who is to say that some of these medieval Welshmen did not turn left instead at the Tennessee River to a paradise of game and fishing, where the land undulates and echoes the landscapes of home, where they might have left scant reminders of the old country in teaching sticks and rock engravings, before their people fully integrated into native tribes?

The prevailing attitude toward such theories, as this one that our findings now suggest, is one of disdain. We will keep our secrets. Our discoveries may come to light one day, but for now I hold them close, the better to keep this place protected.

For myself, I need no further proof of scientists, nor corroborations of other sets of long-dead bones. My own proof confronts me occasionally, just as it first did the night Ruby Alice stood and danced atop the hidden bones, knowing they were there though no one had told her.

Phoebe said she saw a fog blow in from the overlook

then. I saw something else, a blue shadowy figure, that of a man dressed in a simple tunic with a bow and a quiver of arrows on his back. I had seen him on the road that day of the storm, dripping wet as he walked the fields at the base of the mountain.

That Halloween night, he hovered next to Ruby Alice a moment, then he walked to the rock wall and stood on the watchtower, looking out across the valley to the water below, before dissipating into the fog.

Now, from the same spot, I look out over Tullulah and the world. Homer and I go there often to think. Certainly, we're free to do so anywhere on the mountain with no worry of being disturbed. Still, there is something special about the lookout. As fall nights grow colder, the leaves' varied and luscious colors stand out more against the chilly morning fogs. Soon, it will be too cold to stay very long. I treasure the moments while I can.

Boo sits with us on occasion. I see him seated on the wall, always near Homer. He rarely makes himself visible, yet I feel his presence in the house and am comforted by it. I adore him and always feel a certain warmth around my heart when he appears. We watch together, share a look of appreciation at the wonder of a hawk's flight or the way the last rays of afternoon sun bathe the treetops and rock outcroppings in indescribable shades of red and gold. And though he doesn't know it, his own beautiful face, so full of innocence and goodness, brings me just as much happiness as the glories of nature around us.

I do miss Michael, in spite of my conflicting thoughts. Phoebe would be quick to point out that, at my advanced age, Michael is surely my last chance for a loving relationship and I should pursue him in earnest. She's probably right. Her exact words were I should "grab him while he's hot."

Still, I am not quite so advanced in age that I've stopped learning. The discovery of the bones and all its related experiences taught me several things. In regard to Michael, I've learned that no matter how wonderful a once in a lifetime chance is, its rarity isn't reason enough to take it. It must be right, no matter what color the moon, even if it might never come round again. Whether Michael and I will develop a closer relationship, I couldn't say. We would see.

As pessimistic as that might sound, I have also learned to be more open to possibilities. Phoebe once said that, though she had no proof, she believed she had a small amount of Indian blood, that it made no difference to her whether or not proof could be found of it in books or records. She feels it and that is enough.

I find the elements brought together by Cal's box #2 make me more inclined to accept that. A fact that hasn't been recorded on paper or in stone, or has been hidden for generations in deep woods worlds away from obsessive note-takers, is still a fact. In such cases, a telling blood may be all that remains of a fact's history, with the only records in feelings imprinted deeply into genes.

That's not the reason I feel so attached to this land. Yet just as medieval Welshmen may have settled here because the hills and valleys reminded them of home, I do wonder if the land of my childhood calls to me here as well. At times, it feels like an echo in my soul. It reverberates through the mountain and moves my heart in the way of lush orchestras or a hundred strong male voices singing an ancient tongue. High on the watchtower's bluff, looking down on the river valley and across the great expanse of thick autumn leaves and evergreens, I breathe in the world as it once was and give thanks for the joy of its riches and for being here, surrounded by its beauty.